The Miracle Railway

Cenarth Fox

First published in 2022 by Fox Plays
Melbourne Australia

www.cenfoxbooks.com
www.foxplays.com

ISBN 978-0-949175-68-7

Cover design by oliviaprodesign
Cover photo by Andrew Watts
Weybourne Station, North Norfolk Railway

With grateful thanks to those who helped

Ken Wheatley
The Great Eastern Railway Society

Mike Rea
Elsenham Village History Society

Andrew Watts
Norfolk's Disused Railways

Dedication

To my father, Allen William Fox
for an introduction to railways

The Station Lad

Chapter 1

The man knocked gently. At midday he should be at work and, my God, how he wished he was. From inside, footsteps sounded. Would he throw up? The door opened and the lady of the house felt a chill grip her skin and bone body. This man would never call unless there was serious news and here he stood in the middle of the day. Scrunching his cap, his face told her everything. Would *she* throw up? A young girl pushed past her mother and stared at the man making him feel even worse, if that were possible. He spoke.

'I'm terribly sorry, Missus.'

He swallowed his next sentence as the woman stifled a scream, fighting hard to not frighten her deaf daughter. Emily excelled at reading body language and lips, and sensed bad news despite her tender years. An accident in a fairground when she was six broke bones in her ear. One ear was deaf and the other had little hearing.

'Is he ...' asked the woman, her hoarse whisper fading causing the child to sense her mother's distress. The girl stared at the man who nodded, wanting to leave the details till later, preferably never.

'But it's the boy's birthday,' whispered the mother and wife, tears coming alive. Emily felt a new pain with her mother unintentionally squeezing her so hard.

'I'll be on my way, Missus. His body was taken to the undertaker, and someone from the company will be round tomorra with his pay and bits and bobs, and of course we'll pay for the funeral. Is there anything else I can tell you?' he asked praying she'd let him go.

The deceased had often told his wife of the dangerous machinery where he worked. She didn't want to hear the gory, graphic details. 'Thank you, no.'

'Please accept my condolences and know your husband was a highly respected employee. There'll be a grand turnout at his funeral.'

The widow continued suppressing her grief. She nodded sending tears flying, then led her daughter inside and closed the door. Outside, the visitor breathed normally and hurried back to work.

1

'What's happened, Mummy?'

In that moment, Connie grew a new backbone, suppressed her sorrow and opted for a soft version of honesty. 'Daddy's been in an accident at work. He's poorly and may not get better.'

'Has he died?' asked Emily, staring at her mother so as to read her lips. The child saw the man say the word *funeral* and knew its meaning. Her mother cried and lost her voice. Cue the widow's grief.

The child's disability gave her a remarkable inner strength, a greater resolve to face life whatever hardship came her way. She suffered a double whammy when, a few years previously, the London-based Royal School for Deaf Children, once known as the Asylum for the Deaf Children of the Poor, upped sticks and moved to Margate in Kent so the students could benefit from the sea air. No-one knew how that helped the London-based deaf children.

Connie didn't answer Emily's question. 'Get your coat; we're going to see Grandma.'

The girl ran to get ready while her mother looked at the wrapped birthday present her husband prepared for their son. The cake she baked sat quietly in the bread bin, its twelve candles unlit and now not wanting to burn bright or ever on such a sad occasion.

What a way to remember your birthday. Your father died.

The present was a new fishing rod and even though well wrapped in brown paper, anyone could guess the contents. John Miracle, recently deceased, always took his boy fishing on the Sabbath. They picked their favourite spots on the Thames, and one in particular on Regent's Canal. On special occasions, and this Sunday was obviously special, they'd set off to fish in the Tottenham marshes.

'I'll be 12 next week, Dad,' George kept reminding his father. 'Can we go to the marshes, please?'

'Only if I hear from your teacher you've been the best student in your class.'

'Would second-best be good enough?'

The boy's smile pushed his father to respond in kind. The two loved one another and for Connie, this was the heart breaker.

She thought. *How can I tell the boy? Far worse, how will he handle the news?*

Connie's mother lived about a hundred yards away in the next street in the unique housing development, the Noel Park Estate in Wood Green, North London. Florence was frail and Connie's brother, Fred, an unmarried Londoner, steadfastly and proudly lived with his Ma having done so his entire life.

Using her own key, Connie opened the door and called.

'It's only me, Ma.'

There was no need to ask where her mother might be, it was always the kitchen. Same chair, same shawl, same fire in the same stove and same kiss as her daughter bent to greet her.

Emily gave her grannie a kiss and saved her mother the bother of breaking the news. 'Daddy's dead and he's going to have a funeral.'

Florence gasped and in shock stared at her daughter. Connie struggled to speak and settled for nodding.

'What happened?' whispered Grannie.

'Don't know and don't want to,' replied Connie. 'His boss came and told us. It was an accident at work and I didn't ask for details.'

'But it's George's birthday,' whispered Florence with her hands on her cheeks. 'It'll break the lad's heart. You need to be home for when he finishes school.'

'I can't, Ma,' whispered Connie, the pain in her chest forcing more tears. 'I'll ask Fred to tell George.'

'But he doesn't finish his shift till 6.'

'I thought he could get a sort of special leave, for a family tragedy or serious incident. You know how George loves his Uncle Fred and it'll be bad for the boy if he sees me blubbing like a baby.'

'Perhaps you're right,' murmured Florence.

'If I can leave Em with you, I'll go to the station now and ask him.' She paused desperate for support.

Grannie reached for her granddaughter and, in so doing, spoke in a louder voice. 'Come here, young lady.'

Emily leaned against her grandmother for a hug with feeling. For years Florence was told there was no need to raise her voice to Emily but there are people who can't or won't be told.

'I'll be back soon, darling,' said Connie. 'Be good for Grannie.'

'She's always good,' said the old woman and pointed to the biscuit tin as the young widow left the old widow and slipped away.

Liverpool Street Station in 1910 was 36 years old and one of London's busiest. Being close to the Underground station of the same name, passengers poured in and out of the premises. Connie's brother, Fred Carmody, spent his entire working life in the employ of the Great Eastern Railway Company starting more than 40 years ago, and today held the prestigious position of station master at this prominent London location.

Connie hurried along Bishopsgate trying to keep her emotions under control. Fred and his sister were always pals. She knew he would do anything for her and especially her kids. *Help me, please Fred.* The brothers-in-law too got on like a house on fire. She thought. *Should I be the one to tell my son his father is dead? Am I being unfair asking my brother to perform such a terrible task?*

She reached the ticket barrier where the ticket collector recognized her and smiled. 'Hello, you're the SM's sister. How are you?'

'Not well, I'm afraid.' The man's expression instantly changed. 'I'm sorry to hear that.'

'There's been a death in the family and I need to speak to Fred.'

The man whistled and a lad porter ran towards the barrier. He was told to find the station master and have him come to the barrier immediately. The lad took off.

'Would you like to come onto the platform, Missus?'

'Thank you but no. I'll speak to my brother away from the crowds.'

'As you wish, Missus, but now if you'll excuse me, please.' A train pulled in and the ticket collector became busy.

People poured out of the station and headed into London. Connie paced up and down away from the throng. She heard her brother before she saw him.

'Connie,' called Fred now worried. This was not a social call and his sister would only come to his place of work in an emergency.

She told him as best she could. The ticket collector glanced at his boss and saw him embrace his sister. It was a tough time; bad news.

'Of course I'll tell him,' said the SM. 'Let me get some cover. Wait here and I'll be back directly.'

Connie felt what couldn't be called happiness but more like relief for the first time since she heard the heartbreaking news. Fred was as good as his word and in a few minutes walked through the barrier and escorted Connie to his and their mother's home.

Rather than wait for birthday boy George to come home, Fred went to the lad's school to give the boy the news as soon as possible.

Still in uniform, the SM reached the front of the school. He stood away from the gate being observed by a few mothers who wondered what a man in uniform, an important man with a cap bearing the words *Station Master*, was doing so far from a station.

A bell was heard followed by many footsteps, chatter and the odd squeal. Children appeared and disappeared. Fred scanned the students. He spotted his nephew deep in conversation with a pal.

'George!' called Fred.

The boy responded to his name and knew the voice. A smile spread over the lad's face giving his uncle a deeper feeling of dread.

'Uncle Fred,' exclaimed the birthday boy shaking hands with his much-loved uncle and waving goodbye to his chum.

'Hello, young man, and many happy returns of the day.'

'Thank you and this is a wonderful surprise. But have you come all the way from Liverpool Street just to wish me a happy birthday?'

Fred's face told all. The boy sensed danger and trouble sneaked inside his soul.

Guiding his nephew, the uncle took the boy into a park making small talk about possible presents. They sat on a bench. People walking dogs and a woman pushing a pram walked past. Fred hoped his plan would work. Once he would have asked for divine support but having served in the Boer War and witnessed horrors, Fred could now rightly be described as a born-again atheist.

'I have sad news, George.' The bearer of cruel tidings decided to speak plainly and did so. 'It's your Dad, my boy. There's been an accident at work and I'm so sorry to tell you he's been killed.'

The look on George's face was something his uncle would never forget. It wasn't fear, anger or sadness but disbelief. The boy could not comprehend the fact the father he loved with all his heart would never take him fishing again. It was too hard to accept, incredible.

Fred put his arm around his nephew and spoke quietly. 'I know your heart is breaking, George, but now you have the hardest job any young boy can face. You have to be the man of the house. Your mother and sister need you to be brave and strong and to carry on.'

The boy did what was natural; he cried. Fred felt sick.

He's a child, you fool. Asking a lad to be a man the moment after his life has been shattered is cruel and plain bloody stupid.

Fred said nothing. He pulled his nephew even closer and shed a tear himself. There they sat, united in grief, as the afternoon sun slipped behind a cloud causing a chill to settle upon them.

What a birthday present for the now 12 year-old George Miracle.

The duo reached Florence's place where the greeting between the boy and the females was moving. Emotions spilled out with tears and hugs being oddly mixed with birthday wishes from Grannie.

Connie decided. Having a celebration in their house with all her late husband's belongings was wrong. 'I think we should have your party here at Grandma's place.'

'Excellent idea,' said Fred. 'How about I take George and Em and we collect the presents and the cake?'

Emily clapped her hands and a second feeling of relief washed over Connie. Her daughter's show of enthusiasm, of getting on with life made Connie's heart less painful. The heartache at her husband's sudden demise slipped to the back of her mind as she worked to make her mother's home the perfect venue for her son.

'What about Mrs Entwhistle?' asked Emily, remembering their next-door neighbour who was always invited to a Miracle party.

'She can't walk around here,' said Flo. 'She's more frail than I am.'

George's face lit up. 'I could get Mr Bidden to take her on his cart.'

The others stared at George. He loved to ride with and help the rag and bone man, and George knew old Bidden would do him a favour.

'Worth a try,' said Fred. 'Right, come on you two. The train on Platform Number 1 is about to depart.'

The trio set off and Connie and her mother knew the best thing for everyone was to keep busy. Stop grieving. It's the boy's birthday. Prick the sausages, make some mash and hide the presents although not necessarily in that order. Oh, and happy birthday, George.

Chapter 2

What a sight. The elderly Mrs Entwhistle seated on the back of the rag and bone cart with Emily beside the old girl, and George up front with the driver as they travelled the mighty distance of 120 yards. The passengers, presents, cards and covered cake sat between old clothes, a massive horse collar, and cutlery oddments from a kitchen drawer in a deceased estate. Uncle Fred walked between the houses carrying the brown paper-wrapped fishing rod.

Once the guests arrived, Connie's heart continued to cop painful jabs but the change of venue helped. Having the party in the room where the deceased husband and father once sat, spoke and even sung only a few hours ago would have been heart-rending, even cruel.

The food was plain but wonderful. Fred enjoyed a bottle of beer, his mother and sister sipped a sherry, while the children drank homemade lemonade, and Mrs Entwhistle stuck to tea.

'How do you take it, Mrs Entwhistle?' asked Fred.

The children answered for their neighbour. 'Hot and wet,' they cried together reprising her oft repeated joke. The mood lifted again.

George ate and drank too much, and the adults knew his unusual behaviour was the result of the suffering he endured and tried to cover but couldn't. He missed his father more than the others could imagine. He raced outside and threw up in the backyard. Uncle Fred followed and waited till the boy stopped vomiting.

'All gone, lad; 'tis better out than in.'

The sincere but forced smile on the railwayman's face told the boy he was loved. George washed his face and they returned to the front room.

When the birthday boy removed the brown paper from his present, his tears took over. It was the best and worst present at the saddest time of his life. He loved the rod but couldn't handle the fact he would never go fishing with his father again.

'Your Dad picked it out for you, George,' said Uncle Fred. 'He showed it me last week and asked if he thought you'd like it.'

Without meaning to, Fred brought a new sadness to the gathering. Mentioning the absent father dragged the issue front and centre. Fred hated himself wanting to bite his tongue then did so as a form of punishment.

Mrs Entwhistle, she of pauper status, took out a small oddly wrapped object and called to George. Her action changed the mood yet again.

'ere you are lad and a very 'appy birfday an' all.'

George smiled despite his misery. 'Thank you, Mrs Entwhistle,' he said as everyone watched him unwrap his present. When said gift appeared, silence took over.

'It belong me old man,' she said. 'I cleaned it proper like.'

George held up the late Mr Entwhistle's favourite pipe. The boy placed it in his mouth and, folding his arms, took a pose, and magic happened in Grannie Carmody's parlour.

The adults laughed or made witty comments but little Emily hit the nail on the head.

Pointing at her brother and with even sharper wisdom than Solomon, announced, 'George is our new Daddy!'

Lightning struck everyone except Emily. On the day when the husband, father, brother-in-law, son-in-law and neighbour, suffered a horrendous accident at work and was killed instantly, the saying, "The King is dead, long live the King", bounced around the room.

On the day George Miracle turned 12, he acquired presents including a new fishing rod and an old pipe. Surely that makes him an adult. Good luck to you, son.

The boss who broke the shocking news was right. There was an excellent turnout for John Miracle's funeral. The service, at St Mark's in Lymington Avenue, was packed. The church, in irreverent terms, was a barn which was fine considering the number of mourners.

Being the third son in his family, the vicar did the right thing; oldest son to the Law, second oldest to the Army and number three to holy orders.

The priest spoke well, kept emotion under lock and key to protect the grief-stricken family, and did a splendid job shaking hands with heathens and atheists who made up the majority of the congregation.

London cemeteries in 1910 were full, overflowing or filling fast.

Connie, with help from the leading station master in London, obtained a burial plot in Highgate Cemetery. Here a hardy mob from the deceased's place of work, joined Connie, her children, close family, and cousins only seen at weddings and funerals, at the grave site. To rub salt into the Miracle wounds of unhappiness, it poured.

Grannie made it to the church but Fred took her home before the burial. 'I think Connie will take me up on the offer with George,' said Fred to his mother.

'What choice do they have? They need every penny they can get.'

'I mentioned them coming here and she wouldn't have a bar of it.'

'Me neither. But they might have to shift to a Second Class house and have Emily share with Connie.'

In the Noel Park Estate there were five classes of house and not a single pub. A second class house had only two bedrooms.

'I'll have a chat to the boy after the cemetery. Bye Ma.'

He kissed his ageing mother and left, travelling by train to Highgate and walking to the cemetery.

Burials on rainy days were a perfect fit. Mourners concentrate less on their grief as they pull their coats and umbrellas closer. Connie wanted her children at the graveside. Maybe it was a hangover from Victorian times, and with John Miracle in the ground, the widow and her children returned home with Uncle Fred by their side.

Back in the Miracle house, drying his clothes before the fire, Fred noticed the dwindling supply in the coal bucket. 'I'll slip out back and get some more,' he said.

'We need to go easy on the coal,' said his sister. 'What little money we were given from John's company needs to go a very long way.'

There was no answer to that so he looked at Connie indicating his nephew. She gave the merest of nods and Fred addressed the youth.

'George, young man, it's time we had a chat.'

Quick as a flash, Emily spoke. 'When can I have a chat?'

'As soon as I finish with George.'

'Girls should go before boys,' stated the eight year-old, 'because it's always ladies before gentlemen.'

The adults paused. Solid logic packs a punch and when coming from a child, and one who is deaf, makes it a white flag time.

Fred went to Emily, gave her a hug and stared at her face. 'I promise Miss Emily Jane Miracle, that I, Mr Frederick Michael Carmody, will make time to discuss the meaning of life with you for as long as you like starting no later than 15:30 hours this very day.'

The child was both satisfied and perplexed. 'Is your name really Frederick Michael Canterbury?' Fred and Connie grinned for the first time all week.

'I'll be back in two shakes of a lamb's tail, Em,' said Fred leading George to the parlour where they sat.

'Is this about me working on the railways?' asked the boy giving his uncle a second jolt at the maturity and understanding of a child.

'It is,' he said.

'Ma told me it would be better if I leave school and help the family by earning a wage. She said you might be able to help me find a job.'

'Your Ma is right. The money your Da brought home paid for the rent and food for your family. Now his money is no more and you will help your Ma and sister if you leave school and start work.'

'Will I be able to get a job?'

'Can you work hard?' The boy nodded. 'Then you will get a job.'

'On the railways?'

'On the railways with your Uncle Fred.'

George thought hard. His life changed and continued to change. 'Thank you, Uncle Fred for all the help you've given Ma and Emily and me. I hope I can make them and you proud.'

Fred stood and extended his right hand. The boy took it. 'Do you know why we shake hands with our right hand?' George was surprised and shook his head. 'Because in the olden days, as is the case today, most men were right-handed and drew their sword with their right hand. By offering to shake hands with their right hand, a man was saying to another man, "I come in peace". He couldn't draw his sword while his hand grasped the other man's hand.'

George's mind became a sponge. He learnt a lot and quickly.

'What work will I do, Uncle?'

'You'll start as a station lad at Liverpool Street. It's where I work and I can look out for you and be there to help if you need it.'

'What does a station lad do?'

'All sorts. He fetches and carries parcels, sweeps the platform, helps passengers who are lost, and always keeps out of the way of station masters who are all silly old duffers.'

George spotted Fred's eyes twinkling. 'I thought duffers were placed at the end of the line to stop trains running out of track.'

Fred wasn't sure if the boy was clever and mocking him. 'They be dumb buffers, young man, I be dumb duffer.' They both grinned. 'Work hard, George, and you'll be promoted to lad porter.'

'And please, Uncle, what does a lad porter do?'

'The same as a station lad but he gets sixpence more a week.'

The next morning Connie and Emily walked to Noel Park School where George was a student. Mother and daughter waited outside the head master's office on the hardest bench in London.

Mr Brisket, known to many as Mr Biscuit, opened his door and invited the visitors inside.

'My dear Mrs Miracle, once again I offer you the condolences of everyone at our school on your tragic loss. If there is anything I can do to help your boy, you only have to ask.'

'Thank you, sir, there is. I wish for George to leave.'

'Leave?' Mr Brisket took it personally if any of his pupils left.

'We need the money, sir, and we hope my boy will obtain employment with the Great Eastern Railway Company.'

'I see. Well the term ends next month and ...'

'I'm sorry, Mr Brisket, but George has an interview at Liverpool Street Station at 8 o'clock in the morning.'

'Tomorrow?' gasped Mr Brisket.

'We'll be most grateful if you can write my son a reference, sir. His teachers have always spoken highly of his behaviour.'

'Indeed, indeed.' He stood and looked at Emily and raised his voice, another adult not understanding how deaf people can read lips and thus understand. 'And how is your daughter getting along?'

His jaw dropped when the daughter replied.

'I'm very well, thank you, Mr Biscuit.'

He copped a double whammy. The deaf child clearly understood everything the head master said and then, as politely as one could be, called the gent by his nickname.

Well done, Em.

Connie worried that Emily's "mistake" might impact her brother's reference. She need not have worried as George arrived home after his last day at school with a note which thrilled his mother.

'Let me see,' protested Emily as her mother read George's reference and tears welled in her eyes.

The girl struggled with vocabulary and pronunciation. 'What does *exemplary* mean?' she asked.

George froze at his mother's response. 'Are you all right, Ma?' he asked. She replied by hugging her son as Emily became further stumped, this time with *exceptional*.

George didn't need a rooster or his mother's urging to rise and shine. Next morning, he was up with the lark, washed and dressed and entered the kitchen to discover the thickest piece of toast ever seen, and beside it, an egg standing to attention in his father's egg cup.

His mother fussed putting George a little on edge. Eating from his father's egg cup didn't help.

'Uncle Fred will be here any minute,' said Connie. 'Remember your manners, son, and I'm sure you'll get the job.'

'Yes Ma.'

'And take your dad's comb and fix your hair before you go in for the interview.'

'Yes Ma.'

Emily arrived yawning. The front door was knocked. Connie looked at her daughter. 'Door,' she mouthed and Emily skipped up the hall. Her squeals announced the arrival of the station master.

There are milestones in every family's life. This was a Miracle one.

'Morning all,' said Fred appearing with niece. 'How's the new railwayman?'

'I'm well, thank you, Uncle Fred.'

Connie's nerves appeared. 'Now Fred, don't go counting your chickens. Wait till his interview's finished.'

'We haven't got any chickens,' said Emily.

After breakfast, Connie and Emily led the long-serving railwayman and the would-be railwayman to the front door.

George hugged his mother and sister and they waved until uncle and nephew turned the corner. Fred Carmody spent his entire working life on the railways. As a childless bachelor, his sister's children were his surrogate offspring. If he could help George or Emily, nothing would be a trouble.

Chapter 3

Nepotism didn't come into it but having an uncle who was the top man at a top London station certainly helped. George got the job and thought his heart was fit to burst.

A station lad was the lowest of the low. They were the youngest, least educated and lowest paid employees. The one possible piece of good news being the promise if they worked hard and showed respect to all, and especially to the travelling public, they might, just might collect a tip or two.

None of that mattered as George tried on his uniform and, dressed to the nines, knocked on the door bearing the sign *Station Master*.

'Come in,' called Mr Carmody and the look on his face was priceless as his nephew did as ordered.

'Well, well, well,' said Fred coming from behind his desk extending his hand. 'Welcome to Liverpool Street Station, Master Miracle.'

'Thank you, sir,' said George tingling with excitement and trying but failing to match the strength of his uncle's grip.

'You look grand in your uniform, George. Kindly keep it like new.'

'I will.'

'And you should call me Mr Carmody when we're at work. Calling me Uncle Fred might encourage your workmates to give you a serious serve of sarcasm.'

'Yes sir ... I mean yes, Mr Carmody,' said George not being familiar with the word *sarcasm*.

Fred grinned and slapped his nephew on the back. 'Come and I'll give you a tour of your place of work.'

George produced his own grin as they went exploring.

The Great Eastern Railway Company operated out of Liverpool Street Station. Many years earlier, the GER used a station at Shoreditch, in a not-so-affluent part of London. The company wanted to attract smart and well-to-do passengers who worked in the financial hub of the city called the City of London, hence the move to Liverpool Street.

13

It was a big station, opening in 1874, and by 1900 was not only one of the biggest and busiest stations in London but in the world. It was built on the site of a hospital for the mentally ill and some called the station Bedlam. Below ground was another Liverpool Street station although this was part of the London Underground, and in time played host to a number of underground lines. Busy, busy, busy.

The above ground station towered over London streets. It looked impressive with its many platforms, serving both mainline and local stations, and stretching out beneath a mighty vaulted roof with what seemed acres of glass. The station master ruled over hundreds of staff and George Miracle was but a number in this mass of employees.

As uncle and nephew wandered around, George saw staff members nod or touch their forehead giving a salute to the boss. 'Good morning, sir,' became a constant greeting. Many staff members took note of the youngest employee being escorted by the boss.

Who's the new kid? Why is he with the SM?

They soon learnt.

A passenger train arrived as George and his uncle were on one of the mainline platforms. Smoke spurted and steam spat from the locomotive built in the nearby Stratford works. The train arrived from Norwich. The smell and sight of the engine gave George a burst of pleasure. He felt a tremor with the hairs on the back of his neck up and dancing. Was there steam in his blood?

Passengers threw open the heavy doors and were on their way even before the train stopped; late for work no doubt. Fred waited as scores of travellers hurried past. George wondered why he and his uncle stood in this spot forming a minor obstruction on the busy platform. Fred knew why and led his nephew to the locomotive.

'Now George, the passengers are the reason we come to work. Never forget we are their servants.' George nodded. 'But as important as they are, no-one is more important than two giants of the railway.'

Fred turned the boy to face the locomotive.

'Morning, Mr Carmody,' said the driver leaning out of the locomotive's cab and who needed a damn good wash. So did the loco.

'Good morning, Alf,' said the SM. 'Good run?'

'Not bad. There was a cow on the line by Eccles Road, and them gates at Ipswich are still not right.' He looked at George. 'Your boy?'

'Nephew,' replied Fred. 'Station lad starting his first day.'

'Welcome, son. I'm Alf and this 'ere big lump is Lord Fauntleroy better known as Shovels.' The fireman stepped forward and grinned. His teeth were not pristine but shone brightly in his blackened face.

George didn't know what to say. He muttered, 'Hello' as he stared at the driver and fireman. Both needed a scrubbing. Alf looked like he'd drawn white rings around his eyes with the rest of his face grey fading to black. Shovels was black all over with the filthiest hands on the Great Eastern Railway.

'Been on a footplate before, son?' asked the fireman.

George seemed to have lost his ability to speak. Shaking his head he muttered, 'No, sir.'

Alf beckoned to the boy who looked at his uncle and boss. Fred nodded but issued instructions to his nephew. 'Touch nothing and when you've finished driving the train to Norwich and back, report to the head porter, Mr Peters.' He winked at his nephew and left.

George thrilled to live every schoolboy's dream of riding, well standing, on a footplate and it was on his first day within 10 minutes of starting work. A tour of the loco's dials, levers, gauges and whatever was an experience he'd find hard to forget. The firebox door was opened and the heat made his eyes water. The enthusiasm, fun, knowledge and kindness of his new fellow workers, set his body aflame. When he thanked and said farewell to Alf and Shovels, a tiny thought slipped inside his head.

Thank you, Da. You dying has made all this happen. Trust me, I'll do my very best to make you and Ma proud.

Fred sent a telegram to his sister. It read, *The boy done good.*

Opening partly in fear, Connie read the message and put a hand to her face making Emily both curious and concerned. In her unusual speaking voice, she asked, 'What is it, Ma? Has someone else died?'

Connie felt pain but quickly recovered, shook her head and handed the telegram to her daughter.

Her reading skills were excellent, probably aided by her disability. She queried the wording. 'Is George the boy?'

'Yes and the message means he's now working on the railways.'

Emily smiled and clapped. 'Good old, George,' she cried and the word *old* hit her mother hard.

At night, around the kitchen table, with a supper of cold meat and bubble and squeak, George held the floor with spellbinding tales of his first day as a station lad. He could have been an entertainer.

His tour of the footplate sounded as if he actually drove the locomotive. Mother and sister wanted to interrupt and ask for more details but off went the youthful railwayman at full throttle.

Carrying the suitcase of a posh lady with a fox stole around her neck saw him earn his first tip—a penny. George made it sound as if he'd scored a fiver. Being able to explain the situation to befuddled passengers gave him an air of superiority. He demonstrated.

'Certainly, sir,' he said pointing. 'There's the Great Eastern Hotel. Turn around please and proceed through the ticket barrier.'

Connie purred and Emily's eyes shone. The man of the house was sounding forth and doing so in style.

When it was time to retire, George asked if he might stay up a little longer. 'I need to learn the station names, Ma. I need to become so good I can be promoted to lad porter.' His mother agreed to his staying up late. 'Will you test me, please?'

He handed his mother a piece of paper on which he'd listed stations then began to recite. As he rattled off the names with barely a hesitation, his mother struggled to keep up. He spoke with confidence and enthusiasm.

'London Cambridge Ely Thetford Wymondham and Norwich. Then London Brentwood Colchester Ipswich Haughley and Norwich.'

He looked at his mother in hope. 'How did I do?'

'Very good, George, and for your first day, you were excellent.'

He drew a deep breath and looked at his mother's face in the flickering lamp light. She couldn't read as well as her son. She didn't know the correct pronunciation of some of the stations. She did know her heart was racing. Her boy's enthusiasm pushed her to weep for joy. He'd stepped up since the crushing blow of losing his dad.

He was now the man of the house and his mother could not have been happier with her son.

Chapter 4

Christmas was always a happy time in the Miracle home. Alas, not so in 1910 with the beloved patriarch not there to carve the roast, make a speech, propose the loyal toast, and then tell a terrible Christmas joke and laugh the loudest at his own punch line.

This year his absence caused all sorts of pain. His absence was physical. They could sense his presence. The family could see him wearing his hat indoors and getting tipsy but never drunk. Uncle Fred and Grannie came round, and Mrs Entwhistle struggled in from next door. It took her longer to reach her front door than to reach the Miracle front door. Her house and the Miracle abode were a pair with adjacent front doors sharing the same porch. They were third-class cottages in the Noel Park estate in Wood Green, North London.

People reckoned it ironic because to build Liverpool Street station, they first demolished many workers' houses forcing the tenants to move to the Noel Park Estate, the one with thousands of houses but not a single pub.

One of the enjoyable aspects of this Christmas celebration was the success of George and his new job. The station lad had indeed done good. Did he get favourable treatment because his uncle was the top man? No, he would stand or fall on his own efforts. Did ambitious staff reckon currying favour with the SM's nephew might help them climb the ladder of promotion? Hardly, he was a lowly station lad.

Fred called upon the new man of the house to tell tales of dealing with passengers at Liverpool Street. George stood, rattled off his first experience, and beamed when greeted with applause. He was quickly becoming a man and one of importance. Off went George again.

'Thank you, Uncle Fred, I mean Mr Carmody.' That too triggered a laugh. 'How can I ever forget the large Yorkshire gent who grabbed me and complained? George slipped into a Yorkshire accent. "I've lost it, son, it's gone," he whined. I asked him what he'd lost.'

George again spoke with a rich Yorkshire accent. 'The wife bought it me at start of season. She'll kill me if I go home baht at.'

George spoke as himself. 'Well sir, if you'll describe what you've lost, I can help you look for it. The gent became even more agitated.' George mimicked the passenger.

'Eee by gum, it cum all way from Orstraylia.' The man held out his hand. 'It were 'ere, in me 'and, not five minute ago.' George continued as himself. 'Now I'd been told the customer is always right.'

'You mean always reet, lad,' added Fred only to be shushed.

'What colour was it, sir, I asked trying another method.'

The young Yorkshireman continued. 'Colour?' he gasped. 'Since when 'ave cricket umpires worn pink or purple caps?'

'I raised a finger like so.' George demonstrated. 'There's a white cricket cap tha on thee head, sah.'

'What? The passenger from Yorkshire blurted, reached up and grabbed the headpiece then fumbled in his waistcoat pocket and, would you believe it, gave me three pennies.'

'Thruppence?' chorused the adults in disbelief.

'I didn't know if it was for finding the cap never lost, or as a bribe to make sure I never repeated the tale.'

'Well you have now,' said Grannie and laughter exploded.

The mood seemed happy enough. From time to time Connie glanced towards the door expecting, hoping in vain, her husband would enter. And despite his outward bubbling nature, George too became the clown who cried on the inside. *I miss you, Da.*

'Tell us again about the feline hero of Platform 4,' said Fred.

George lost his enthusiasm. 'I've told it already, Uncle Fred; it must be at least three times.'

Emily gave an order. 'Tell it again.' She softened and begged. 'Please, George, please.'

He nodded. 'I was sweeping near the end of Platform 4 when I heard a scream. I rushed along the platform where a little girl, a bit younger than Emily ...'

'How much younger?' asked his sister who'd asked the same question every time she heard the tale.

'I don't know, Em.'

'Last time you said 6.'

George agreed. 'She was 6 and crying hysterically. Her kitten slipped from her grasp and dropped onto the tracks. The train was about to leave. I shouted to the guard telling him to hold the train!'

Emily knew the tale backwards, to her she was the little girl, and corrected her brother who chose to omit a significant part.

'Where was his whistle and green flag?' she demanded.

George sighed. 'His whistle was on his lips and his flag above his head, about to be waved.'

'Go on,' said younger sister.

'The guard heard me shout, and watched as I raced away from him along the platform, climbed up to the cab and yelled at the driver. Then I ran back to where people were gathered. We could see the kitten on the track beside a wheel of a carriage. It froze. I froze.'

George paused for breath. 'Go on,' urged Emily.

'One onlooker suggested a broom handle to poke the kitten and get it to move. The girl was horrified and I pointed out if it ran out the other side, the 14:38 Up was due in a minute and would squash the tiny animal.'

'Don't frighten the kitten,' said Emily suspending disbelief and living in the present.

'The guard arrived and I told him to hold my ankles. I knelt and he lowered me from the edge of the platform in the narrow space between the carriages and, after a few scary moments, I grabbed the kitten, and the guard lifted me back to the platform.'

Emily applauded. 'Tell us about the kiss,' she teased her brother.

George sighed. *Do I have to?* He did. 'The little girl gave me a big kiss, the kitten scratched me a second time, and the girl's mother gave me sixpence.'

Applause broke out and Emily adored this latest version of her favourite story. She surely would ask for it again.

'You're missing the best part,' said Fred.

George hesitated. 'All right, if I have to. The station lad in question was summoned to the office of the station master where he was congratulated in person then given a warning.' The word *warning* grabbed their attention. George imitated his uncle. 'If you continue to behave like you did today, young Miracle, you'll find yourself being promoted to lad porter.'

The sigh and laughter from everyone made the spirit of Christmas come alive in the small and crowded front room, the parlour. There were presents for all with Mrs Entwhistle again winning the prize for best recycled tat.

Having his own money, this was the first Christmas George could buy presents for his family although cash was not required for one gift. His present to Emily had a hidden back story.

He was sweeping behind a bench on Platform 1 when he discovered a child's toy. It looked like a homemade doll. It was small, well-worn and filthy needing a bath. George couldn't see any likely owner. He finished sweeping before taking the toy to Lost Property.

The porter in charge, 2 or 3 rungs higher than George, did a nice line in being surly.

'Wotcha want, kid?' snapped the toady Thomas Trembath.

'I found this child's doll, sir, and have brought it in as lost property.'

Trembath gave it a cursory glance. 'It ain't worth two farthings. Chuck it.'

'But sir, it might have great sentimental value to a child.'

'Sentimental?' scoffed the porter. 'I bet you can't even spell the word. No son, you can take your toffy words and your crappy doll and get lost.'

George persisted. 'Please sir, if you could hold it for a day or two in case a passenger comes asking, I'll be most grateful.'

Trembath glared at George, snatched the doll and tossed it on a shelf containing enough umbrellas and gloves to sink a ship. Some of the gloves were a pair but many were single and most of those were right-handed. Make of that what you will.

Three days later, George returned. 'You again,' sneered the toad.

'I wondered if the child's doll has been claimed,' asked George in a polite way.

Trembath turned, grabbed the doll and threw it at the station lad. Being soft, it bounced off George's chest. He picked it up and turned and left. It was not like George to omit his thanks but Trembath's rudeness deserved a nothing response.

George took the doll home, washed it, had his mother do some repairs then wrapped it and, on Christmas Day, gave it to his young sister. She cried. To her it was beautiful. Emily's reservoir, full to the brim with love for her father, now transferred her love to another man in her life, her big brother.

Sadly, George and his Uncle Fred soon found they shared something in common. Both lost a parent on a significant day. George's father died on George's birthday, and Fred and Connie's mother died on Jesus' birthday.

Christmas at the Miracle home went well. Despite it being the first without John Miracle, the family and Mrs Entwhistle felt warm inside and out. George helped Mrs Entwhistle to her bedroom in the terrace next door then helped his uncle guide his grandmother home.

At the end of the street with only 20 yards to go, Fred stopped. 'We'll be right from here, lad. You pop off home to your Ma and sister. Merry Christmas.'

'Thanks Uncle Fred and Merry Christmas,' said George who kissed his Grannie and walked home. It was the last time he would see her.

In the morning, Fred took her a cuppa first thing and found his mother dead in her bed. Her health was so-so and the doctor believed her heart simply wore out. In non-medical terms it's called old age.

Connie lost her husband and mother in the space of four months.

But the black clouds did have a silver lining. With Mrs Carmody laid to rest, Fred insisted the Miracles leave their rented home and move in with him. He lived in a fourth-class house which included a smaller second parlour used by Grannie as her bedroom, and being on the ground floor made it convenient with no stairs for Grandma.

Grannie's room was fine for Connie and the three bedrooms upstairs meant the children enjoyed their own room. This move brought much needed and welcome financial relief for Connie with an added benefit; Fred made sure the station lad was never late for work.

Spring lifted people's spirits. The four residents and Grannie's cat, Trixie, at 24 Darwin Road kept on with life. George worked hard as a station lad and the odd tip put a spring in his step. Connie earned a few bob taking in sewing and Emily found a retired teacher to help with her signing and tutoring. For George, life at Liverpool Street was never boring when funny and tricky situations came his way.

He spotted a woman struggling to board the 17:26 to Cambridge. She was a first-class passenger carrying many parcels bought on her day out in London.

'Can I help, madam?' asked George approaching the passenger.

Her face lit up. 'Oh thank goodness,' she replied and offered packages to the boy. He now struggled. They weren't heavy but odd shapes and numerous. He dared not drop anything in case the contents might break although hats and girdles don't usually shatter.

He followed the woman into the carriage. She found her seat but didn't sit choosing to direct the employee like a musical conductor.

'That one can go up there and those two round ones can sit there on the empty seat. I'll have that soft parcel on my lap.'

George could hardly position certain parcels until the woman placed her bottom on her seat. Outside, a fellow employee, Henry "Bruiser" Bentley, a chap with the loudest voice in Liverpool Street, bellowed. 'All aboard, train departing on Platform 2.'

George felt an urgent need to move and was about to do so when the woman gave additional orders. He couldn't dump the passenger's goods and scarper. Pointing at the largest parcel, she announced. 'This one should be up on the luggage rack but please do be careful.'

A whistle sounded, its shrill tone bouncing off any surface it could find. Carriage doors slammed shut. Bruiser nodded to the guard who did a semaphore-type routine with his green flag.

The hiss of steam from the loco was the final nail in George's coffin. He was off on the Down pass to Cambridge.

The woman, who remained standing, found the moving train more than she could handle and when the journey commenced, lost her balance falling back onto her seat. Thump. She squealed, George died, and the unwanted adventure began.

He settled the passenger, bade her farewell but was called back to receive the princely sum of one penny.

'For your trouble, young man,' she said.

George maintained the same polite response to any person who gave him a tip, be it a farthing or a florin. Waiting at the end of the carriage, in his mind, he tried listing the stations on the line. Bethnal Green Junction was next and then he reckoned Hackney Downs. He tried to think which would be more likely to offer him the quicker way back home. He took the first stop and soon boarded a London Up but all the way back to Liverpool Street, worried if anyone would have noted his absence. He worried in vain. He was not that important.

Another incident produced a much happier conclusion when in summer, passengers and staff sweltered on a particularly hot afternoon. Mind you people in Madras and Melbourne would consider this London weather cool.

George spotted a well-dressed older man with head slumped and seemingly about to faint. The station lad nipped around other sweating passengers and took hold of the man's arm.

'Would you like to sit, sir? There's a bench over here.'

The gent nodded, deeply grateful for such kind and practical assistance. With the man seated, George continued.

'You rest, sir, and I'll fetch you a glass of water.' A smile from the man and George took off. It was a cup not a glass and the passenger drank the lot. It helped his recovery.

'You are most kind, young man,' he said, 'and one good deed deserves another. Do you have a family?'

George hesitated for a moment then answered. 'I have a mother and a sister, sir, oh and an uncle.'

The man removed a business card and a fountain pen and wrote on the card before handing it to his helper.

'Here are four complimentary tickets to the matinee on Saturday at the Empire. Present this at the box-office and I hope you and your family enjoy the show. The music is by the American chap, Berlin, and the show is *Everybody's Doing It*.'

He managed to stand, again helped by George. 'Now I believe this is my train.' He raised his hat. 'Good afternoon, sir.'

As he walked with a slow but steady gait, George followed and opened the carriage door for the passenger.

'God bless you, young man,' he said and entered the carriage.

George pocketed the card and resumed his duties. Later, when not so busy, he studied the writing. On the back, in a wobbly scrawl he read, "4 comps DC Sat mat". He didn't then know comps meant complimentary tickets, that DC meant Dress Circle and Sat mat was Saturday matinee. The printing on the front of the card read:

Mr Randolf Moss
Producer
Moss Empires Ltd
55, Broadway, London

At night, the conversation around the kitchen table in the Carmody/Miracle household was one of non-stop excitement. Fred asked subtle questions wanting to know the background to the gift of the theatre tickets. His heart warmed at the way his nephew tackled his job. Emily and George would soon attend their first theatrical production, and Emily in particular couldn't stop talking.

The show proved a brilliant adventure with all four guests re-living it over and over. Emily seemed to experience the music through her body and thrilled at the dancing and costumes.

George entered his second year at Liverpool Street, and one afternoon a young man stopped him on the platform.

'Are you a porter, boy?' asked the man.

'I'm working to become one, sir. Can I be of assistance?'

'You can. I need you to distract a person.'

Immediately George worried. There were criminals in the station, in every station. Pickpockets were good at distracting victims making the theft of items so much easier.

'I'm not sure what you mean, sir.'

The man removed a coin. 'Here, I'll give you a shilling if you do exactly as I ask.'

The offer of a shilling shocked the boy. His mother could make good use of that coin. It would mean a selection of food for the family with perhaps change left over. He thought. *But what's the catch?*

'You are most generous, sir, but first I need to know what you plan to do. The station is a busy place and any disturbance to the passengers is not allowed.'

'I understand,' said the man. 'But what if I promise not to break a single railway company rule or a single law of the land?'

George continued to worry. Agreeing to something he couldn't control might jeopardize his position or prevent his promotion to lad porter. The man held out the shilling. George weakened.

'Very well, sir but what am I required to do?'

'As I said, distract a passenger. I want you to engage in conversation with a person for about half a minute.'

'How, sir? I mean what should I do?'

The man snapped. 'Oh don't be so contrary. Think of an interesting topic and engage the person in conversation. Talk about the weather or the train timetable, anything. Well? Will you do it?'

George nodded and the man relaxed. 'Come with me.' He led George behind a newspaper kiosk. 'See the young lady with the large white hat?' George spotted her. 'Distract her for 30 seconds. Now go.'

George was pushed out amongst the passengers. Without looking back he approached his target. He stopped beside the lady and coughed politely. She was looking for someone and ignored George.

'Pardon me, Miss,' said the station lad and the woman turned to him. 'There has been a delay in the next train to Cambridge and as you are waiting on this platform, the company wishes to apologise for any inconvenience.' Two lies.

'But I'm not going to Cambridge.'

'Oh,' said George desperate for the 30 seconds to expire. 'Well there has been a minor accident at Tottenham and in fact all trains will be delayed for at least ten minutes.' Two more lies.

Now he was lying without thinking, and as he tried desperately to keep the woman distracted, the 15:29pm from Tottenham pulled into the adjoining platform.'

She pointed to the information board then to the newly-arrived train, and then finally to George. 'Are you unaware of the workings at your own station?' she asked.

George failed. She was distracted but now she was annoyed. Angry passengers make complaints and George could well receive a black mark against his name. Black marks delay promotion and even bring on dismissal. Before he could say another word, the whirl of bagpipes burst out on the platform. Everyone turned to look at the source of the distinctive Scottish sound.

From behind the piper appeared two wee lassies in full highland dancing outfits. One carried a beautiful bouquet of flowers and the other a tray with an ice bucket holding a bottle of champagne and two glasses. The musical party came closer stopping a few feet in front of George and the passenger. The woman in the big white hat forgot all about the station lad. Curious passengers gawped with many milling around.

From behind a group of interested passengers, George's man appeared, dropped on one knee and held up a small box within which rested a glittering diamond ring.

George stared spellbound as the woman with the big hat gasped.

'My darling girl,' said the man, 'will you do me the great honour of becoming my wife?'

The woman could only nod and shed tears as the man rose and kissed his sweetheart. Passengers clapped and cheered. The flowers were presented, the champagne cork popped, and George needed to react fast as a shilling spun through the air heading his way.

The happy husband-to-be sent a letter to the station master mentioning the unnamed station lad who helped with the proposal. Instead of a black mark, George copped a commendation.

The assistant station master entered Fred's office holding the letter from the budding bridegroom, a Mr Hamish McGregor. 'Just arrived in the latest post concerning a certain nephew of yours,' said the ASM, Jack Rogers.

Fred read the missive and smiled inside. 'The boy done good.'

'He has to be made up to lad porter, Fred. He's polite, works hard, knows his timetables and he's never late.'

'He doesn't have a choice. If he's still in bed when I get up, all hell breaks loose.'

'I know he's family, Fred, but what lad with his record wouldn't get promoted to lad porter?' Fred hesitated. He hated nepotism 'How about you take a day off and visit a few SMs down the line? I'll do the business with George, and with you not here, he'll feel he earned it.'

Fred took his time, nodded and spoke. 'I'll go visiting tomorrow.'

Chapter 5

From station lad to lad porter was hardly a big promotion but to George and his family it felt wonderful. For the boy, now a strapping teenager, it meant the world. The fact his uncle was out of London when the announcement was made only added to his pride. His mother and sister now considered George as important as Uncle Fred but then again they were biased.

'It's a little more money, and I can aim for a promotion to porter.'

'What's a pronotion?' mispronounced Emily. Her mother corrected her and explained. 'George is doing well in his job.'

'Will he be the station master when Uncle Fred dies?'

A swift correction was needed as the front door opened and the SM arrived.

'Evening all,' he said hanging his cap on the hook behind the kitchen door. 'Now a little bird told me about a promotion today.' The uncle extended his hand and forced the nephew to step forward. They shook hands for a long time. 'Congratulations lad porter George Miracle. Richly deserved and may it be the first of many promotions.'

'Thank you, Mr Carmody,' said George catching the gleam in the SM's eye.

'He's not Mr Carmody?' responded Emily. 'He's Uncle Fred.'

'I am indeed,' said Fred giving his niece a hug. 'Now what have you been up to today, young lady? I want a full report on your life to date.'

Connie served the meal, Emily spoke and didn't stop, and George sat and purred thinking about his new title. Life was okay with this family, no, better than okay.

George continued his love affair with the railways and those who worked thereon. He made friends with some and ignored those who ignored him or treated him with disrespect. As 1911 came to a close, the lad porter continued to serve the Greater Eastern Railway Company and their passengers with professionalism and pride.

Over supper one night early in 1912, Fred issued a request. 'Tomorrow morning, George, before you come to the station, I want you to collect my fountain pen please. It's been repaired.'

'Yes Uncle.'

'The shop's in Kensington High Street. Here's the receipt.'

Next morning George maneuvered his way around London and arrived at Kensington High Street, a busy place especially during business hours. Today it was bedlam, akin to a war zone. George stood on the pavement and gawped. *What is happening?*

There were police officers, firemen, pedestrians staring, and builders, tradesmen and shopkeepers all in conversation, with everyone as shocked as George. Many were angry.

He spoke to a constable. 'Excuse me officer, what has happened?'

'It's them suffragettes; hundreds of 'em. They've only gone and smashed more than 200 windows. And why? So women can have the vote. What would women know about politics and government?'

George thanked the constable for the facts although not for the criticism, and went in search of the stationer's shop. He reached the boarded up premises. It's difficult to trade with your display window smashed.

'Come back tomorrow,' said the shopkeeper dealing with a glazier.

The suffragette protests continued. Westminster Abbey suffered minor damage when a bomb fizzed yet scared the life out of those inside. Another bomb exploded, this time in the male toilet at Oxted railway station in Surrey. It too proved a bit of a dud.

But burning the words *Votes for Women* into the grass of expensive golf clubs with their hundreds of male members, and setting fire to the contents of letter boxes provoked outrage.

Some protests did real damage. The pavilion of the attractive cricket ground in Tunbridge Wells went up in smoke, and a shocking fatality occurred at Epsom racecourse when a suffragette ran onto the track during a race and was killed by a horse owned by the King.

On many occasions, suffragettes travelled by train. They held rallies with hundreds attending. George and other railway staff never knew if the women from whom they collected tickets or helped on and off trains were leaving to firebomb a church or force their way into the House of Commons or No. 10 Downing Street.

Two suffragettes once boxed themselves up in a parcel and had friends post the living correspondence to the residence of the Prime Minister. They couldn't fit through the letter opening and were returned to sender.

From angry suffragettes, the British and certainly Londoners got a foretaste of violence and conflict with more to follow.

In April 1912 when a passenger boarding the Titanic asked a ship's officer, 'Will this ship sink?' his reply was simple.

'Madam, not even God can sink this ship.'

No-one ever laid claim to making such a statement, and if it was uttered, the speaker probably joined the masses who slipped beneath the waves. And anyway, God was not required as an iceberg did the trick aided by the captain's rash decision concerning speed.

The news of the Titanic's demise rocked the world. George saw the newspaper posters as he came to work, now as a lad porter.

TITANIC SINKS

All London talked about it—passengers, railway workers, the royal family and the man on the Clapham omnibus—everyone including the Miracle family.

On the day after the terrible news broke, George was taking a parcel to the parcel office when something caught his eye. On a sunny morning, under the mighty glass roof at the Liverpool Street Station, a gleaming object lay almost hidden beneath a bench on Platform 1.

Placing the parcel on the bench, the boy knelt and picked aside a cigarette packet which the wind deposited beside the shiny object. Almost hidden behind the rubbish, George picked up a beautiful pocket-watch with its chain intact. The golden timepiece and chain seemed to George to be expensive. So what thief would discard his ill-gotten gain? What owner would hide his valuable object? And how did the object get under the bench in the first place?

George collected his parcel and pocket-watch and headed first to the room for parcels and then to Lost Property. There his bête noire lounged behind the counter. Thomas Trembath refined his surly attitude over the years.

'Not you again,' he scoffed. 'Found more useless tat have we?'

Without speaking, George carefully removed the watch and chain from his jacket and placed it on the counter. Trembath's attitude changed in an instant. He studied the watch.

'Where did you steal this from?'

Wary of possible repercussions, George still gave the young man a taste of his own rudeness, 'Well if I nicked it, I'd hardly be handing it in as lost property.'

Trembath glared at the lad porter and reached for an official form. 'Fill this out,' he snapped and tossed a pencil towards George.

With form complete, Trembath inspected it then unlocked a safe and placed the watch inside. The safe door closed tight.

'Wotcha waiting for; a medal or a chest to pin it on? Get back to station sweeping, Sonny Jim.'

George understood, still hated the bully, and left without speaking. He'd never discussed the surly Lost Property porter with Uncle Fred and decided to maintain this silent routine. He kept his powder dry.

The next day, in his office, the assistant station master found himself dealing with a young woman close to tears. 'Now then Miss, please take a seat and compose yourself, and start from the beginning.'

Between sobs and dabbing of eyes, she explained. 'I bought a beautiful pocket-watch with a gold chain for my fiancé as a wedding gift, and now it's lost or been stolen. I remember looking at it here at the station while waiting for my train. I put it back in its black velvet bag and then in my handbag,' she said holding up her bag. 'But when I arrived home, it was gone. I thought I might have dropped it in the street. I searched everywhere. I wasn't robbed and no pickpocket could have reached it inside this bag. I don't know what I'm going to do. Our wedding is on Saturday week.' Her tears flowed again.

The ASM didn't like her chances of ever seeing such a valuable item again but naturally tried to help. He led her outside to a bench in the corridor. 'Please wait here, Miss, while I investigate further.'

As he headed out into the station the thought, *a waste of time* settled in his mind. Whoever found the watch, if dishonest, would have pocketed the timepiece immediately meaning, for the young woman, it and her money were gone. But if found by someone honest at this station, it would be in Lost Property.

The ASM headed for the obvious place to investigate. The surly Metcalf would always address a senior member of staff with the utmost respect. He reached for the log book listing items received.

'Pocket watch you say, Mr Rogers?'

'Yes, with a gold chain attached.'

'I'm sure I would have remembered such an item, sir.' Metcalf ran a finger down the page then onto the next one. 'Pocket watch, pocket watch, pocket watch.' He stopped. 'Sorry, sir, no such item.'

The ASM suspected same. 'If such a watch is handed in this week, I want to know about it immediately.'

'Yes sir,' said Metcalf revelling in his Uriah Heep persona.

Rogers went to the canteen, the room where staff took their break to drink tea, eat their lunch and relax. The ASM wrote a brief note about the missing pocket watch, and pinned the note to the staff noticeboard. He returned to his office and informed the young woman the precious pocket watch could not be found at Liverpool Street. He asked for more details including a description of the watch and where it was purchased. She gave the information but left dejected giving up all hope of ever seeing the gift again.

Later, George passed the staff noticeboard and read the pocket watch message. He knocked on the ASM's door.

'Excuse me Mr Rogers but I found a gold pocket watch and chain yesterday, and took it to Lost Property.'

Rogers called the boy in and bade him close the door. 'When and where did you find it?' George answered naming the spot which was where the distraught woman said she last remembered seeing the timepiece.

'Was there any carry bag by the watch?'

'No sir. I was rather taken by the beauty of the timepiece.'

'Describe the watch and chain in as much detail as possible.'

George did, Mr Rogers took notes and then sent the lad porter back to work while he, the ASM paid another visit to Lost Property. Mr Surly slipped back into his Dickensian character role.

'Metcalf, please check your records again. A staff member informs me a gold pocket watch was found on the station and handed in here yesterday.'

The porter shook his head and reached for his log. 'I'll search again, Mr Rogers, but I doubt it's in the book, and, as I said, I would certainly have remembered such an expensive object.' He looked long and hard then stopped. 'No, as I suspected, there's nothing, sir.'

'Lad porter Miracle is certain he found a watch and gave it you.'

'Ah, well there's your answer, Mr Rogers. Miracle has a habit of finding and keeping so-called lost property.'

Alarm bells sounded for the ASM. The nephew of his boss recently gained promotion, albeit minor. Members of the travelling public had written to the SM praising the work of George Miracle. Now comes an allegation the boy is a thief, allegedly guilty of the most serious and sackable charge of stealing.

'Kindly explain,' said Rogers.

'Well he stole a child's doll not so long ago. I saw him with it and challenged him. Miracle reckoned it was of no value so kept the doll.'

'And you say you challenged him?'

'Of course, sir, but most of us lower ranks see how the lad porter Miracle uses his position as the SM's nephew to do as he likes.'

The ASM paused, thinking. *Is this the boy I know? And if the stealing property claim is true, his career will be ruined and his uncle devastated.* 'Say nothing of this to anyone, no-one.'

Metcalf nodded. 'Of course I won't, Mr Rogers.'

The ASM departed in a hurry and Metcalf smirked.

A station lad was summoned to find George and have him report to Mr Rogers. The ASM worried. He wanted the truth but then again he didn't because if the lad stole lost property, any property, he'd be instantly dismissed, station master's nephew or not.

George arrived wondering why. He soon knew. 'I've been to Lost Property, George,' said Rogers, 'and there is no report of a gold pocket watch being handed in yesterday or at any time this month.'

George couldn't speak. His short career in the Railways taught him a few home truths. Crooks and ne'er-do-wells were alive and well in busy London locations with Liverpool Street Station a hotspot.

He knew what he'd done; found the watch, handed it in and filled out a report. The ASM probed.

'I did find and hand in a gold pocket-watch and chain, Mr Rogers.'

'Tell me what happened in the Lost Property room.'

George explained.

'This form you completed,' asked Rogers, 'was it in a pad?'

'No, it was a single sheet, sir.'

'And what happened to the watch?'

'Mr Metcalf placed it in a box then locked it in the safe, sir.'

'And then you left?'

George nodded, his heart beating faster.

'Have you ever found anything on railway property and kept it?'

Now George felt sick. His father often impressed the importance of always telling the truth. George wished his Da hadn't made such a point because confession time now loomed large.

'I have, sir.'

Rogers too felt sick. 'It's a sackable offence, George.'

The boy fought hard to stop tears breaking free.

'Might I be able to resign, sir, rather than be sacked?'

'What have you stolen?'

George told him. 'It was a child's doll, sir, ripped and filthy. I think it'd been in the weather for a week or more. I took it to Lost Property, and Mr Metcalf called it rubbish and told me to throw it away.'

'He didn't accept it?'

'He did after I pressed him but when I went back to see if it was claimed, he laughed and threw it at me.' George paused. Now he confessed. 'I took the doll home, sir. My mother repaired and washed it and I gave it to my sister as a Christmas present.'

Rogers felt a thousand times better. 'Resume your duties, say nothing of this to anyone, and report back here in one hour.'

George added confusion to his heartache. *Am I sacked? Am I about to be sacked? Do I come back so Uncle Fred can be here to witness my execution?*

George returned an hour later. The ASM collected his coat and cap. 'We're going out. Follow me.'

They left the above ground station with George none the wiser. They descended and caught the Central Line on the Underground. George remained nervous tasting bile.

If I'm being dismissed, why am I travelling around London with my uncle's second-in-command?

As the train pulled into Bond Street, the ASM spoke briefly. 'Out here.' They took the stairs to the surface and turned into Bond Street. Only then did Mr Rogers speak.

'I want to discover the truth, George. I've not mentioned any of this business to your uncle. I need you to observe and say nothing unless I ask you to. Do you understand?'

George did and he didn't. 'Yes sir.'

As they walked along Bond Street, the ASM looked at shop numbers. He stopped. 'In here.' The uniformed railwaymen entered.

The jewellery shop sold expensive items. George would never be a customer. 'Good afternoon, gentleman,' said a smiling, impeccably dressed attendant. 'How may we be of service?'

George wondered who he meant by "we".

'Good afternoon,' said Rogers. 'We are employees of the Great Eastern Railway Company at Liverpool Street. Yesterday a passenger informed us she lost a pocket watch she purchased from your shop.'

The gent stiffened and his teeth disappeared. The word "shop" stuck in his craw. Emporium, definitely and establishment yes but shop? Never. 'I see,' was his curt reply.

Rogers handed him a slip of paper. 'These are the customer details. Are you able to confirm the purchase please?'

'If the watch has been stolen, surely it's a matter for the police.'

The ASM kept calm and refused to reveal the reason he and George were standing in the shop. 'The watch has been lost, sir. If you prefer, we can report the matter to the police and have them call on you for confirmation.'

George admired the answer. The gent, he would have hated the word shopkeeper, gave a silent snort and examined his bookwork. He sniffed. 'A person by that name purchased a gold pocket watch and chain two days ago.' He paused. 'Now, is that all?'

It was an impolite way of saying, "Get out and never darken my door again".

'Thank you,' replied Rogers maintaining a reasonable manner. 'If the watch was found by a dishonest person, where might it have been taken?'

Goodness me! Asking a reputable jeweller to provide the name of a fence was akin to a slap in the face for the purveyor of exquisite items.

He adopted a suitably snooty expression. 'We have no knowledge of such individuals. Good day.'

He omitted the word "gentlemen" and turned away. Rogers led George outside. In the street, the lad porter spoke.

'Do I understand, Mr Rogers, you are not convinced I stole the pocket watch?'

'I am still investigating, George. Now, let's go back to the station.'

They set off towards the Underground but after a few yards stopped when they heard a voice behind them.

'Excuse me.' George and Rogers turned to see a young man, well-dressed but without a suitcoat, approaching. 'Gentlemen, I was in the back of the shop and heard you asking about a fence. I may be able to help.' The investigators stood fascinated.

The young man gave them a name and address, apologised then turned and ran.

Rogers looked at George. 'This way, young man, the game's afoot.'

The address was in a shady part of the city, and the pawnbroker gave himself airs and graces by calling himself a silversmith. A few old cups and saucers and a motley collection of trinkets adorned his front window. This would never pass muster in Bond Street. The railwaymen entered, their arrival announced by a tinkling bell.

From the rear of the shop an oddly-dressed man, going to seed, entered with the filthy cuffs and collar of his shirt begging for a wash.

'Good day, gentlemen. What can I do for you?'

Rogers gambled pretending he knew certain facts. 'We're here to collect the gold watch our colleague Metcalf gave you to sell yesterday.' The pawnbroker froze and Rogers knew his hunch worked. Wearing GER uniforms reinforced their position.

The pretend silversmith's voice changed. 'Who are you?'

'You know we work with your friend. You know Metcalf stole the watch and wants a minimum price meaning you haven't paid him anything—yet. He'll be up before the magistrate in the morning as will you unless we get the watch here and now.'

'I know the Law,' sneered the pawnbroker. 'If a person loses a gold watch and later finds it in a pawnbroker's business, the matter must be referred to the magistrate. The police can do nothin'.'

'But we can. Metcalf is cooked and will name you as his accomplice. Give us the watch and your name will never be mentioned. It's your choice, Mister, only you must decide now.'

The pawnbroker took the easy way out and fetched the watch and chain. Rogers examined it noting the markings to those provided by the young woman. He turned to George.

'Is this it?'

George knew. 'Yes sir, definitely.'

Rogers addressed the pawnbroker. 'You may have lost a supplier of stolen goods but you've saved yourself a stretch in prison.'

Out in the street, Rogers offered his hand which George shook. 'I apologize, George. I should never have doubted your word.'

George didn't speak. He couldn't but then no words were necessary. The look of relief on his face said it all.

Back at Liverpool Street, Rogers took the lad porter to see the boy's uncle. When the story was explained, the station master struggled to control his pride. With love, he hugged his nephew.

George was asked to wait outside. The SM and ASM discussed the matter and then George was invited to join the group heading to Lost Property. The ASM led two constables with George tagging along in the guard's van, so to speak.

The look on Metcalf's face was worth a photograph. The ASM didn't mince his words.

'We've recovered the watch you stole, the watch the lad porter Miracle delivered to you two days ago. Your fence co-operated. You are now dismissed from the Great Eastern Railway Company and these police officers would like a word.' George watched as the stunned thief suffered in silence. 'Oh, and good riddance.'

The police moved in taking an arm apiece. Metcalf froze. But there was more. The ASM continued.

'Normally a new staff member learns the ropes by spending time with the one departing but in your case, Metcalf, that won't be possible.' Rogers indicated George. 'Meet George Miracle, the youngest acting porter ever to be put in charge of Lost Property.'

It was hard to tell who looked more stunned; George at his new promotion and responsibility or Metcalf at his arrest.

The owner of the watch discovered a seam in her handbag had come adrift allowing the soft bag with its watch and chain to slip out unseen. The bag blew away. But all's well that ends well and she delighted in giving her fiancé the gift to celebrate their wedding.

Chapter 6

George did well working in Lost Property. His uncle's heart copped jabs of pleasure when he saw how his growing nephew became such a reliable and knowledgeable employee.

But happiness in the Miracle home and elsewhere would soon be thrown into disarray as politics in Britain and elsewhere turned nasty. Of course conflict has always existed, and wars began once tempers, stone throwing and revenge were invented.

But up until 1914 there had never been a worldwide conflict; wars yes, world wars, no. That was about to change.

With Britain declaring war, the suffragettes put aside their campaigning for the franchise, and instead worked hard to help the war effort any way they could. They would return post war.

And another change would involve George Miracle and his chosen profession. In World War One, the railways became busier than ever.

Violence begets violence. Different groups argue about borders. Some reckon they "own" a parcel of land. Others demand the return of land they consider stolen. Action causes *reaction*. You steal my country, you kill my countrymen, then I will return fire and with interest.

In 1914 a number of great European powers rattled sabres. Britain, France, Russia, Germany, Bulgaria, Italy, and Austria-Hungary were the main pugilists ready to enter the ring and slug it out.

Negotiation and appeasement failed and the stage was set for an almighty conflict. Several young Bosnian Serb assassins armed themselves and prepared to strike. Initially they made a mess of it.

It's hard to believe World War One kicked off because a chauffeur turned right instead of left.

The future Emperor of Austria and his wife were being driven from one Sarajevo event to another when his car went the wrong way. 'Reverse!' was the cry and in so doing, the car stalled. A teenage Bosnian Serb assassin, not expecting his target, panicked when the intended victim's car stopped a few feet away.

'My God, it's him!' gasped the killer, drawing his revolver as he raced onto the road and fired. The Archduke and his wife were killed and World War One began. The assassin died in jail from tuberculosis while the chauffeur found it hard to get a job reference.

Sitting around the kitchen table in Wood Green, North London, Uncle Fred, his sister, nephew and niece discussed the news.

'What's it mean, Fred? Is Britain really at war?' asked Connie.

'We are. But I heard military chaps at the station today say it'll all be over by Christmas.'

'Well don't you get any ideas about joining up,' said his sister.

'What's joining up?' asked Emily now nearly 12.

'Never you mind,' said her mother who turned to George. 'And as for you, young man, you are far too young to even think about being a soldier.'

Fred tried to calm the situation. 'The boy and I are going nowhere. The government will need the railways more than ever now. We'll be as busy as bees.' He spoke to George. 'You concentrate on your next promotion.'

George said nothing. His role of acting porter with responsibility suited him well. It meant more status and hopefully a long and successful career. Could he ever rise to the heights of his Uncle Fred and become a station master?

As for this new war, this world war, the men Fred overheard on the platform were hopelessly, woefully wrong, and the over-by-Christmas war still had a long, long, long way to go. This war changed the station, the country and its people.

The number and type of passengers using major stations such as Liverpool Street boomed. Men, even young men barely two years older than George Miracle, gathered on platforms in uniform and carrying their kit. They came from Norfolk, Suffolk, Essex and Cambridgeshire before heading off to other stations and trains. The acting porter watched them.

The soldiers smoked, drank cups of char, laughed, and said goodbye to family and friends. George continued to observe. Young women, he guessed to be sweethearts or wives, were often in tears. Their menfolk were off to war. Would they ever return? Was this "it'll all be over by Christmas" malarkey true?

When the war began in 1914, the British Army numbered about 400,000 men. By the time the carnage was called off in 1918, the Army numbered 10 times that figure. Many, most of those soldiers needed rail transport, and George's busy life became busier.

He didn't work solely in Lost Property and would spend time on the platforms, collecting tickets, giving advice and carrying things. One day, he watched passengers disembarking. From behind, even on a busy platform, he heard a distinctive voice.

'Hey, George! Over here.'

He turned to see a beautifully-dressed, middle-aged gent wiggling a finger. George moved to him.

'Good afternoon, sir. May I be of assistance?'

'Indeed you may,' said the man in a broad American accent. 'I need my luggage transferred to the Great Eastern Hotel. Where is it?'

As George loaded the gent's cases on a trolley, he explained the nearby location of the hotel.

'It's right behind you, sir.' The visitor spun around and saw the huge lettering on the front of the hotel—GREAT EASTERN HOTEL.

'Oh, gotcha, now I see.

'If you'd kindly follow me, sir,' said George and set off.

'Okay, George, take it away.'

The acting porter set off with his passenger close behind. 'May I ask you one thing, sir?' asked George.

'Sure thing, George, fire away.'

'How did you know my name?'

'Your name?'

'Yes sir. I'm George but how did you know?'

'But I don't know your name. I wouldn't know you from Adam.'

'Yet you called me George, sir, my name.'

The man laughed and stopped. George stopped.

'Back in the States, young man, we call porters who work on our railroads, George. They're all referred to as George.'

The real George smiled and again set off pushing the trolley. 'Do you think I might get a job in America, sir?'

The gent hesitated. 'You might do but you'd be the odd man out.' George looked puzzled. 'You might have to change your skin colour.'

George pondered the comment and, with the doorman holding

open the hotel door for him, picked the cases off the trolley and followed the American visitor into the lobby.

'Now George called George,' he said, 'I ain't sure about your English money but I hope this here will do.' He handed a florin to the lad who smiled.

'You are most kind, sir.' He saluted. 'I hope you enjoy your stay in our country.'

And then the English George called George almost skipped his way across the concourse and back into the station. *A florin; wow!*

He headed to Platform 1 where a group of soldiers stood together smoking. George didn't know much about ranks within the army but these men looked like officers. They wore ties and caps rather than hats, and their uniforms were suit-like and smart.

Standing apart from this group was another soldier. George spotted him. No officer's cap for him. With his kitbag and rifle, the young man stood away from the edge of the platform as if hiding.

George wondered. *Why is this chap alone? Is he lost?* Their eyes met and George found himself drawn to the soldier. 'Good day, sir. Can I be of assistance?' asked the acting porter.

The soldier spoke in a refined, educated voice but appeared humble even worried. 'Thank you, I'm fine and it's damned civil of you to ask.'

'I take it you're off to fight.'

The man nodded. 'I've enlisted, done my training and my unit is leaving for France.'

'You won't get a train from here for the south coast, sir. Depending on where you're going, St Pancras or Waterloo would be your best bet if you're catching a troop train, sir.'

'Thank you, I know those facts. I popped in to use the gents and am waiting for my officer colleagues to make a move.' He nodded towards the group.

George sensed the soldier was troubled but knew asking about it to be none of his business.

'If there is anything else I can help you with, sir, please ask.'

'Thank you, again, most kind.' George smiled and turned to leave. He took two steps before the man called.

'Wait.' George stopped. The soldier moved away from the officers forcing George to follow. 'There is a task you could do for me.' George waited. 'Can you tell my family I'm off to France?'

'Of course but could you not do so yourself? As a complete stranger, I may not be believed. I can show you where to send a telegram or to make a telephone call.'

The soldier looked sullen and shook his head. 'Thank you but if I did tell them they would move heaven and earth to stop me.' He paused. 'I think one or two of those officers over there might know me or my parents. I'm lying low so they don't see me heading off to the Underground. Once my troop train departs, I'll be indebted if you would call at my parents' home and give them the news.' He reached into his pocket and removed a small leather wallet. 'I'll pay you of course.'

George raised a hand. 'Please, sir, there is no need. But are your parents here in London?'

'Yes, in Hampstead, a short walk from Hampstead Heath station. Here's the address.' The man handed George a card with an address.

'I can't today, sir. I don't finish my shift until 7pm so tonight would be too late. But I'm not working first thing tomorrow so could call in the morning on my way to work.'

The young man grabbed George's hand and shook it vigorously. 'I am in your debt, sir. You are a gentleman, and I owe you a drink.'

George wondered what he'd let himself in for. 'Is there anything special I should say?'

'Only what I've told you but I should warn you my parents will not be best pleased and will ask many questions. My mother in particular will be angry. You see I have a place at Oxford and she wants me to take it now. They agreed to me enlisting but only if I took my degree first before going to war. It's their way of keeping me at home.'

George became fascinated with the tale. 'My name is George.'

'Snap,' said the man as they shook hands. 'George Carruthers.'

'George Miracle,' replied the acting porter.

'I do believe George Miracle we are kindred spirits. Am I right? Do you wish to serve your country?'

George's heart thumped. 'I do but can't enlist, I'm only 16.'

'But your work on the railways is essential, vital. You are doing your duty on the home front and together we can help Britain win this damn war.'

George felt inspired. He admired this young man who seemed but two or three years his senior. 'I will visit your parents in the morning.'

'Excellent. By the time you spill the beans, so to speak, I'll be on my way across the Channel. And again, thank you for your kindness.'

They looked at one another. Neither knew what to say. George Miracle spoke. 'Then I'll let you get on and wish you good luck and most of all, good health.'

For the rest of his shift, George kept thinking about his namesake in uniform, with rifle in hand, setting off overseas to fight and to kill or be killed.

Could I do that? I've never even fired a gun. If I enlist, what will my mother and uncle say? And will this war really be over by Christmas?

He said nothing about his chance meeting with the youthful soldier. At home, over supper, he asked the station master how long the war would last.

'I have no idea, George.'

Connie jumped in. 'Stop asking about the war, and stop thinking about enlisting. I've told you before, George Miracle. We need you here at home.' Her look left George in no doubt.

'What's enlisting?' asked Emily.

Fred tried to explain and Emily went back to her fried potato.

George needed a decent lie, something believable. Going to work so early when his shift didn't start for hours looked suspicious. His Uncle left first thing leaving George to be grilled by his mother. He lied.

'I promised an elderly lady I would call to say her lost parcel is found and ready for collection.'

'That's not your job,' replied his inquisitive mother.

'She promised me a shilling, Ma, and you have always told me how every penny counts.'

He kissed Emily and his mother and set off. He took the train to Hampstead Heath. In the summer, this station became very busy, especially on weekends, with families arriving to visit the heath.

From the station he set off and asked a local for directions. Soon he arrived at the home of George Carruthers' parents. George Miracle peered through the garden to a massive house in the distance.

Having lived his entire life in a terrace in the relatively new estate of Noel Park in North London, George's experience of massive houses with massive gardens came to nothing.

The front gates for a carriage or motor car were monumental. To open the single gate for pedestrians, he needed to put his back into it.

Then, once inside the property, the garden proved a challenge. Following a path he set off. A packed lunch might come in handy.

A man's voice from behind the bushes scared the life out of him.

'Where do you think you're going?'

George froze. He looked in the direction of the voice then stepped back as the bushes parted and a huge man with terrifying whiskers appeared.

'Good morning, sir,' said George coming in peace.

'Well?' boomed the man. His question remained unanswered.

'I've a message for Mr and Mrs Carruthers from their son, George.'

His reply stopped the man who was dressed like a gardener, with collar and tie of course, and who held a large pair of pruning shears which George imagined as a weapon.

'It ain't Mr and Mrs but Lord and Lady Carruthers so even if you are who you says you are, at least get their names right.'

'Thank you, sir, and I apologize. May I continue?'

The gardener sniffed then set off. 'This way,' he grunted.

He led George through the garden and arrived at an immaculate area of lawn with croquet hoops to one side and a tennis court on t'other. A water fountain sat centre stage gurgling in the key of C.

At the rear of the house, the gardener opened a door and yelled. 'You there, Mares?'

Mary the housekeeper appeared and the interloper was discussed in the third person.

'Come with me,' said Mary, and the acting porter, having wiped his boots on a door mat which he would have needed more than a year's salary to buy, took a tour of the mansion. It screamed old money.

Having traipsed along two corridors, George entered a third and stopped beside a door. 'Wait here,' said Mary and disappeared. Moments later she returned, indicated with her head and gave a command. 'In there.'

George thought he was dreaming. All this grandeur and palaver

43

just for a simple message. *Why didn't I send a telegram?* He entered the magnificent library and saw who he assumed to be the parents of young George Carruthers, standing and staring at him. They looked anxious, angry and expectant all at once.

Lady Carruthers wore the trousers, literally. 'You know my son?'

George's railway training kicked in. 'Good morning, sir and madam,' he said. 'My name is George Miracle and I work for the Great Eastern Railway Company employed at Liverpool Street station.'

Her Ladyship lost whatever patience she once possessed. George thought sparks came from her lips. 'How do you know my son?'

His Lordship spoke in a softer and far more restrained manner. 'Let him speak, my dear.'

Cynthia Carruthers sat fuming but took her hubby's advice. 'Go on,' she spoke looking straight at George.

Having been wrong with titles before, he wasn't sure if the son was a mister, master or even an honourable so opted for the third person.

'I met your son at my place of work and he asked me to deliver a message to his parents and so here I am.'

'What message?' snapped Her Ladyship.

George gripped his cap to stop his shaking hands being exposed.

'Your son has sailed for France to fight for … '

'No!' howled the mother slapping the settee in a mixture of rage and fear. She pointed at her husband. 'I told you he would do this. He's tricked us. He never had any intention of going to Oxford, and it's your fault; you useless pathetic excuse of a man.'

Surprisingly his Lordship weathered the abuse hurled at him by his so-called loving wife. He wanted details and spoke to George. 'Please sit.' George hesitated and Her Ladyship snapped a command. George sat. 'You say you met our son at Liverpool Street station.'

'I did, sir.'

'Under what circumstances?'

George explained the meeting in as few words as possible.

'Did he pay you to come here?'

'He offered, sir, but I declined.'

'Why?' asked His Lordship, believing all working class people did nothing for nothing.

George found his breathing returning to normal. 'Do you mean why did he offer to pay or why did I decline?'

Her Ladyship exploded. 'You insolent, working-class weasel.' She spluttered as her blood pressure continued to climb.

George wanted to leave. He stood. 'I wanted to help your son because I was impressed by his courage and desire to serve his country. He made me proud to be British. Now if you'll excuse me, sir, madam, I'll return to my work.'

He didn't wait for permission but turned on his heel and left. The door magically opened as he approached, and the housekeeper stood back as he departed.

She looked at the titled couple but his Lordship waved her away. Mary caught up with George as he reached the kitchen. 'Wait here, boy.' She left.

Boy? I'm an acting porter with responsibilities, Miss, likely the youngest on the railways. Please don't call me "Boy".

He didn't wait, headed into the garden and sailed past the gardener before walking back to the Hampstead Heath station.

At work and at home, he said not a dickey-bird about meeting Lord and Lady Carruthers. For him, the matter was closed. He would never hear from the rich folk on the hill again, and thank goodness for that.

Next morning he set off for work extra early, and as he approached the entrance to Liverpool Street, he spied the newspaper poster beside the chap selling papers.

'Morning Alf,' said George giving his usual wave and greeting. Alf waved back and went on selling his papers. Then the world seemed to stop spinning as George stopped as if shot, changed direction and returned to the poster. He stared at it.

Hampstead Murder
Lord Dead

Chapter 7

What a start to the day. George bought a newspaper and hurried to the gents' lavatories. Inside a cubicle, he closed the door and studied the article. The paper shook because George's hands shook; his whole body shook. Gents entered and left. George kept reading. The first paragraph put his brain in a spin.

> Lord Cuthbert Carruthers, of Tudor House in Hampstead, London, was found dead in his home last night. A burglary is believed to have taken place and police suspect foul play.

There were many more paragraphs but George struggled to read. He wasn't hot but still perspired. He folded the paper, opened the cubicle door and set off to start work while still in a daze.

'Morning George,' said a lad porter as they passed on Platform 4, and the younger worker was surprised to get no reply, not even an acknowledgement. It appeared George was sleepwalking.

He stumbled through his time in Lost Property. Items were brought in and people arrived in the hope of finding their belongings. George did the necessary. The morning dragged. He decided. He needed to tell someone about his time with the newly deceased Lord Carruthers. He considered his uncle then decided the assistant station master might react in a different or rather better way.

'Come in,' called ASM Rogers. 'George,' he said with a smile, 'what brings you here? You've not got another crime to solve?' The look on George's face grabbed the ASM's full attention. He gasped. 'Don't tell me you have?'

George gave his boss chapter and verse from meeting Private Carruthers here at work to sitting in the Hampstead library with the new recruit's titled parents. George placed his copy of the *Daily Mail* with its front page story on the ASM's desk.

'Bloody hell,' gasped Rogers continuing his reaction of gasps.

'What should I do, sir?'

'Well before we continue, George, have you told me everything? I mean you didn't sneak back to Hampstead last night and stab, shoot or strangle His Lordship?'

Of course it was a joke although George thought there was a whiff of being serious in the question.

'I'm sorry, sir, but I can't see anything funny in this terrible incident.'

The senior man felt ashamed. 'Of course you're right, and I apologize for the tasteless remark.'

'But there's another horrible situation, sir. The young man who asked me to visit Hampstead, to inform his parents he'd sailed to France, has gone to war and doesn't know his father is dead.'

'You're right again. Okay, the first thing we do is tell Mr Carmody. Come on.'

George struggled to believe his life's latest adventure, if that's what it was. He tried to help a stranger and was now possibly involved, albeit indirectly, in a murder. He hoped at least the worst was over and prepared his replies for Uncle Fred.

As they approached the SM's office, the acting porter and the ASM nearly died. Two London Bobbies stood in the corridor outside the Mr Carmody's office. When George and the ASM entered, his uncle was not alone. A man wearing a suit and an overcoat stood.

The SM looked in shock. 'Inspector O'Reilly, this is the assistant station master, Jack Rogers and the young man is acting porter George Miracle.' He looked at his stunned nephew. 'George, this gentleman is a detective from Scotland Yard and would like a word with you.' Fred and Jack looked nervous, George bewildered.

His mind collapsed. It went all mushy, becoming a blur. *Why have the police come to Liverpool Street Station?* The Inspector addressed the acting porter.

'George Miracle, I'm arresting you on suspicion of conspiracy to murder Lord Carruthers.' He called. 'Officers!' and the two uniformed constables entered the room. George lost his ability to speak. The SM and his deputy let their jaws drop. George was accompanied by the three police officers and marched out of the station.

What?

George's police record was non-existent. He was certainly not known to the police. Now he was arrested, placed in handcuffs, escorted from the station and taken to Scotland Yard headquarters. He didn't weep; he was too scared.

Fred collapsed in his chair, his hands on his face. 'What am I going to tell his mother?'

The ASM shook his head. 'Fred, it can't be true, it can't.'

'The inspector said Lady Carruthers named George as the stranger who came to her house. She claimed he spoke rudely to His Lordship, the man who was murdered. The police believe the boy discovered the layout of the house and then passed this information to the burglars who, when disturbed by His Lordship, murdered the gentleman.'

Rogers raged and stood up for his favourite porter. 'Spoke rudely? And from that the lad is charged with murder? Fred, he went there as a favour for a soldier. This is absurd!'

'He's not been charged, only arrested and for conspiracy, not the actual killing,' explained his distressed uncle. 'But why was he there in the first place? What favour?'

Rogers explained the background and the message.

Fred fumed. 'What? Is that all?'

'Yes and now we need to help the boy. He needs a solicitor, Fred. He's alone and will be terrified.'

Fred grabbed his coat and cap. 'I'll go. You're in charge, and if any director turns up, I'm out inspecting timetables, tickets or trains—anything.'

The SM entered the office of Turnbull and McCready, solicitors and barristers at Law in Middle Temple. This legal company worked for the Great Eastern Railway Company handling its legal matters.

Fred asked to see Mr McCready. When the solicitor was told the station master from Liverpool Street was outside, he appeared.

'Good morning, Mr Carmody. This is most unusual to have you call in person,' said the solicitor as they shook hands.

Fred was shown into the legal man's office and explained the situation. McCready didn't hesitate. The two men left for Scotland Yard.

Being gentlemen and of the professional class, the inspector willingly met them. McCready spoke on George's behalf. Fred added his piece by saying the boy was at home with his family, including his uncle, all evening.

The inspector's interview with George had failed to convince the officer the suspect was even indirectly involved in the murder. When George explained how young George Carruthers made his parents furious by sailing for France, the detective saw another and new side to the case.

His Lordship was definitely murdered but George Miracle was released without charge.

That night when told about George's "adventure", a furious Connie took aim at her brother. 'You allowed your nephew, your own flesh and blood, to be arrested.'

George butted in. 'It's all right, Ma. The police let me go without charge.'

'They shouldn't have arrested you in the first place.'

'What's arrested mean?' asked Emily.

Connie ignored her daughter and continued attacking her brother.

'You're the boss of the station. Why didn't you protect a member of your own staff? He's still only a child for God's sake.'

'*I'm* still only a child,' said Emily, ignored for the second time.

'It's done and dusted, Connie. And you should be proud of the lad, helping a new soldier in his time of need.'

That made the mother even more irate. She turned to George. 'And I've warned you, George Miracle, your responsibility is to your family first and the railways second. Forget about playing soldiers.'

Emily wanted to know about any toy soldiers her brother might own but must have kept hidden. Connie's response frightened the girl who chose to say nothing.

A silence settled in the kitchen until Fred spoke although knowing he would cause another fuss.

'I think George should change stations.'

The acting porter snapped to attention.

'What do you mean?' demanded Connie thinking another London station might be the location.

'Lots of staff saw George being escorted away by the police. The story will be all over the station. He'll be teased and a few nasty workers might stir up trouble. It will be good for George to get away and work in a new place for a while, meet new people, and gain new experiences.'

Connie's anger cooled a tad while George's curiosity warmed.

'Which station, Uncle?' he asked.

Fred hesitated knowing his sister would explode—again.

'I think a good place would be Norwich Victoria.'

'What?' shouted Connie, and Emily's eyes widened. 'Norwich is a hundred miles away.' It was 97.

Earlier that afternoon, Fred made a phone call to an old friend. Now the result of the telephone call could be revealed.

'George, the SM at Norwich Victoria is a longstanding friend of mine. He's in need of a reliable acting porter to work with passenger and freight trains, and there's a spare room at the SM's railway house. You can start this week.'

George tingled. Connie didn't.

'You can come to London for a weekend once a month,' said Fred.

'Once a fortnight,' snapped Connie and they agreed the compromise. As George packed his case preparing to leave the family home for the first time ever, the murder in Hampstead remained unsolved.

Inspector O'Reilly pondered the lack of tears by the widow at her husband's demise. Suspicions mounted but evidence, if it existed, remained hidden. No evidence meant there was no arrest. One definite fact was known; George Miracle had nowt to do with it.

Two days later, Fred and Jack Rogers stood on a Liverpool Street platform with George in his coat and cap and holding his case. The 09:17 to Norwich, pulled by an S69 Class, 4-6-0 built in Stratford, hissed ready for departure. Both senior men had discussed young Miracle's job status the day before. Jack Rogers wanted to promote the acting porter, his uncle didn't.

'He's far too young. No-one gets promoted to porter at his age.'

'Fred, we're desperately short of staff thanks to this damn war.'

The SM knew that was true. They reviewed George's outstanding record and Fred reluctantly agreed.

'Okay but let's keep it quiet.'

On the platform, the two senior railwaymen shook hands with

George, and the ASM delivered the good news.

'We have decided to make you up to porter class, George. You are no longer acting.'

A smile appeared naturally as the former acting porter looked at his uncle who nodded.

'Thank you, gentlemen,' said George, 'and I'll do my best to make you proud of my work.'

A guard blew his whistle and George climbed into a third-class carriage—there was no second class—looked out the window and waved as the train departed.

Sitting facing the engine, he watched the London suburbs replaced by the countryside. This was a stopping train and the trip took almost three hours.

At journey's end stood Norwich Victoria station giving arrivals a look of modest grandeur with an interesting history; its booking hall once housed a circus. Because of its architecture, it could be called a showing-off station, although its major fault was its proximity, not being in the heart of the cathedral city. When George arrived, passenger numbers were declining.

He waited until the other passengers alighted before stepping onto the platform. The crowds dispersed and George looked along the near-deserted station. A man dressed in a station master's uniform stood grinning and beckoned to the young man. George approached.

'You even look like your uncle,' said Albert "Bert" Ramsbottom. 'Welcome to Norwich, young man. Good trip?'

'Yes, thank you, sir,' said George, relieved and quietly excited.

'I believe congratulations are in order, *Porter* Miracle.' George smiled his thanks. 'Okay dokey, young man, follow me.' They set off. 'We're a tad smaller than Liverpool Street with our two platforms alongside your dozen or so in London. But we're busy with freight and have half a dozen passenger trains a day.'

They reached the ticket gate where Fred introduced the new arrival. 'Porter George Miracle, meet Porter Mickey Upton.' The men shook hands and George felt better already. 'Mickey does the Down as well as the *Up*ton trains,' grinned the SM who cracked the same so-called joke to every new arrival.

There were smiles all round and George entered the station

building and met various fellow employees. Bert gave him a slip of paper with an address.

'Back in the early days of building the railways, many companies provided accommodation for staff. Have you ever been to Swindon?'

'No sir.'

'The Great Western built streets of terraces with medical services, a church, library and even a pub for their workers. Mind you, working in their machinery sheds, most of the Swindon men were deaf by the time they reached thirty. There's no such village in Norwich but the SM is given a house as part of his position. My housekeeper is expecting you. Settle in then come back after lunch and we'll get you sorting, sweeping and stamping.' He grinned. 'Now, any questions?'

'No, sir, and thank you,' said George feeling wonderful. With suitcase in hand, he set off.

'Hello, you must be the new porter. I'm Miss Woods but everyone calls me Daisy. Come in.'

George's first meeting with the SM proved terrific. This second meeting with his housekeeper topped it. He was shown his room, big double bed, big cushions, high ceiling and windows with a view over the city. He unpacked his meagre belongings and returned to the kitchen for a doorstop sandwich covered in butter produced on a nearby farm, and topped with homemade blackberry jam with fruit picked for free from Norfolk hedgerows. The whopping mug of tea doubled as a foot bath. What a start.

With a full belly, he set off for his new station. In Norwich, with not a soul knowing anything about George's indirect involvement in the murder of Lord Carruthers, sarcasm and teasing didn't exist. He was here to gain experience in a station outside the capital.

His first task involved shifting parcels. He was working at Norwich Victoria with a clean slate and a large dose of enthusiasm.

Chapter 8

The first world war raged and while planes and, towards the end of the war, tanks were used by both sides, much of the fighting involved infantrymen often described as cannon fodder. They dug trenches and, living in the most appalling conditions, shot, shelled and gassed one another in the hope the enemy would surrender first.

In 1915 many terrible battles took place in France and in 1916 an even worse act of insanity known as the Battle of the Somme dragged on for months. The death toll, on both sides, shocked the world.

News reports reached Britain listing massive casualties. Uncle Fred and family discovered the truth as did the whole country.

One thing changed for porter Miracle in Norwich; his fortnightly weekend trips to London became monthly trips. Connie saw her son growing into a strapping young adult, being happy and successful but George's absence hurt his family, the women particularly missed him.

On one trip back home, George suggested Emily and their mother do the travelling and come to Norwich. Emily clapped and agreed almost begging her mother for approval. It became a possibility.

When alone with her brother, Connie expressed her fear about George joining the army.

'He's too young,' said Fred.

'And what if the government introduces conscription?'

'No need. After Lord Kitchener's poster appeared all over the country, more than a million men have volunteered.'

'I've already lost my husband, Fred. I'm not going to lose my son.'

In Norwich, George won the respect of SM Ramsbottom and many fellow workers. His landlady, Daisy, fussed over the young man. Most nights, after their evening meal, the elderly SM would sit for a while in front of the fire burning coals from Newcastle before retiring. George and Daisy enjoyed one another's company and would indulge in cocoa and toast as a late night feast. They chatted about all sorts, with George having told the lady his life story covering his family, work and his now neglected hobby of fishing. He did omit his activity involving the late Lord Carruthers from down Hampstead way.

'Do you have a family, Daisy?' asked George in all innocence and certainly not prying. She hesitated and he wondered if he'd been impolite. He spoke first. 'I'm sorry, Daisy, please don't feel you have to tell me anything.'

She sat still, pensive and paused then whispered. 'I want to.' George went to respond then bit his tongue. The light in the room came from the coal fire in the grate. He waited. She struggled with her face scrunched and scared. Finally she spoke.

'My parents threw me out when I was your age, sixteen, because I was pregnant.' Silence filled the room. 'I had a baby boy. I was not married and the father who promised to marry me, left and I never saw him again.' A tear appeared in her eye.

'I'm sorry,' said George in a soft and caring voice.

'I couldn't keep the baby and ...' Her voice cracked. 'I gave him away to a married couple who wanted a child.'

She dabbed her eyes. George risked making her sadness worse.

'Do you know what happened to him?' Daisy shook her head. It was too hard to speak. 'Would you like to know?'

His question seemed to sting her, as if he'd slapped her face. She jerked her face towards him looking confused even angry.

'Why would you ask that?'

The mood of their "chat" swerved. It became like a train, slipping and swaying on the tracks as the locomotive prepared to derail.

In a panic, George fought to save the train. 'I meant no harm, Daisy, I spoke without thinking. Please forgive me.'

The loco recovered. Daisy didn't speak for a while staring into the dying embers. 'I don't talk about it but I still think about it—every day.' She paused again and fell silent. 'Every day,' she whispered. Still George didn't know what to say. 'But yes, I would like to know.'

The porter was in unknown territory, the topic a foreign language to him. He took a punt. 'Could I help?'

It was another of those slap-in-the-face moments. Daisy stared at him. No-one ever asked such a question before. Mind you, no-one ever knew about her lost child before. 'Would you?' she whispered. 'I mean, could you? What can you do?'

George struggled. 'I've searched for many lost parcels and things but I've never searched for a lost baby.'

She became angry once more. 'He wasn't lost, he was given away.' She spoke louder punishing herself. '*I* gave him away.'

George cringed. His simple question caused pain and distress. His mind raced. *Why did I ask such a question?*

'I'd like to help, Daisy. Is there a government department, a church, business, charity; someone who looks for adopted children?'

It was not the question but the way he asked it which saw Daisy weep freely. The topic she'd never forgotten but never spoken about now swamped her mind. Until now she had never planned anything. Now the young boarder sitting beside her in the dimly lit room offered to help. His words created a tiny pinprick of light at the end of the darkest and longest tunnel. It appeared for the first time. For Daisy with her decades of suffering, a pinprick of light was brilliant; it was hope.

'I'll see what I can find out, Daisy,' said George, 'but please don't expect a miracle.'

She stared at him. 'But you're a Miracle.' He smiled at her pun.

She told him all she knew; the baby's name, his birthday, where he was born and where she gave him away, and a description but not the names of the couple who took him. She was never told their names. 'But those other facts, I can never forget.'

He moved to her, bent and kissed the top of her head. She didn't look up but grasped his arm and wouldn't let go. When she did, he whispered, 'Goodnight, Mother,' and slipped away.

Daisy sat there in the dark with her throat blocked and her eyes flooded. *Where is my boy now? Does he know his Mum exists?*

As George enjoyed his breakfast next morning, Daisy placed an envelope on the table beside his plate. *My son* was written on the front. George looked at Daisy. She whispered.

'It's a letter I wrote to my son not long after I gave him away. I'd like you to give it to him, please.'

Goodness, she is serious, thought George. 'Of course,' he whispered. *But what if I can't find him? What if he's dead? What if I find him and he wants nothing to do with his birth mother?*

Life at Norwich Victoria suited George to a tee. The mix of passengers and freight brought variety to his tasks. His education in railway working kept growing. He befriended many co-workers. One driver asked if he ever planned to join him on the footplate. Surprised, George laughed but the idea settled in the back of his mind.

Could I become a fireman, a driver?

His monthly weekend in London went too fast. Uncle Fred wanted to talk shop, his mother probed his living conditions, and Emily wanted to show him her drawings. She clearly missed her big brother.

'Next month, Ma,' said George, 'you can bring Em to Norwich.'

Emily clapped, excitement shining from her face. Fred looked miffed. 'What about me? I'll be alone with no-one to cook me supper.'

'You can all come,' announced George. 'The SM's house is huge.'

So the plan was made and George returned to Norwich on the Sunday evening pass from Liverpool Street. He said farewell early giving the excuse he wanted to call on chums in London who were now absent friends. He became good at telling lies.

Instead, he called at the vicarage of St Mark's, close to where he lived. The only other time he entered this church was for his father's funeral. A woman answered the door.

'Good afternoon,' said George asking if he might have a word with the vicar. He soon sat with the reverend gent asking for help in his quest to find a baby, adopted in 1879.

The massive, tricky and seemingly impossible task began.

Heading home to Norfolk, a passenger left a newspaper on his seat. George picked up the paper and read reports of the war. He groaned. He remembered the unit in which George Carruthers served and read reports of many casualties. George thought of his namesake. The chap was only 2 or 3 years older than him. Yet there he was, if still alive, in the trenches, eating, sleeping, and trudging through mud and blood to reach the latrines in-between firing and being fired upon.

What am I doing for my country? I'm swanning around on trains, sorting lost parcels, and helping confused passengers.

He was on a stopping train and each station brought with it the locomotive sounds of hissing and puffing, wheel-spins, the clanking of carriages, the opening and slamming of doors, the cries of the station staff, whistles being blown, and the footsteps of people rushing to catch their train.

George knew the stations to Norwich by heart. He knew much of the timetables operated by the Great Eastern Railway. While sitting at Diss, he knew a freight express train was due to pass at this time heading deep into Essex. He heard the approaching train. His senses crackled and panic set in; the speed and sound of the approaching freight train slapped his face. *That's too fast! That's way too fast!*

The sound grew louder; it became too loud, too quick. He choked, his breath locked in his throat. He stood and froze, not knowing what to do. Other passengers saw his fear and became distressed.

'What's wrong young man?' asked an elderly woman.

'Get on the floor!' yelled George then repeated the order twice as loud. The sound of the loco wheels crunching the ballast came first followed by the explosive crunching of freight cars against the platform and then against the stationary train, his train.

Passengers on his train and the platforms screamed. There were no passengers on the freight train although desperate swearing, possibly prayers, exploded on the footplate.

Windows on the carriages shattered. 'Get down!' screamed George again as he lay flat beside the seats. Glass fragments and splinters of wood exploded landing on everyone. It was a violent storm, an on-going explosion, a living nightmare. When would it end?

The smashing sounds continued. A speeding train takes forever to stop. A derailed speeding, heavy-laden freight train takes longer to stop and once it does, the screams of the terrified keep going.

Wagons piggy-backed their neighbours. The locomotive rolled with its wheels in the air and steam, fire and boiling water ran free.

Once the debris stopped flying, George was on his feet. Groaning led him to passengers. He used his basic first-aid skills and kept speaking to assure people help would soon arrive.

Station staff entered the train, calling to locate those in need of help. The SM came across George and saw his uniform.

'You all right, son?'

George nodded, not being able to see the blood on his face. Some was his own and some from fellow passengers. The able-bodied struggled to help the injured and dying.

The emergency services arrived to discover a war zone. George read about the horrors in France and wondered if this was as bad.

Darkness fell but the recovery work went on. In Norwich, as elsewhere in the country, the news broke of the rail disaster. The death toll kept rising. A temporary morgue was set up in the waiting room on the platform with the badly injured ferried to hospitals.

In Norwich and in London, two station masters heard the news.

Fred didn't know what to say to his sister, and Bert, knowing Daisy was keen on the lad, feared bad news would knock her for six. The SMs held their fire.

It took a policeman to stop George from his mighty rescue work. The young man suffered from exhaustion and it showed.

'Right, matey, enough,' said the constable taking George's arm and helping him out of a carriage in which he'd been working.

In the ticket-box office, George drank a mug of piping hot tea with a decent slosh of brandy. Then he collapsed.

The news hit the nation hard. With massive casualties across the Channel, to then have a self-inflicted tragic event on home soil, rubbed salt in the raw wounds of those already grieving. The families of the dead and wounded at Diss suffered their own grief as did those who lost their son, brother or father on Flanders Fields.

George's mother and his Norwich housekeeper rejoiced in the news of his survival. He returned to Norwich and resumed work but as a changed man. The crash experience stung George to his core. He said nothing to anyone but decided. If he could survive a terrible incident, and his countrymen abroad constantly copped that type of hardship daily, then he could play his part in fighting for his country.

The official enquiry into the crash called many witnesses including the Norwich porter. George spoke well with his current and former SMs attending on the day he took the stand.

Fred felt enormous pride watching his nephew. Returning to London, the station master told his sister her son was no longer a boy. 'He's a man, Connie. His father would be wonderfully proud of him, and you've done a brilliant job in raising the lad.'

Connie's feelings were mixed. Proud, yes, but near terrified thinking he might behave recklessly and volunteer.

The official cause of the accident was excessive speed by the driver of the freight train, and poor maintenance of the tracks right before the station. Potholes below the ballast can cause the tracks to move.

The GER directors discussed the accident and the coroner's report. The terrible publicity caused angst, and the financial costs sent shudders through shareholders.

The directors worked hard to protect the good name of the company, and one way of gaining positive publicity was to praise and promote employees who did their bit for king and company.

One employee given a certificate of gratitude was George Miracle, now confirmed in the company publications as promoted to porter.

Christmas was a sombre affair with thousands of British casualties in the Great War. George returned to porter duties in Norwich, and during his monthly visits to London, he worked on his special mission—helping find Daisy Woods' long-lost son.

After months of letter writing, personal visits and detailed research, George grew ever closer to striking gold. He persuaded SM Ramsbottom to allow him to catch an earlier London train on Fridays enabling him to spend a few hours in the city before heading home. On those monthly Friday afternoons, George searched records in churches, hospitals and government departments. He reckoned his eyes changed colour as he poured over the census information from 1881 to 1911. Finally, magically, George hit the jackpot.

The war raged and George began to feel he had two families. Of course he loved his mother, sister and uncle but now had formed a strong bond with his landlady. He found a special present for a special person, his dear housekeeper, Daisy.

He found the "baby" Daisy delivered had been christened Oscar Wilding, and today was a middle-aged man, a broker for an advertising agency in the City, with a wife and three children living in Cricklewood, North London.

George suffered from shock and disbelief. He bubbled with excitement and groaned with despair.

How will I tackle this? Daisy will be thrilled. But what if her son wants nothing to do with her? It will all be a waste of time.

He made a plan. He wrote a simple and respectful letter to Mr Wilding in Cricklewood using his Wood Green address, not so far away, almost a neighbour in fact. He briefly explained the facts about Daisy and her son, asking if he might call on Mr Wilding suggesting a date and time. He posted the letter days before he was due in London.

If he got a letter by return asking him to stay away, the search would fail. George couldn't wait for the weekend.

'I'm home,' he called back in Wood Green. Then he saw it.

Emily came bouncing along the passage. 'There's a letter for you, George. Have you got a girlfriend?'

He laughed, kissed his sister and collected the envelope from the hall stand. The neat handwriting suggested an educated person.

'And what would you do if I did?' he asked.

Emily called. 'I told you, Ma. He *has* got a girlfriend.'

George tore at the envelope, opened the letter and gasped. It came from Mr Oscar Wilding of Cricklewood stating he is indeed the adopted son of Daisy Woods and the most wonderful news of all was he would love to meet his birth mother. When can this happen?

Oscar's enthusiasm oozed from the page.

George purred but chose to say nothing to anyone, especially Daisy, afraid something might go wrong before the Cricklewood meeting could take place. He decided to meet Oscar first.

His family never did take up the offer of a weekend in Norwich, and on the Sunday before heading back, he travelled across London and stood outside a certain Cricklewood address. A gentleman, presumably the homeowner, worked in his garden.

'Mr Wilding?' The man looked at George and knew exactly who he was and why he was there. 'I'm George Miracle.'

Dropping his spade, the gardener hurried to his front gate. 'Come in, please,' said a nervous Oscar. Inside, George met Daisy's daughter-in-law, Mrs Miriam Wilding who knew the whole story.

'My husband has talked about his unknown birth mother for years. You have done him a great service, Mr Miracle.'

'Please, call me George.'

He explained his situation in Norwich and how boarding with Daisy led to the search for her long lost son.

When George handed Oscar the envelope containing Daisy's letter, tension in the room came out to play. It was hard to breathe.

To George's joy, Oscar and Miriam read the letter with delight. Both wept and hugged one another, their happiness on show. It quickly became a group hug with George welcomed to the family.

The letter explained Daisy's predicament at the time, how she hated having to give away her baby, and how she stated she would never stop thinking about her little boy.

'When can we meet her?' asked Oscar.

George felt teary too and kept seeing Daisy's face and pictured how she would look and behave when told the news.

'I suggest you and your wife come to Norwich for a day trip. You can catch a morning train from Liverpool Street, spend time with your mother and then catch an afternoon train back to London.'

'How wonderful,' exclaimed Oscar. 'But when can we go?'

'Next Saturday should be fine.'

Oscar's enthusiasm shone. 'I'll buy the tickets in the morning.'

George suggested a future plan. 'I could bring Daisy to London on my next visit, and she could come here and meet her grandchildren.'

When is too much happiness never enough?

'Would you have a photograph I could show to Daisy?' One with the whole Wilding family was found. George's heartrate sprinted.

He enjoyed the trip back to Norwich. Once in a while he remembered a Wilding response and broke into a big smile. Some passengers would look at and wonder why this young man was so happy.

He arrived at the SM's house and greeted his boss and the housekeeper. He said nothing while Mr Ramsbottom was present wanting Daisy to feel comfortable. The usual routine of Bert retiring and George and Daisy having a hot drink before bed continued.

'Daisy, please listen, I have wonderful news.' She looked at him sensing danger or sadness. He cut to the chase. 'Your son is alive and well and wants to meet you.'

He watched her and panicked. The shock hit her hard. *Is she having a heart attack?* She turned white. He held her hands.

'Are you sure?' George nodded. 'This is not a terribly cruel joke?'

'I've been to his house, Daisy. I've met him and his wife.'

It took Daisy an age to stop crying, to stop breathing fast, and to fully comprehend the situation. 'But does he want to meet me?'

'He does, Daisy and so much so, he and his wife are coming to Norwich next Saturday to spend the day with you.'

The mother, now grandmother, covered her face with her hands and let out a sort of cry. It was unbridled joy but unusual and loud. So loud, station master Ramsbottom popped out of bed, waddled downstairs and appeared in the doorway in his pyjamas.

George so wished he owned a camera. He did have a photo of the middle-aged "baby" and his family and Daisy studied it for ages.

George explained the news; the old SM fell back into a childhood delight and grinned so hard his wrinkles ran away. Next Saturday, the SM and the porter stood together when the Down London pulled in.

Daisy's boy and his wife were given a warm welcome and escorted to the station house. Daisy sat in the parlour fretting, patting her new hairdo, twisting a handkerchief and rehearsing her lines.

She heard the key. Her heartrate exploded. George opened the door and called. 'Daisy, there's someone here to see you.'

There was a pause because Oscar felt as much emotion as his mother. He exhaled and entered and the mother/son greeting hit George's eyes with a vengeance. He wept as much as the others.

Tears, hugs, apologies, promises and plans appeared. Life stories were told. George loved being a part of the reunion and felt at home with this reunited and his new family.

Once the initial greeting ended, George went to leave to give the trio time alone but all three objected. 'Oi! Where do you think you're going, Mr Miracle?' almost demanded Daisy. George stayed.

No time to waste became the order of the day. Next Christmas would be the best ever. Daisy tearfully accepted an invitation—or was it a demand?—to spend it in London with her new family.

Going home to his family for Christmas 1915 gave George a special inner glow. The fact Daisy sat next to him as she travelled to be with her boy and his family in London, made the trip even more special.

But despite his happiness, deep down George suffered doubts. A dark, foreboding secret he dreaded, gurgled away in his gut.

The Wildings were at Liverpool Street to collect their special guest. George wished them all a Merry Christmas then headed home.

His 18th birthday kept edging nearer and he wanted to enlist. He knew such a move would cause heartache for his mother. Doing anything to hurt her made him feel ill and knew she would fight tooth and nail to keep him at home. George decided the best thing to do was to say nothing and enjoyed Christmas with his family.

The Soldier

Chapter 9

General Kitchener, the soldier with the longest list of awards, the longest handlebar moustache, which doubled as a bar bell for spindly recruits, and the famous pointing finger exhorting you to volunteer, knew two facts. The war would never be over by Christmas and to win, Britain needed a massive influx of new soldiers.

His campaign, beginning in 1914, saw more than a million men join the Army within 12 months. But the continual massacres across the Channel meant still more men were required, desperately so.

In January 1916, only months before George Miracle turned 18, the government signed into law the contentious Military Service Act of conscription. It meant single males aged between 18 and 40 were required by law to join the armed services.

There were exemptions for men in certain occupations which included locomotive drivers and firemen, and station masters. Vicars and widowers with offspring were likewise excused as were some others. But clog dancers and cigarette manufacturers, even those who supplied fags for officers, saw their appeals rejected.

For the first time ever, you could apply for an exemption by registering as a conchie, a conscientious objector, but if you did, you were warned to look out for the flak from anyone and everyone if it became known you refused to bear arms.

The issue of conscription was talked about long before it became law in 1916. Like the whole country, Connie heard about the new legislation. All the arguments she prepared to use to keep her boy in the railways were wheeled out. Surely he would be exempt. Surely the country needed the railways more now than ever in this terrible conflict. George may be of age but he must never be conscripted.

He came home on his monthly visit from Norwich. He caught the train to Cricklewood and slipped around to Oscar's house. Young Mr Miracle was the bearer of homemade gifts for three delighted grandchildren, home for half-term, from Grandma Daisy in Norwich.

Back in Wood Green, George's family was always pleased to see him. Fred came home from Liverpool Street wanting to know all the rail news from the mainline to Norwich. Emily found a new teacher and was desperate to tell big brother about her signing progress.

Only Connie stayed quiet behaving like a swan—all calm on the surface but paddling madly out of sight.

'Now Ma,' said the son and heir, 'I suppose you've heard about this new conscription law. When I turn 18, I'm required to enlist. I think I'll go to the recruitment centre in Whitehall.'

Connie prepared the evening meal and as she spoke, refused to make eye contact with George. She turned desperate. 'Men with certain jobs, and essential workers, are excused,' she said.

'Yes but handling parcels, collecting tickets and sorting lost property does not qualify for an exemption, Ma. At Liverpool Street or Norwich, I'm nowhere near the most important member of the Great Eastern Railway Company.'

Connie dreaded those answers. 'Your uncle is exempt,' she snapped. Her mind filled with images of her only son floundering in France with German machine gunners salivating over who would slaughter the new recruit.

George didn't like humiliating his mother but knew the facts.

'Come on, Ma. Uncle Fred has one of the most important railway jobs in the country. And anyway, the cut off age limit for conscripts is 40.' He looked at his uncle. 'I remember your 55th birthday, Uncle Fred, and I'll be surprised if you've been getting any younger.'

The men exchanged smiles and Fred winked but they knew the lady of the house was devastated.

The meal was hot but the atmosphere frosty. Before leaving on Sunday, George took his sister to visit places in the city. Anywhere with big brother George was fine by Emily. They ended up in Hyde Park which would have horrified their mother. Here hundreds of men gathered preparing to go to war.

'Don't tell Ma we saw all those soldiers,' said George. Emily read his face as well as his lips. She felt a shiver, understood and nodded.

Fred spent his weekends with his feet up reading the week's newspapers. Connie moped around leaving the siblings to have a grand time. Walking home, Emily looked at her brother.

'Do you have to be a soldier, George?'

He didn't need to speak. Their eyes met. He gave a brief nod.

'You have to promise me one thing, George.' He looked at her. 'You have to promise me you won't get killed.'

He thought about his answer. 'Okay, I promise.'

She liked the answer and they came home bubbling. Their mother and uncle sat without a smidgeon of "bubbling" between them.

George went back to Norwich where the railways were flat out transporting men and machines for the war effort. He counted the days until his birthday. He told the people who were close to him of the decision he made some time ago. He would enlist.

In Norwich, saying goodbye to the porters, the men in the sheds, the footplate crews, cleaners and others became emotional. These folk from the cathedral city became solid pals. They knew George was about to be conscripted. They thought it but never spoke aloud; *will I ever see this young man again?*

To farewell the SM and Daisy took time. Mr Ramsbottom was close to retirement and war was not for him. His handshake left George in no doubt he was sent off with the best of wishes.

Daisy counted George as one of her own. He was the reason she found her long-lost family. He was her hero, her knight in shining armour. To Daisy, he was part of her family. She kissed George with feeling and couldn't say anything loving so settled for a threat.

'You make sure you bloody well come back here, George Miracle, or I'll never ever speak to you again. Do you hear me?'

A rough translation read something like, "I love you, my darling boy, and I'll pray for you every day". Of course Connie sang from the same hymn sheet.

His 18th birthday party was the saddest on record. Talk about pretence. Even Emily struggled to come to grips with her big brother going away to fight in a war. Her mother warned her to not mention the army, war, soldiering, rifles or anything related thereto.

Connie's way of handling her grief was to talk about anything other than her son becoming a soldier.

On enlistment day, Fred announced he would walk with his nephew to the recruitment office on his way to work. At the front door, George hugged his mother and sister. Connie fought like blazes to control her tears but Emily let them flow.

To his mother, George even looked like a man. He wore civvies with coat, collar and tie and the hat his father wore for years.

The men left and Connie closed the door so quickly, it struck Emily. 'Ow, Ma!' she yelled and rubbed her stinging elbow.

Both the men in their immediate family were gone; father dead and son, according to statistics, as good as dead. 1916 was not the best time to be alive as a soldier on the Western Front.

As they walked, Fred chatted about life at Liverpool Street, trivial matters so as to not discuss the war and the horrific death toll of British troops, of all troops. People were still reeling from the news that in one day, *one day*, tens of thousands of men were killed. Even the word *slaughter* seemed inappropriate, inadequate.

Talking about his nephew's future seemed cruel. Near Whitehall, uncle and nephew faced one another. For fear of breaking down, Fred refrained from hugging the nephew he loved.

As they stood fifty yards from the army recruitment office, Fred refused to look at the group of men waiting outside on the pavement.

'I know your mother would appreciate a line now and then,' said the station master.

'Of course,' said George. Neither knew what to say next.

Fred extended his hand. 'Right then, lad. Remember there's a porter's job for you at Liverpool Street once you're back in Blighty.'

They shook hands. Fred's throat grew tight. He patted his nephew, turned and set off to work. He couldn't bring himself to look back.

George glanced at the men, like him, about to try and become soldiers. He moved towards them. They chatted, smoked but most, all refused to admit, deep down, they were terrified.

Nearly all conscripts were untrained soldiers. To make them effective, they needed skills and knowledge. This meant living in army accommodation for weeks with no four-poster beds or cups of tea from the maid in the morning, and drills, drills and more drills.

First they needed to pass inspection. George joined the others and next to him stood a nervous young man about George's age, fidgeting. They shuffled forward awaiting their turn.

'Will we pass?' he asked. 'I heard they reject blokes under a certain height.'

'We'll be right.'

'I'm five nine. You?'

'Five ten.' George held out his hand. 'George Miracle.'

They shook hands. 'Patrick Murphy.'

'You don't sound French,' said George and Paddy took a second to twig. As he laughed, a loud voice bounced off the corridor walls.

'Next two.'

They glanced at one another and entered an office. There were two men in long white coats, an orderly and two tables decorated with items of medical equipment.

'Strip to your waist,' snapped the orderly. They did.

The elderly doctors gave them the once over. Young chests were measured; anyone short of 34 inches was in trouble. Their height and weight were noted, and their heart and lungs checked.

'Any diseases, son?' asked a doctor.

George shook his head. 'No sir.'

Paperwork followed by more paperwork was completed until both recruits were given the medical all-clear. George and Paddy were in.

France, Belgium or Gallipoli were not the next station down the line but an army compound in Hyde Park. George acquired a uniform when he joined the GER. This time the kit looked more elaborate.

The kitbag, a large canvas, sausage-shaped bag full of goodies including a blanket, toiletries and waterproof gear could be carried easily. But when your hands and arms clasped your uniform—always a size too big—holding your boots, headgear and other bits and bobs, proved tricky. Forget marching with all those goodies.

Standing outdoors laden down with their new gear, George and a motley group of new conscripts tried to form a straight line while a burly sergeant wandered up and down practising snarling. George remembered a couple of railway officials who liked the sound of their own voice so wasn't intimidated. Paddy, on the other hand, worked in his family's florist shop and suffered the shakes on his first day.

They left the kitchen sink behind but with everything else either on their body or in their kit bag, George and the other conscripts were bundled into a truck and driven to London Waterloo station. As they waited for a troop train, George observed the station staff.

'This where you used to work, George?' asked Paddy.

George explained his time at Liverpool Street. He wondered when he'd next be employed on the railways—if ever.

Salisbury Plain stretches out over vast swathes of Wiltshire. It became famous for an odd collection of giant rocks with Stonehenge one of the most famous landmarks in Britain.

Long after the edifice appeared, the military bought hundreds of square miles of Salisbury Plain and used the area for training. Trees and people were few and far between. Many buildings were built for military personnel, and even an aerodrome or two appeared.

Wiltshire was a foreign county to George and Paddy but both would soon get to know many a blade of grass on Salisbury Plain. Here they trained for the war in continental Europe.

But in 1916, the army faced a tough assignment. The war, now called The Great War, saw casualty numbers soar. The top brass believed the way to win was to have fewer dead than the enemy; thus the need for fresh cannon fodder. As old boys from Harrow or Eton, the top brass may have been inspired by the Bard.

"Once more unto the breach, dear friends, once more; or close the wall up with our English dead."

Now the more training the new recruits received, presumably the better their chance of continuing to fight, or rather survive, once on the battlefield. But time was of the essence. 'We need them now!' cried the leaders at the front.

George, Paddy and their fellow conscripts were put through the wringer. Up early, cold showers before physical workouts followed by war games on Salisbury Plain. Those in charge were shocked at the spindly physique of so many recruits.

For George, the training was straightforward until he came to the weapons of war—rifles, machine guns, gas and grenades.

George's father loved fishing and the boy could attach a fly, cast a line and use a net while still in short pants. But until he turned 18, George had never handled a firearm; not even an air rifle. Give him a broom and a platform and the boy was a natural but guns? Nothing.

Killing was another unknown activity for George. For a peaceful young man with an interest in locomotives and railway timetables, George copped a smack. Not only did he need to learn how to strip, clean, load and fire his standard issue Lee-Enfield rifle, he had to master the cut and thrust of a bayonet.

George baulked at killing anyone. He found shooting from a distance the least upsetting. But standing toe to toe with the enemy, a fellow human being, and thrusting a razor-sharp bit of steel inside the other chap's belly, literally turned George's stomach. Lunch or a full breakfast followed by bayonet training did not a pleasant time make.

Mind you, he and the other recruits could have skipped bayonet training and not missed much as, due to the development of war machinery, far fewer casualties were caused by face to face fighting.

Paddy bought into the idea. Encouraged, or rather ordered by a ferocious officer, Paddy charged at a straw-filled dummy, screaming en route, and plunged the bayonet into the artificial enemy. Paddy's roar at the denouement gave George the inspiration or rather the Dutch courage. He bit the bullet and charged. His mother would have died.

One afternoon they were playing war games on the Plain. Their group would run forward, flatten themselves behind a small rise, and then, lying on their belly, take aim at the imaginary enemy and fire.

All went well. The cries of the officers, the firing of rifles and field guns gave the area a realistic atmosphere of war—less the dead bodies, shattered limbs and the outpouring of blood and intestines.

George's group was given the order; fall back. *Retreat* was a word officers avoided whenever possible. With the cacophony of sound, it was hard to hear but George did. He smacked Paddy's shoulder.

'Come on, Pat, we're falling back.'

George bent low and ran. Smoke flares set off by officers to simulate a war zone confused Paddy. He too took off but almost at right angles. George saw his friend disappear in the wrong direction.

He screamed. 'Paddy!'

The cry caused young Murphy to stop and thus saved his life.

A team of officers on horseback and towing field guns came thundering across Salisbury Plain. If Paddy had kept running he would have been skittled, smashed by the galloping entourage.

George ran to the trembling soldier. 'Come on, this way,' he yelled rescuing the passenger from the tracks as the express roared past.

Chapter 10

The sergeant's voice boomed through the barracks. 'This is your last chance in Blighty to write to your family. We leave for France at O six hundred hours. So get your head down.'

Paddy looked at George. Both sat on their stretcher in their barracks, their new home away from home. It had come to this. After three months of basic training, these once raw recruits were now fit, fighting men. But were they ready for war? Possibly. Were they scared? Of course. Who wouldn't be?

'What will you say to your mother?' asked Paddy starting to write.

'What I always say,' replied George. 'I'll tell her about the food, the weather, the good officers, the crazy ones, and, of course, I'll tell her about my best mate.' He pretended to look puzzled. 'Damn, I've forgotten his name.'

Paddy laughed and they wrote, both pondering their future. Would they survive? Would they be wounded? George knew about disability with his sister Emily being deaf. The recruits saw trains coming home with nurses caring for wounded soldiers, some of whom would be disabled forever.

They wondered if such a fate would befall them. Would they become a cripple, be blinded or even go mad? As he wrote, George's mind filled with thoughts of death and destruction. He could be killed on his first day. Was this his last night on Earth?

Both young men, 18, found it hard to sleep. When they did, it wasn't the peaceful slumber of a baby. In the wee small hours, Paddy tossed and turned.

'You awake?' he whispered.

'No,' whispered George.

'What time is it?'

'Go to sleep.'

A loud voice, with an Irish accent, two beds along, settled the matter. 'If you blokes don't shut up, I'll feckin' well put ya t'sleep.'

Silence returned as the clock ticked inexorably to departure hour.

A soldier never enjoyed a lie in and when off to fight in France, he needed to be up, shaved, dressed and fed, pronto. George and Paddy said little. Normally they'd talk about drills or war games or whatever they'd face on the day. Not today. Today was different.

After breakfast, men were lined up and inspected. Were they dressed correctly? Did they have all their kit? What about their rifle and ammo? Officers stopped in front of any soldier they suspected of being slipshod or lazy. George took it as both a challenge and a point of pride to pass any and every test. It must have been his immaculate uniform and attention to detail when on duty at Liverpool Street.

The troops were never told anything in advance. The less a Tommy knew before he was sent over the top, the better. An officer addressed the men. At the last minute, they were told the travel plan.

'We take the train to Folkestone and from there, the ferry to Boulogne. Then we expect the unexpected. Trains run late in peace time so anything can happen in time of war.'

George wanted to comment on train punctuality but didn't.

'So in France we catch a train to the front if the track hasn't been destroyed, the bridges blown or if the locomotive breaks down and we're missing the necessary spare parts.'

Troops needed encouragement. This officer failed. He became Captain Negative and highlighted misery.

'If the trains aren't running, we'll climb aboard a lorry, and if they break down or get bogged, we'll bloody well walk.' He studied the mass of faces. 'Are we clear?' A few men muttered. The officer steamed and spat his question. 'I said, "Are we clear"?'

'Sir,' sounded the reply en masse.

'Move them on, Sergeant,' said the officer, and this convoy of conscripted soldiers, including George Miracle and Patrick Murphy, headed for the railway station. No longer a porter but a passenger; George went to war.

Getting there involved life on the ocean wave. It was hardly months at sea but crossing the English Channel proved too much for several soldiers. They threw up, in most cases overboard, as seasickness stirred heaving stomachs.

George proved a good sailor. He comforted Paddy who turned green around the gills. 'I think drowning's the cure,' he moaned.

'I would normally say "chin up, old man",' said George, 'but right now, "chin down" is your best move.' He yelled. 'Not into the wind!'

Sighting the French coast, George told Paddy his worries would soon be over. Paddy didn't believe a word of it or rather, didn't care.

They disembarked, walked to the rail head and waited for their train. If ever they needed reminding this war delivered death, it was when the train they were expecting arrived from the front with wounded en route to Blighty. Orderlies and nurses fussed over men on stretchers or with crutches, with many wrapped in bandages. When said bandages completely covered a soldier's head, one shuddered to think about the condition of the poor bugger's face.

With the wounded removed, George, Paddy and the other conscripts boarded the train. A few wanted to walk knowing it would take longer. Failing a shelling, this train would get them to the killing fields much quicker.

Few were interested in the scenery, and travelling home was the time to make jokes. Heading into battle and possible eternity helped concentrate the mind. No gags with the next stop being Hell.

They disembarked and set off on foot for the front line and the trenches. Ah, the trenches. If freezing or blistering temperatures, mud, overflowing latrines and rats weren't bad enough, you could always count on German shells and bullets to keep you on your toes. Mind you, losing your toes was another prospect when living in the trenches. By standing in water for so long you could develop trench foot, a disease where exposure to moisture saw your feet turn blue or red and which, for some, meant amputation. General Kitchener never promised luxury.

The Brits were not alone in predicting the war would be over in a few weeks. German generals reckoned they'd rout the French and be home for Christmas. Six months passed and both sides adjusted their expectations, settling in for the long haul.

In Europe, from Belgium to Switzerland, both sides excelled at digging. Trenches were essential giving troops protection most of the time. These open excavations became home.

Depth was important. No-one fancied having to duck as they traversed their trench. German snipers stared across no-man's-land ready to pick off any tall or silly Tommy.

Several yards in front of each trench was a fence of barbed wire. Between your fence and the enemy's fence was a barren landscape known as no-man's-land.

Trench walls were lined with planks or sheets of corrugated iron to keep the sides from collapsing. Trenches were made with bends as shrapnel didn't usually travel around corners; some even zig-zagged.

There were steps for standing on, enabling you to fire at the enemy, and to be shot at, and climbing ladders so as to exit your trench and run towards rattling machine guns which delivered millions of casualties. Too bad if you were injured and left lying between the two lines of barbed wire, or worse, left lying *on* the fence of barbed wire. Still, you can only be killed the once. Instant death definitely seemed preferable. There was even a satirical song about where you could find the old battalion; "They're hanging on the old barbed wire".

On top of the trenches were sandbags, to absorb bullets and shrapnel and any other flying implements of death.

Bathrooms were basic with latrines offering nothing in the way of privacy or home comforts. The stench and rats kept you company. In any month the rain made soldiers miserable, and in winter, so too did the snow and ice. Sleeping quarters became a slit in the wall or for officers, a bed within a cave. It's true; war is hell, but it could be more of a purgatory for an officer.

And into this world of slaughter and stupidity, George Miracle and Patrick Murphy now set foot. Good luck, lads.

The location of the rail head was flexible. Its present position meant the troops alighted two miles from the front line. They couldn't see any fighting but even hard of hearing soldiers could hear it. The artillery sounded close. It *was* close.

'Gas masks,' shouted the officer. 'Have them ready, and keep your tin hat on your head.'

George pondered his kit. During training he learnt about chemical weapons and their possible horrible consequences. Hearing about sudden changes in wind direction put the wind up him, so to speak. Such sudden weather changes meant there was danger from your own side. You could score an own goal and be gassed by a fellow Tommy.

'Two ranks,' shouted the officer and George and Paddy finished up side by side. 'Company, by the left, quick march.'

This wasn't parade ground activity. There was no need to keep in step. This was move in the same direction and get to the front line as quick as you can without being killed *before* you arrive.

George didn't expect a welcoming party. The men in his area of the trench were experienced having been there for weeks, months, even years. Their uniforms provided excellent camouflage being the colour of mud.

'You wanna get yourself mucky, son,' said a corporal with a fag end growing out of his bottom lip. 'Fritz is real keen on fresh meat.'

When the NCO left, George and Paddy scooped up mud from beside the boards they stood on, and rubbed it on their uniforms.

On Salisbury Plain, the sounds of artillery were loud but didn't have fear attached. German artillery came with fear gift-wrapped. When a shell landed nearby and dirt splashed into the trench, George didn't need an invitation to flatten himself against the trench wall. He soon discovered this wasn't an odd occurrence as the enemy's artillery worked overtime.

The former porter stood not far from a soldier who used a box telescope, a periscope for troops who wanted to spy without being shot. The soldier saw George and beckoned to him.

'Come and have a look, mate.'

Being naturally curious and desperate for something to do to break the monotony, George placed his Lee-Enfield rifle against the trench wall and approached.

'Thanks,' he said. 'I'm George.'

'Donald,' said the soldier and indicated the device.

Not knowing what to expect, George peered into the "periscope". *So that's what they mean by no-man's-land.*

Years of countless shells splintered and smashed the trees and destroyed the remaining vegetation. Pieces of wood helped the mangled lines of barbed wire stand tall along the horizon. It *was* the horizon. As far as the eye could see George stared at mud and it surrended years ago. Donald explained.

'That's our wire in front. About a hundred yards beyond is their wire close to the German trench. We don't know if we copied Fritz or he us but it don't matter as lawyers for both sides ain't speaking.'

George peered, taking it all in. He thought his eyes were playing tricks. He stepped back, shocked.

'Are those bodies on the barbed wire?'

Donald nodded. 'Some are there for days. We've had the odd truce so both sides can collect their dead. We leave the odd horse even if we're starving. The birds and rats get first dibs.' George grew up fast. 'The dead men are lucky. The chaps who lie there wounded learn how to die in agony.'

George switched to war tactics. 'How do we take their trench?'

'We've tried going over the top which only reduced our mess bill. Dead soldiers don't eat as much. I think our present plan is to stay here and wait till they grow old, run out of sauerkraut and die.'

George knew the soldier was using humour to disguise despair. Donald's eyes told a story. They were dead, cold and impenetrable.

'How long have you been here?' asked George.

The Tommy sniffed. 'What year is it?'

George didn't think a simple question would shock him so much. 'It's October 1916.'

'Damn,' spat the soldier, 'I was sure it was 17. My captain reckons we'll win in 18 so if he's right, we're only stuck here for two more bloody years.'

Only? George arrived two hours ago and already 1918 seemed an eternity away.

Their quiet "chat" ended in a split second. Donald threw himself at George and shoved him to the boards on the floor of the trench. It scared the newcomer witless.

'Get down,' screamed Donald. 'It's a Minenwerfer.' The sound dominated. Donald pointed up. 'Look.'

To George, looking anywhere didn't appeal but again his curiosity dragged his eyes skywards. Against an overcast sky, he saw this German bomb, big, black and, unbelievably, rumbling and tumbling as it plummeted to Earth.

'If it lands anywhere near us, we're dead,' yelled Donald.

Staring into the face of death, George chose being killed from behind so buried his face in the mud. A wave of soil rained down and only when the ground stopped shaking did George and Donald resume their abnormal normal life.

'We call 'em mine throwers. They're small cannons that lob mines over short distances,' said Donald not bothering to "clean" his uniform. 'Last month, one of their bombs scored a direct hit in our trench about half a mile away. They collected all the large body parts but we're still finding bits of flesh and bone.'

George felt a chill. 'Can't we get our artillery to bomb theirs?'

'We can try and do but accuracy's the key. Fritz moves his mine throwers and doesn't have the decency to tell us when and where they're located. Do you know how far away their heavy artillery is?' George shrugged, having no idea. 'If your rifle can kill a German a thousand yards away, their big guns are way out there on another planet.'

George grew up in five minutes.

'What do the officers say is our plan?' he asked.

'Not sure but we reckon it's either attrition or suicide. Either they run out of ammo or food before we do or we get sent over the top and flood their trenches with our bodies.'

George felt sick. His letters home would have to be the biggest pack of lies ever created. His mother, every Tommy's mother lived in blissful ignorance. They knew millions died but not how.

Chapter 11

George settled into the war routine. A Tommy would spend up to a week in the forward trench where the enemy bombarded your hole in the ground with lethal monotony. When he did stop shelling, George felt tempted to call out his thanks.

"Much appreciated, Fritz; feel free to take an extra-long breather!"

Relief for George and his mates came when they were sent back to a rear trench where a soldier could rest for 3 or 4 days.

In writing to his mother, George never once mentioned the overflowing latrines or the size of the massive rats. He did describe his bed as comfortable. It was a space, a slit he dug into the trench wall, high enough to avoid getting flooded when the rains arrived.

As for food, it was nigh on impossible to get a hot meal. Like the field hospitals, the field kitchens were as far from enemy fire as possible. By the time any hot food arrived, it was no longer hot.

George needed to upgrade his domestic skills. He learnt how to make a stew with carrots, onions, potatoes and the ubiquitous bully beef. In a patch of dry ground, good luck in finding that, he dug a hole for his fire, the stove. His saucepan was his mess tin.

He'd cook the chopped vegetables in the Gelatin from the corned beef, and discovered overcooking the bully beef was never wise. It became a pink mush. With water for stock his stew was ready and at least the food was hot.

Once the weather turned cold, anything hot became a godsend.

Army rations provided the bare minimum, and if you wanted anything special, you might get lucky at the canteen situated a mile or more behind the lines near the field kitchen.

George remembered his Uncle Fred coming home one night with a can of Campbell's tomato soup from Fortnum and Mason. It was 1910 and the first time the American product was on sale in England.

How he would love a can right now in 1916. Another favourite was HP sauce and this "luxury" could be purchased so George used some of his pay to buy a bottle of the brown liquid.

When he met up again with Paddy Murphy, they went halves on certain items. Sharing helped pass the boredom and saved money. But eating together was not always possible as one stood guard while the other ate his grub.

If together and not on duty, they played games. Collecting pebbles or making your own with solid mud meant they could play Checkers.

They knew life was crook when the winter set in and the bread the Army baked changed flavour. The flour came not from wheat but turnips. The vegetables were dried and ground, and tasted worse than bland. In his letters home, George never mentioned turnip bread.

In London, when George's letters arrived addressed to his mother, Fred and Emily demanded each precious page once Connie finished reading every word two or three times. It was nearly Christmas 1916.

The generals, the decision-makers, gave orders from afar. They saw the ever-expanding casualty lists but persisted in their method of sacrificing troops in the hope the enemy's dead would outnumber their own. Did they boast? 'Our slaughtered men are fewer than those of the Boche.'

At least one prominent person tried to persuade the top brass to change tactics. Sir Arthur Conan Doyle, creator of Sherlock Holmes, urged the military to copy the outfit worn by the Australian bushranger, Ned Kelly. Shields too could be used urged the author.

Prime Minister, David Lloyd George, nailed the truth when he described the British tactics as, "hammering away with human flesh and sinews at the strongest fortresses of the enemy".

In the trenches, the men kept wondering and talking about the next attack. 'What's the word, Sarge?' asked a conscript, now a seasoned soldier.

'I know as much as you do, and when I know, you'll know.'

George chatted with men who were now his mates. 'Has anyone here gone over the top?'

'I have,' said a Tommy with a London East End accent. 'I used up a lifetime's worf of good luck in ten bloody minutes. I saw blokes mown down all around me. I tell ya, the screamin' is somefin' I'll never f'get.'

George thought about what he was about to say. Every man knew defeatist talk or criticism of orders was a court martial in waiting.

'Why do we go over the top like we do? Why do we run at the

Germans who machine gun us with ease? If the reports from the Somme are true, we're target practice for the Boche.'

The others were shocked. One challenged him.

'What, you reckon we should stroll over singing *God Save the King?*'

'No but is there another way to capture a German trench without sacrificing so many of our boys?'

George clearly meant business. Now the mood turned serious. Another soldier, Reynolds, took exception and abused George.

'I admire your guts, Miracle. You're the first soldier I've heard admit he's a coward.'

The mood grew darker still. In the huge battle which was World War One, a much smaller conflict started in a British trench. George provoked anger, hatred even and knew he'd now have to fight another foe. Before he could scramble to his feet and physically defend his good name, his pal, his best mate, Paddy Murphy took control.

'Now come on lads, this is ridiculous. George is no coward; he's as brave as the best of us. An' no-one makes a better bully beef stew. So let's be saving our strength for killin' Fritz.'

Paddy winked at George who nodded his thanks. The anger settled a little but continued to bubble. The situation changed when their officer, Captain Alan Laidlaw, came along the trench.

'Right chaps, you take over guard duty in ten minutes.'

The officer turned to leave but stopped when Reynolds spoke.

'Captain, what should we do if we find one of us is a coward?'

George winced, as much as when the Germans fired their Minenwerfer bombs.

The officer stared at Reynolds. 'Explain.'

Reynolds didn't hold back and pointed at George. 'Private Miracle here doesn't want to go over the top.'

No-one spoke. A strange silence settled in the trench. The Captain turned to George. 'It's not a crime to be scared, Miracle. When the time comes, I'm sure you'll do your duty.'

'I'm not ashamed to admit I'm scared, sir, but I do wonder why we attack the way we do.'

'He's a coward,' hissed Reynolds.

Laidlaw became curious and challenged George. 'Go on.'

'Why don't we try other tactics in order to capture their trench, one that doesn't almost guarantee massive casualties to our side?' He paused wanting permission to continue. The Captain nodded. 'Why not send fewer men and have them crawl or slide at night rather than charge and run by day? Have one group cause a disturbance and draw fire, and while the Germans are distracted, a second group cuts their wire and attacks their trench. If it doesn't work then only a handful of our men may die.'

'Will die,' said a soldier.

The captain spoke. 'We've tried night raids before, several times. The idea's not new.'

'Yes but why not something new to destroy their machine guns, sir?'

Laidlaw spoke. 'So you reckon we send over an artillery barrage, and then a few men crawl out towards Fritz?'

'No artillery barrage, sir.'

'What?' almost exploded the officer. 'You need cover, man.'

'But the cover tells the Germans we're coming, sir. They know our tactics. Once our big guns open up, their machine gun crews are on standby ready to fire. Our tactics don't seem to change. We're predictable. Why not try something different, sir?'

Without realizing, George challenged his captain who needed time to think. He was not used to the lower ranks having ideas, let alone coming up with proposed tactics. The others were fascinated. Reynolds boiled with fury. The man he accused of cowardice seemed brave even reckless. George struck the killer blow.

'I'd be prepared to go, sir,' he said.

A split second later, Paddy spoke. 'Me too, sir.'

Laidlaw froze. Here were two of his men, not even NCOs but privates, suggesting a daring plan, an initiative for his unit, and offering to risk their lives to see it through. He needed to make a decision; tricky for many officers.

'I'll need to send this up the line.'

'Why, sir?' asked George in a respectful way. 'We could go tonight, the two of us. If we destroy their machinegun, it'll make a later charge so much safer.'

George's logic battered the officer. His training kept him on the straight and narrow. Refer up the line before making any decision but here, now, his men, well one of them, urged him to be daring to try and destroy the enemy another way.

'I'll think about it,' he said. 'But if you go, you'll be better off with three men.' He looked at the group in their mud-covered uniforms. He stared at Reynolds. The accuser felt sick. He'd painted himself into a corner. The man he called a coward volunteered to make the ultimate sacrifice. Coward? Hardly. Reynolds owned his mistake and gave the smallest of nods.

'Good man, Reynolds,' said Captain Laidlaw and walked away.

The three volunteers struggled to control their bodies with shaking becoming easy.

Darkness settled and George stood on guard duty fighting his own thoughts. *I've signed my own death certificate. How will my stupid sacrifice help my mother and sister? How will they feel when a telegram is delivered to 24 Darwin Road? Private George John Miracle has been killed in action. If I don't get home alive, Daisy in Norwich will never speak to me again. What have I done?*

'Time's up, private,' said Paddy informing his pal they were relieved.

'Any word from the captain?' asked George.

'About what?' replied Paddy trying to keep George relaxed.

George stared at Paddy and walked past him to his bedroom suite further along the trench. Reynolds stepped forward.

'You've got your wish, hero,' he said and George froze. 'Your suicidal raiding party leaves at O two hundred.'

George couldn't speak. Hero was not the word he would have used. Bloody fool more like. Captain Laidlaw arrived.

'Permission granted, Miracle. A small raiding party is to approach the Boche trench to the south of their closest machine gun. You'll deploy as many Mills grenades as possible. I hope you all play cricket as throwing grenades is key. We'll be ready with covering fire to help you get back in one piece. If you knock out the machine gun, we'll consider a raid. You go at O two hundred hours. Any questions?'

George shook his head. 'No sir.'

'Good show. Get your grenades and sort out your roles.' He walked away and George looked at Paddy and Reynolds. *Am I in charge?*

'What's the drum, skip?' asked Paddy accepting George as leader.

Reynolds interrupted, assumed command and called the shots. 'I'll

81

scout ahead and cut the wire. You two throw the bombs.'

The others didn't object and wondered if Reynolds took on the front position to prove he possessed bravery to burn. The trio prepared. Was it for death or glory or both?

The distance between British and German trenches varied. In one area the trenches were hundreds of yards apart; in others, barely a cricket pitch separated the two "teams". In some places you could hear your enemy chatting, laughing or screaming in pain. For George and colleagues, their no-man's-land measured about a hundred yards.

With no moon thanks to cloud cover, visibility was a few yards if that. Captain Laidlaw stood beside the ladder. 'All set?' The black-faced trio muttered their assent. Talkative could never describe any soldier about to enter no-man's-land. 'Good luck, keep your head down and get back sharpish once the grenades explode.'

George grabbed the ladder but was pushed aside by Reynolds. 'I'm first,' he said and climbed steadily. They all knew German snipers watched and waited. Daily, one or two Tommys copped a puncture in their tin hat and died in an instant.

Despite the darkness giving their spirits a lift, they knew the outline of a slithering body might still be seen, and a German sniper always shot first and never bothered asking questions later.

There were disguised gaps in their own line of barbed wire making their passage to the swamp beyond easier.

Reynolds separated two sections, slid through the gap then gave a short soft whistle. George and Paddy slid forward and out into the valley of the shadow of death. They froze peering into the gloom. Reynolds closed the gap then joined them.

'Ready?' he whispered.

The others tapped his shoulders and off he went.

This was no-man's land, treeless, grassless, stinking mud. A few of the bomb craters were so big they housed small lakes. Most craters doubled as temporary cemeteries with bodies or parts of bodies asleep on crater walls. A dead horse provided reasonable cover, its carcass stopping German bullets.

In daylight and under moonlight, the place looked like the surface of the moon whatever that looked like.

The trio slithered through mud and around corpses. The revolting stench of death forced them at times to hold their breath. Touching a dead comrade sent a shiver through your body.

They stopped a few yards short of the German wire.

'I'll cut their wire,' whispered Reynolds. 'Give me five minutes then follow and chuck your bombs. I'll give you cover until you get back here. Our boys will give us covering fire to make it back. Okay?'

George and Paddy nodded and checked their watches.

Reynolds set off.

He reached the German wire. The silence seemed loud, the Brits waited for a flare pistol to explode revealing them as sitting ducks to the waiting Germans. Reynolds found a place to cut the enemy's wire. A snap of the tool sounded like a rifle shot. Where were the German shouts? All three froze waiting for the snipers' fire. No response.

Watching their watches and listening for any sound made hearts work harder. Could the Boche hear British hearts?

'Five minutes,' whispered George pointing to his watch. Paddy nodded and both spoke softly as one.

'Good luck, mate,' which provoked a grim grin, and together they slithered towards the German wire. Through the gap they went then froze. Where was Reynolds?

They peered through the gloom thinking they could see and hear him. A few yards to go but sliding through mud made a sound. A German light shell rocket with a flare on a parachute would flood no-man's-land in light and have withering fire end their raid and their lives. George looked across at his mate.

"Bombs," said their eyes,' and George felt for the grenades in his satchel. The plan was to have them placed on the ground, pull two pins then throw both. While the grenades did their deadly business, they would pull two more pins, throw them then flee. They were 30 yards from the Germans so with heads down, they should be safe.

Both men carefully put their bombs on the ground. They looked at one another and George raised his hand to give Paddy the signal.

As George's hand started to drop, an almighty scream exploded. Reynolds leapt to his feet and screaming, ran at the German machine gun firing as he went. His bayonet then became his only weapon.

His scream woke the Germans in front and his colleagues a

hundred yards behind. Sleeping soldiers awoke in a flash.

George didn't hesitate and yelled. 'Throw y'bombs, Paddy,' and did so with his. It took a few seconds for the grenades to explode and for the Germans to open fire. Way behind them, the British in their trench were ready and joined the party.

George and Paddy pushed themselves into the mud as possible shrapnel from their bombs plus bullets from Mauser and Lee-Enfield rifles went pinging across the mud.

With all their grenades set free, George slid around and headed to the crater. 'Paddy!' he screamed hoping his mate would join him. He did and they "swam" through the mud and slid towards a crater.

How they'd get from there back to their trench could wait. First, survive by finding relative safety.

George gathered speed and dragged himself head first into the crater. Paddy followed and George helped him to the bottom. The battle exploded above as they cowered in the mud.

Paddy looked at George who saw fear or pain in his friend's eyes.

'Paddy? Are you hit?' George scrambled up close to his mate who didn't speak. A flare broke in the sky above and George clearly saw Paddy with blood all down the side of his face and a dark patch on his shoulder. 'Lie still,' demanded George fumbling for a bandage.

Paddy lifted a hand. It hurt to do so and more so to speak. 'I'm gone, George. Leave me, go.'

'Shut up,' snapped George desperate to help his pal.

Paddy coughed blood. George despaired. He ignored the Great War above and around them. Another flare turned night into day. George found a bandage but didn't know where to place it.

'Stop,' croaked Paddy grabbing George's arm forcing him to freeze. 'Shoot me,' begged the dying man in obvious agony. 'Now, please, shoot me. George ...'

Blood gushed from his mouth stopping his speech. George could no more shoot his pal than stop the war. His despair became a physical pain. He looked into Paddy's eyes and watched the light fade and fade then disappear. Movement and a smattering of dirt into the crater distracted him. Lying flat above him, George saw a German pointing his rifle at the two Tommys.

The Mauser spat and the already dead Paddy was shot. This wrong choice of target gave George the moment to scramble up the crater, rip the German's rifle from his grasp then grab the enemy's shoulders and pull hard. Down slid the Boche. George shackled his desperation to his misery. Enraged, he grabbed his rifle with bayonet and killed a man up close and personal then fell back exhausted.

Sucking in deep breaths, he replayed the last few minutes in his mind. Never mind the artillery exchanges between the trenches, George pictured Reynolds on his suicide mission, and then Paddy dying in the mud beside him.

The German didn't count, until he groaned and George faced another nightmare. The man was still alive. *Should I help him?*

'Help me,' groaned the enemy. 'Erschießt mich, bitte, Engländer.'

For the second time in a matter of minutes, George was asked, rather begged to kill a badly injured fellow human.

What part of my military training covered this situation?

George couldn't do it. He lay in the crater as darkness returned and the firing became sporadic. The wounded German's breathing grew noisy. His lungs were filling with blood or water or whatever. This time he did die. The firing ceased. Despite his mental torture, exhausted, George fell asleep.

Rain woke him. Good solid drops that grew heavy and stung his face. Dawn was a good hour or more away. He squinted through the drops in his eyes. Two bodies nearby didn't feel the rain. George dragged himself towards Paddy.

He tried to close the man's eyes but only succeeded in adding to the mud content of his face. Thank God for the rain. Paddy's head was pointing towards the German trench. George knew what to do. As the rain became heavier, he climbed part of the way up the crater, grabbed Paddy's feet and began dragging the corpse up the crater wall on the British side and back home. It was a long way to London's East End but the first stop was their trench.

At the top of the crater, in the pre-dawn darkness, George couldn't see more than a yard in any direction.

With his back to his own trench and kneeling, he dragged his friend to safety. A step, drag his friend. Repeat. Repeat again. No artillery, no firing of any sort. He couldn't feel his hands due to the cold and rain. His tears were invisible as he spoke to his mate in a normal voice. 'Hang in there, Paddy. Blighty here we come, mate.'

When he felt an object touch his back, the fear nearly killed him. He turned slowly and discovered the British wire. He faced the unseen trench and called. 'Hello. It's me, Private George Miracle.'

A voice was barely heard in the storm. 'What the hell are you doin' out there you idiot? Can't you see it's rainin'?'

Before George could ask for help, two Tommy's were by his side. One held the gap in the wire while the other surveyed the scene.

'You get in, George. We'll bring y'mate.'

The next few hours were a mess for George. He drifted in and out of consciousness. He felt a new pain. When he gained a sense of reality, he realized it was a doctor beside him working on his body.

'Easy, soldier, we're almost done.'

The medical man spoke with a clipped accent, the sort George heard from Liverpool Street passengers wearing a pinstriped suit and bowler hat.

'Where am I, sir?' asked George.

'You're in a field hospital, old man. You copped a bit of shrapnel and we've managed to clean you up. But I don't fancy you'll be playing for Tottenham Hotspur next week. Try and get some kip.'

George couldn't sleep if you paid him. His mind came alive with memories of the last few hours; he didn't know how many. Tears came alive as he remembered Paddy and his horrific death, his begging to be shot.

Did his body make it back to our trench? Has he already been buried? What will I say to his family?

In fact, Paddy was already buried. At least his family could, in years to come, travel to France and lay flowers on his grave marked with an identifying cross. Private Patrick Anthony Murphy.

Hours passed and then days. He felt pain in his hip but lying on a stretcher in the field hospital was not too bad. The trouble occurred when he needed the latrine. Oh my God. The serious pain kicked in. One orderly was not enough. Humiliating best described his lot being held either side by two chaps, taken outside and helped to sit between the boards to evacuate his bowels.

One day he stopped in his tracks when a female nurse joined his support team. 'I'm all right, Nurse,' he said trying to send her away.

'Now, now,' she replied, 'we can't have you falling in, now can we?'

Shit thought George.

He wanted to know his future and asked a doctor. 'What's going to happen to me, Doctor?'

'We think you'll soon be fit to travel, soldier. Back to Blighty for you where the nurses are gorgeous and the weather's terrible.'

'Back to England? But what will I do?'

'Get better.'

Get better thought George. *And then what?*

'With any luck you might even be home for Christmas.' He wasn't and spent New Year in France.

The doctor attended to another of his many patients and George lay there thinking of his family and then his future, if any, on the railways.

In time he did become reacquainted with a steam locomotive and rolling stock when he was wheeled onto a platform in rural France to board a hospital train back to the French coast.

Chapter 12

In 1917 the British government faced a financial crisis, a massive debt caused by World War One. Injured soldiers and war widows needed cash. The widow gave up her husband for king and country, and many of the two million wounded soldiers couldn't return to their previous occupation; many to any occupation. But at least the generous government would look after these damaged heroes and their dependents. Or so you would think.

To tackle this financial crisis, *their* financial crisis, the government hired the best creative accountants and political scriptwriters in Britain who created eye-watering ways to reduce or remove payments to millions of suffering men, women and children.

A democratic government created appalling and unfair policies and applied them to their citizens. Consider pensions. The British Government paid a pension according to limb loss and worse, according to the amount of limb loss.

'You've only lost half an arm, Mister. Right, you'll get less than the chap who lost his entire arm.'

What a way to reward those who suffered defending their country.

Then to many female applicants they said, 'You only married your disabled-through-war-injury husband for his money. Sorry, madam; application refused.'

You could describe George Miracle as one of the lucky two million wounded British soldiers. His right hip copped a shrapnel wound and the field hospital doctors removed most of the metal fragments. 'Sorry, soldier,' said the medical man, 'but you'll be buried with a bit of a Boche bullet in your body. Your ballroom dancing days are over.' But at least George was alive, reasonably mobile and determined.

By the time he was cleared for a return to Blighty in the spring of 1917, he was able to get around, using only a stick. His plan was to chuck the cane and report for duty at the nearest recruitment office.

Of course that never happened. His mobility was good but if he was commanded to run, climb and slide through no-man's-land, he would clearly fail. He might as well be an amputee and/or blind.

He landed in Blighty and was placed on an Up train to Waterloo. From there, he and his fellow wounded soldiers were transferred to hospital.

His family knew he was recovering in a field hospital in France. They didn't know he was back in London, not far from his home in Wood Green.

The First London General Hospital, which then was the largest in the world, became home to thousands of wounded soldiers. George found himself in the Charlotte Ward, a long narrow room with space down the middle dividing two rows of beds. The exterior wall possessed big windows allowing natural light to flood inside.

There were chairs—a luxury in many wards—for those able to get out of bed. A plentiful supply of nurses, moving to and from their stations, kept the place busy. A huge Union Flag hung from one wall and every bed enjoyed the cleanest of clean sheets.

Patients were given newspapers and magazines and allowed, even encouraged to smoke until their fingers turned green and their lungs shrivelled and died.

Once settled, George wrote his first letter posted in Britain since the day he left for France more than a year ago. It was delivered to 24 Darwin Road, Noel Park Estate, Wood Green, and Connie couldn't believe the envelope. It bore her name in her son's hand but was postmarked London. London!

The postman rarely saw Mrs Miracle smile. Now her face exploded.

This couldn't be a death notice from the government. It was from her son, and he must be back in England!

Now 15, Emily spent her days in a government building sorting clothing for recycling, while Fred still ran the railway world at Liverpool Street. When the letter arrived, Connie and the family cat, Trixie, were alone in Darwin Road.

Both their hearts beat faster; the cat's because she'd never seen her mistress so excited. The news overwhelmed the widow. Her boy was alive, safe in a London Hospital, and ready to receive visitors.

But was he damaged? Connie knew George would prepare her for bad news. If his wounds or injuries were shocking, he would make sure she knew what to expect. Surely if he was blind or an amputee he would say so. She was so excited she fed the cat way too much. Trixie didn't mind hoping the mistress felt like this tomorrow. Connie made plans to visit her boy.

Fred and Emily were over the moon. 'When can we go and visit, George, Ma?' begged the young girl, now a young woman.

'He doesn't talk about his body being broken,' said Fred handing back the letter. 'Surely he'd prepare us for a terrible injury.'

'What do you mean, terrible?' asked a worried Emily.

Connie calmed her daughter. 'I'm sure he's okay.'

The daughter wanted answers. 'He can't be okay, Ma. He's been brought home and placed in a hospital.'

'I'll go there tomorrow,' said Fred. 'I'll find out when we can all visit. And Em, you can write a letter to your brother and tell him we'll see him soon.'

She liked that idea but complained. 'Why can't we visit him now?'

George constantly pestered the doctors and nurses about being discharged. They all said the same thing. 'Every patient is constantly being assessed but Rome wasn't built in a day. Be patient, patient.'

George never felt sorry for himself. He knew there were wards in this hospital for men who became blind, lost a limb or limbs and who would now struggle for the rest of their lives. He felt sorry for those men and more so for the ones who would never return. His friend Paddy Murphy often popped into his thoughts. As soon as he was able, George planned to visit Paddy's home and tell his family how brilliant and brave their son and brother really was.

When the mail was delivered and he received two letters, his spirits soared. His mother wrote on behalf of the family and his sister penned a personal and touching letter. He longed to see his loved ones and kept looking towards the entrance of the ward when visitors were allowed.

Then it happened. George's bed, in the middle of the ward, gave him time to see a trio of smiling faces as they approached. When close, Emily accelerated running the last few paces. Sitting up in bed, he copped the full brunt of his sister's frontal attack. She bumped his hip and George couldn't help but howl.

People turned, a nurse arrived and Emily died of shame.

'Please be careful, Miss,' hissed a nurse.

Connie and Fred looked on in horror as Emily couldn't help but cry.

'I'm okay, Em,' said George. He wasn't. 'Please Nurse, I'm fine.'

The nurse surveyed her patient and frowning, retreated. This allowed Connie to approach her beloved boy and they carefully embraced.

'Hello Ma, it's good to see you.'

Connie wanted to speak but choked. Fred stood back with his arm around his despairing niece whispering support. She relaxed a little.

He moved forward with hand extended. 'I could say, "Stand by your beds" but I'm sure it's inappropriate.' The men shook hands and his family observed the soldier's freedom of movement.

George felt for his upset sister and beckoned her to him. 'Come round this side, Em and give me a hug.'

She did ever so gently and felt a new form of happiness. Her big brother was home, alive and seemed to be even more solid and reliable than ever.

'Find a chair, Ma, and tell me all your news.'

Fred took a chair from nearby and his sister sat. George patted his bed and Emily sat. Fred stood. Every station master has decades of being on his feet.

'We don't know what's wrong with you, George,' asked Connie now finding her voice.

'I copped a wound on my hip; couldn't walk for weeks and am only now getting around with a stick.'

'When are you coming home?' asked Emily. Trust a young 'un to say what they think. Cut to the chase did the sister.

'Good question, Em. I keep asking the doctors and I reckon by pestering them so much, they'll give in and kick me out.'

Connie caught her daughter's desire for news. 'Will you be able to go back to work?'

Silence. Fred stared at his nephew. George paused and doubled the tension. 'I'm not sure. I'd like to but unless I can push carts, climb stairs and carry parcels, the company may put me out to pasture.'

Fred's voice sounded low but strong. 'You leave the company to me, young man and concentrate on getting better.'

A nurse rang a bell. George's family were late and so were asked to leave soon after they arrived. But they made progress. Their much-loved and much-missed family member, the prodigal son, had returned to the bosom of his family.

More kisses, hugs and a handshake followed with the visitors continuing to wave as they left the ward.

His family were not the only visitors George entertained at the First London General. Word spread around the country, well, at least as far as Norwich. His former housekeeper, Daisy, danced for joy when told George was home safe and almost well. She quickly sent word to her son, Oscar in London. He didn't need encouragement to visit the man who reunited him and his mother. Oscar, his wife and their children went to see the returned soldier, the porter they grew to love.

Two days later, George looked up and saw an officer in uniform stride into the ward. He stopped at the nurses' station and spoke to the sister on duty. She pointed. The officer, accompanied by a corporal excelling in obsequiousness, strode towards George stopping beside his bed. George felt obliged to salute and did so badly.

'At ease, Private' said the officer.

These two soldiers were not your usual family visitors so naturally patients and staff stopped and stared. George held his breath.

The officer read a document. 'Private George John Miracle, following a study of despatches from your division when serving in France in the week beginning November 24, 1916, for gallantry in attacking and destroying an enemy position, and retrieving the body of a comrade, you are hereby awarded the Military Medal.'

He turned to the corporal who handed his senior officer a small box. The entire ward sat or stood transfixed. Those in far beds strained to see. The officer removed the medal and pinned it to George's pyjamas. As the officer extended his hand and George shook it, every patient and member of the hospital staff in the Charlotte Ward applauded with enthusiasm. A chap who'd lost half an arm, slapped his bedside table with his only hand.

The officer nodded then left leaving the corporal to hand George the box, salute the bedridden private than scamper after his superior.

Patients crowded around and George shook more hands in five

minutes than he could remember. Even better, two of the nurses stepped forward and kissed his cheek. George had developed a crush on one in particular and reckoned he'd dream about her in far more detail after her peck.

Wait till the family arrive. Wait till I show them my medal.

But seeing his family was not the only good news.

An hour later the resident surgeon carried out his rounds. When he reached George, he folded his arms and stared at the patient.

'I'm fed up with your malingering, soldier.' George froze at the word malingering. 'We've only kept you in here long enough to get your damn medal.'

The surgeon's face opened into a grin, George went from panic to pleasure and more so when he heard the magic words.

'Congratulations, soldier, and you're being discharged.' He too stepped forward and offered his hand which George squeezed as hard as he could. 'Good luck and you can pester your family from now on.'

Those around his bed clapped and cheered. The surgeon left and George's favourite nurse appeared. She held a walking stick in one hand and a crutch in the other.

'Do you fancy a stroll around the ward, Private Miracle?' she asked holding out both aids. George pointed to the stick.

He was helped out of bed and grasping the walking stick but with his favourite nurse by his side, they set off. His journey produced even more comments, cheers and clapping. George Miracle stepped out with pride wearing his medal which contained the inscription, FOR BRAVERY IN THE FIELD.

His uncle knew nothing of the Military Medal being awarded. He sat in his office wading through paperwork, the bane of his life, and found his mind drifting towards his nephew's safe return. An almighty crash sent a massive shock through his body. A train crash anywhere was horrendous but here in his London station; never!

Fred was on his feet and rushing out to inspect the disaster. Running towards the platform a second explosion gave him heart palpitations. Another crash! My God, what is happening?

Forget railway accidents, Liverpool Street station was the target of a German air-raid.

While machine guns and later tanks were killing machines in the

Great War, by 1915, Germany added aircraft—zeppelins and bombers—to wreak havoc on mainland Europe and now in England. Air raids were a novelty for Londoners.

A hundred years earlier, the good folk of the village of Waterloo in what would become Belgium, walked three miles to the countryside to watch a battle in which thousands of soldiers died. It became entertainment, a sort of spectator sport. Fast forward a century.

In World War One when a dogfight took place in the skies over London, people ran outside to watch. Fascinated men, women and children looked up and died. Hundreds were killed and thousands wounded. The government had done little to warn its citizens of the need to take cover. Such government inactivity soon changed. It needed too.

In June 1917, Liverpool Street station copped three bombs in a daytime raid. The bombs fell on different parts of the station. One failed to explode but its weight caused significant damage.

The two exploding bombs landed, one on a platform and the other on a train about to depart. 16 people were killed and 15 wounded.

Fred burst onto Platform 1 and nearly died. No derailment, no collision but widespread carnage. He hurried to the wrecked train to do what he could for the dying and wounded victims.

It was 11 minutes past 2 on a sunny afternoon when the war came to Fred Carmody's station.

The whole of London talked about the German air-raid. On the day the station copped its bombs, so too did other areas and hundreds of Londoners were killed and more than a thousand wounded. The Western Front moved further west, striking many UK sites including a Whitechapel whiskey warehouse.

George knew countless tales of hardship amid the horrors in France but now his family and especially his uncle, discovered horrific experiences of their own.

The Porter

Chapter 13

The fatted calf equivalent was half a leg of lamb which cost Connie her pin money and a fair chunk of her savings. There were roast potatoes, parsnips, carrots and broad beans, and finding those was a major task in itself. She steamed a plum pudding and her custard saw the diners demanding seconds. Her boy was home and the whole street knew. It would have been London if Connie had her way.

George felt terrific. His hip gave him pain at regular intervals and on cold mornings it took him a good few minutes of exercise to make ordinary walking bearable. But it was sleeping in his own bed under the family roof that gave him a wonderful feeling of pleasure.

Changes were afoot. Connie swapped her room for George's old room upstairs thus allowing him to avoid the climb. There would be no stairs for the man with a stick and, in addition, he was close to the lavatory. His mother thought of everything.

George's first task was a visit to the florist shop owned and operated by Paddy Murphy's family. Their tears were many but the news of the bravery and sacrifice of their boy, added pride to their grief.

For George, the question remained; *what am I going to do?* He thought about it but not while sitting still. Every day he'd be out the front door and walking. The Army paid a small pension. He gave his mother half and squirreled away the rest.

A week after he came home, Uncle Fred knocked George sideways. 'How about you pop into the station in the morning, George?'

The others saw confusion and excitement on his face.

'Me? Come to Liverpool Street?'

Fred nodded. 'It'll do you good to get out, and there are many staff members who'd like to see you. Most have never met a war hero.'

George never paraded his medal but felt waves of pleasure thinking about his first place of work. 'I'd like to return, Uncle Fred.'

'Good, well wear your old uniform and make sure your Military Medal is on your lapel.'

Connie and Emily beamed while George looked shocked with the news sending his heart into top speed. Speechless, he nodded and smiled but gave a huge grin when Fred asked a simple question.

'You do remember how to get there?'

Wearing his railway uniform, he set off at 10am and found his GER Rail Pass still valid. Besides, who would challenge a man who gave his all for king and country?

The porter on the ticket gate was new but had been told all about the porter turned war hero.

'Good morning, sir,' said the man who was twice George's age. 'You must be porter George Miracle.'

The station master was told of the new arrival and came out to greet his nephew he found chatting with former workmates. George loved the attention and even passengers looked at the fuss being made. Fred walked with him to Lost Property and introduced the new staff members.

Back in the SM's office, George enjoyed a cuppa with the boss. 'I can't get over the change in staff, Uncle Fred.' He frowned. 'I'm sorry, Mr Carmody.'

'There's a war on, George, as if you didn't know. The conscription rules still apply. ASM Rogers refused to accept his right to an essential job exemption and is fighting somewhere in Belgium. We're struggling to fill positions which is where you come in.'

George held his breath. 'I beg your pardon?'

'I've spoken with the company and they're prepared to have you return to work but only on certain tasks. Do you agree?'

'Of course,' beamed George. 'Are you serious? I'm sorry; I mean did the company *really* agree?'

'Working in Lost Property and collecting tickets won't require running between platforms or lumping heavy parcels. You can start in the morning.'

'Why not now?' asked George allowing his excitement to override his manners.

The SM stroked his chin. 'Let's not get carried away. You can get out of bed by 7 and travel to work with me. Now be off with you.'

George forgot he was no longer in the army, stood and saluted. 'Aye, aye, sir,' he said and left beaming. He hesitated at the door and looked back at his uncle. He spoke with emphasis, 'Aye, aye, sir.'

And so the second phase of the young porter's working life was born. He would rest his walking stick behind the counter in Lost Property or hang the stick between the railings at the ticket barrier. Whatever pain or discomfort his injured hip caused was brushed aside in his enjoyment of the job, and being back "on the rail".

Word spread about his war service and gallantry, and many regular passengers greeted him by name. A few used their forefinger in offering a simple salute as he collected or checked their ticket.

Meanwhile, across the Channel and elsewhere around the Globe, the slaughter of the Great War continued to rage.

One highlight for George was a weekend trip to Norwich. Bert Ramsbottom should have retired but due to the manpower shortage, remained the SM. He chortled with delight when George stepped off the 11:26 stopping train from Liverpool Street.

'Grand to see, young man, and if you reckon I'm pleased, beware of our favourite housekeeper.'

'How is the dear lady?'

'When she heard you were back in Blighty, *and* awarded a bravery medal, *and* was coming for the weekend, I thought she was having a heart attack. You'll dine well tonight my boy.'

The elderly SM spoke the truth. Daisy would never forget how George the porter, the lodger, traced the baby son she gave away. To this day, she is known as the favourite Grannie in Cricklewood, and Daisy possessed the deepest love for the man who made it all possible. Her greeting made George cry.

Being able to work at a job he loved, helped George in his recovery. It appeared he would always walk with a slight limp but he knew how lucky, how fortunate he was to be able to see, have all his limbs and not suffer horrible mental problems associated with shell shock.

The war continued although as 1918 appeared on the horizon, people hoped and prayed the carnage soon would cease.

Back in London and sitting around the table one night, Fred cleared his throat in what seemed an unusual manner. The others looked at him.

'I have news.' Silence reigned.

'Are you all right, Fred?' asked his sister.

'No. The company doctor gave me a medical last week and told me my heart is getting old.' He paused and the others hung on his every word. *Is Uncle Fred dying?*

'Being the SM at one of the biggest and busiest stations in London is not wise for a man with a dicky ticker.' Another pause and still none of the others spoke. 'I've thought of a plan. If I retire, my pension will make life a pretty close run thing. I went to see the company secretary with a proposal and he said he'd think it over.'

Emily broke the silence. 'Are you going to die, Uncle?'

Connie gasped and Fred smiled. 'Not this week, young lady.'

George jumped in. 'May we know your plan, Uncle?'

'You may and be assured it includes all three of you.' His family were hooked. 'I've asked for a transfer to a station outside of London. It would employ an SM with a station house so we could all move from London and live in the country.' He looked at their stunned faces. 'What do you think?'

'I'd love to live in the country,' said Emily with a smile to match her obvious enthusiasm. 'I'll be sad to leave my friends but I'm sure I can make new ones in the country.'

'It sounds wonderful, Fred,' added his sister.

George sounded like a wet blanket. 'Will there be a job for me?'

Fred raised an index finger. 'Now we come to part two of the plan. I've suggested to Head Office you could become a permanent porter at my new station so when I retire or drop off the twig, you'll have a job, and housing in the country is always much cheaper than here in London. You and the ladies can become country folk.'

The room buzzed. The others saw how the man of the house wanted their futures secured. Happiness flooded the kitchen. George felt his heartrate get busy. Emily brought the others undone.

'Why are you on a twig, Uncle?'

It took a while for the laughter to settle.

Every day George wanted to ask his uncle if any news had arrived from the company. For the porter, no news was bad news. In his break at work, George scoured the GER rail map looking at stations wondering which might be suitable.

It must be big enough to employ another porter and must have a railway cottage attached. He knew most of the station names and certainly on the mainline to Norwich, as he'd passed through all of them when he worked at Norwich Victoria. He tried to picture what certain stations looked like; signal box, branch line, island platform, goods yard, passing loop, crossing gates, goods shed, etc.

Uncle Fred's plan seemed perfect in theory. George would have an ongoing career in the railways and any disability he suffered would be understood by the man in charge. His mother and sister would have a new life in the country and a roof over their head.

But will it happen and if so, when and where?

In the meantime, life continued as did the war.

One morning George was working his shift in Lost Property. A young woman entered wearing a long, tight-fitting dress with a fur collar and a large, almost too large hat.

'Good morning, madam,' said George. 'Can I help you?'

'I hope so. My name is Victoria Hall. My sister is walking out with a soldier I believe you know.'

George found her fascinating. Who are the people she mentioned, and what relevance do they have to a missing umbrella or lost left glove? When she spoke a certain name, his senses copped a whack.

'My sister's beau is Lord George Carruthers.' She waited for the porter's response studying his face.

'Oh,' managed George, memories of a strange death, a possible murder in a posh Hampstead mansion racing inside his head. 'How is Lord Carruthers?'

'We hope he's alive and well but fighting in France is a terrible and tricky situation. But then you would know what it's like over there.'

How does she know my history?

Victoria continued. 'My sister has received letters from George which have caused her alarm. He hints at a possible solution to the mystery surrounding his father's death.'

Again George seemed lost for words. 'I see.' *But why tell me this?*

'I'm a private investigator, Mr Miracle, hoping to help your namesake, and would like to discuss the case with you, at your convenience of course.'

George struggled. 'I would like to help Lord Carruthers but I'm not sure I can. The police interviewed me, I told them all I knew and that was the last I heard. I don't even know if the authorities discovered what happened to the late Lord Carruthers.'

'I understand but my sister believes His Lordship has vital information and believes you may be able to help him and throw light on my investigation.' She paused. He didn't fob her off and refuse to help but nor did he offer to co-operate.

'May I call at your home, Mr Miracle, for a brief chat, please?

Not keen but with fond memories of the nervous soldier he met on Platform 1 an age ago, George agreed. Miss Victoria Hall made an appointment for 8pm at Wood Green that night.

George said nothing about this encounter. He remembered how his visit to the mansion in Hampstead led to the police arresting him and asking many questions. To escape publicity, he took a job in Norwich. Now, out of the blue, the past has reared its ugly head.

Over supper, he told his family about the encounter with Miss Hall, and how the private investigator would call later. Connie reacted strongly. A private investigator was bad enough but a female! Connie swam in scepticism. 'I don't approve of this matter, George. You should refuse to co-operate.'

'But Ma, I've already agreed.'

Fred kept his cool advising George to stick to the facts and to avoid elaboration. 'The less said the better, George. Okay?'

'Yes Uncle,' he replied and the evening meal was consumed in a sombre atmosphere.

When the front door was tapped, George took a deep breath and headed up the passage. Miss Ward, he assumed she was a Miss, stood there with a smile and held out a gloved hand.

'Good evening, George. May I call you George?'

He took her hand in a gentle grip. 'Of course,' he replied stepping back and indicating. 'Please come in.'

They settled in the front room. It was cool not cold but Connie insisted the fire be not lit. 'This is awfully kind of you to help your namesake,' she said taking out a notepad. 'Would you like my sister to send your regards to George in her next letter?'

What could George Miracle say? 'Please do and I would welcome any news from France of his safety.'

Excellent,' smiled Victoria. 'Now please tell me of the events which brought you and Lord George Carruthers together?'

Does she mean the deceased Lord or his son? He spoke and, contrary to his uncle's advice, gave the woman chapter and verse. She took notes and seemed to scribble as well, rarely interrupting to seek clarification.

Once George finished his version of events, she closed her notebook quickly and stood. 'Thank you so much, Mr Miracle. You've been most helpful.'

George stood. *What happened to calling me George?* 'I hope your sister and Lord Carruthers enjoy good health and much happiness.'

He showed her out. Her smile beamed. He stood at the door until she closed the gate and headed down the street. He closed the door to be confronted by all three members of his family.

'Well?' said Connie.

'Was she pretty?' asked Emily.

'Did you stay on the tracks?' requested the station master.

The next morning George had forgotten the private investigator when his uncle sent a lad porter to find the war hero and have him attend the SM's office. 'Sit down,' said Fred, and George's pulse raced. 'The secretary of the company has approved my request to move.'

George wanted to shout, "Hurrah" or "Wonderful" but said nowt.

'What do you know about Chelmsford?'

George's mind raced. 'Ah it's on the mainline to Norwich, I think between Romford and Witham.'

'Well I have pleasure in advising you we have been appointed to Chelmsford starting the first of next month.'

This time George did give vent to his feelings. He clapped his hands as his mind filled with questions. 'But surely, Uncle, I won't be the only porter. It's a large station with many services.'

'Count it as a promotion, George. From there you can think about working hard to become an ASM. Be positive and congratulations.' The men moved to one another and shook hands with feeling and grins. 'I don't know about the accommodation but if there's no bedroom for you, I'm sure we can find you one of the coal boxes.'

Their laughter drifted as far as Platform Number 1.

Chapter 14

Connie and Emily were over the moon. They made an early start to their packing despite the move being three weeks away. 'What will I do with these, Ma?' became a recurring question.

Every night around the kitchen table they talked about their new life. The unseen station house took up so much of their discussion. The shops, churches, parks and cinemas, if any, all copped a mention.

At Liverpool Street, the news spread. The SM leaving seemed natural with Fred closing in on retirement but news of the war hero moving along with his uncle set tongues wagging.

'With his war injury, it's the only way he can stay in the job,' said someone.

'He won't get promotion out in the sticks,' said another.

George heard snippets of gossip and wondered why people took such an attitude. He felt driven to work even harder and better.

The days ticked by and departure day grew closer. The weekend before they were due to leave—by train of course—Fred and George booked a trip to Chelmsford. They were to visit the station, meet the staff, check the accommodation and get the lie of the land.

On the Friday before, Fred received a phone call in his office. 'Fred, it's Clarrie Jenkins. I'm afraid I have bad news. The move to Chelmsford is off.'

Fred felt sick. 'What! But why, what's happened?'

'The former SM at Chelmsford, thought dead in France, is alive and well, back in Blighty, and keen to resume his old position. The chap was a POW but escaped and made it back to our lines.'

'But, Clarrie,' protested Fred. 'It's all been arranged. The porter and I are to visit the station this Sunday.'

'Oh come on, Fred. These things happen.'

'Not to me they don't.'

The official in Head Office of the Great Eastern Railway Company stuck to his guns. 'You're not listening, Fred. The former SM's a hero, and the whole town is celebrating his return.'

'What will I tell my family?'

'Fred, please, it's *nil illegitimi carborundum*. We'll keep you in mind for another post and as soon as I hear of anything, I'll be in touch. Chin up, old man, we'll find you somewhere ideal. Goodbye.'

The receiver went click in Fred's ear and the trying-to-retire SM sat there with the phone buzzing in the background.

He decided to tell his nephew straight away, the womenfolk could wait. George was summoned and a worried nephew entered the SM's office. This wasn't an invitation to take tea with the boss. Fred waited for the porter to sit before spilling the beans.

'Chelmsford is off, George.' The young man's face took a slap.

'Off, Uncle?' He slipped out of the Mr Carmody habit at work.

Fred related the missing POW tale. 'He's arrived back in Blighty, is reasonably fit and healthy, and the company can hardly give a local hero a transfer. I wouldn't be surprised if the Mayor of Chelmsford has arranged a special reception for their beloved SM.'

George blew air. His guts ached and his hip complained. Everything about this move gave him a thrill—a new location, away from London, working closely with his uncle, seeing his mother and sister taken care of, and a new place to meet new people and learn new skills. Now, in a flash, the offer vanished.

Fred tried to cheer up the disconsolate porter. 'Head office said they'll keep an eye out for another vacancy.'

'But it could be weeks, even months. And can your heart stay healthy in this busy station?'

Fred ignored the last question. 'I'll do the talking at home. Don't say anything until I speak to your mother.'

'And Emily,' said George. 'She was so looking forward to the move.'

Fred grimaced. He knew as much and said nothing.

Connie picked up on George's mood as soon as he came home.

'What's the matter, son?'

'Nothing, Ma, I'm fine. I need to write a letter,' he said heading to his room.

'George,' called Emily going after him. 'Look what I found when I was packing.' She showed him a drawing she did as a youngster.

'Lovely,' he said with limited interest and his sister knew a problem weighed on his mind. Poor actor George made Emily retreat.

Fred arrived with a face like thunder. He removed his coat and hat and called his family to the kitchen. Connie and Emily knew something serious looked set to explode. George had set the scene.

'George,' he called. 'In here, now.'

Even George tasted the feeling of fear.

I know the news. Why is he sounding angry at me?

George entered the kitchen and looked at his glaring uncle. 'Congratulations, nephew,' he snapped being both sarcastic and furious. 'Now you're famous or should that be infamous?'

He tossed the afternoon newspaper on the table. It was open at a page with an article headed, *Mysterious Death of Lord*. George moved in close followed by his mother and sister.

They stared at the article but more at the accompanying illustration. It was a drawing, a good likeness of one George John Miracle.

Connie picked up the newspaper and read. After one paragraph she tossed it on the table. Emily delicately picked up the paper.

Connie let fly at her son. 'I warned you about that woman. She tricked you, George and now you've ruined our family name.'

George struggled to think. His mind fizzed. The byline for the article listed the name Victoria Ward. He gasped. 'She's a journalist.' He looked at his speechless family. 'She said her sister was a friend of the young soldier I met at Liverpool Street.'

'It's almost certainly a lie, George,' said the SM. 'She's conned you into giving details for her article. The police have never solved the mysterious death of Lord Carruthers in Hampstead, and now you're back in their sights. What did I say? The less said the better.'

The porter stared at the illustration. It was an excellent likeness.

'She was scribbling while I spoke.'

'She was sketching you, George,' said his sister. 'She's good although I could do better.'

'Well,' said Fred sitting at the table, 'at least there's one bit of good news. This latest fiasco won't ruin our move to Chelmsford.' Connie and Emily looked confused. Connie smelt a rat.

'What's happened, Fred?'

'The company withdrew the offer this morning. The move to Chelmsford's off.'

'What?' gasped the two females. 'Why?' asked Connie. 'Is it because of George's article?'

'No, the previous SM has risen from the grave of a German POW camp as a hero, and will resume duties in Essex as soon as possible.'

The second sucker punch landed. The females sat as Fred gave them the details. Misery flooded the 4th class house in Wood Green.

After supper, George lay on his bed and pondered.

What did happen to the former Lord Carruthers? Where is George Carruthers? Have I ruined my career with the GER? If Uncle Fred retires or worse, dies, what's next for my family?

He avoided everyone by retiring early, and first thing next morning, grabbed a piece of bread and cheese and left for work before anyone even hopped out of bed. As he closed the front gate, he heard his name.

'George!'

He turned to see a man with a camera take a picture—of him.

For a second he thought about chasing the man but instead turned and headed to the station with an exaggerated limp to match his fury.

He was early for ticket collecting and waved the other porter away. 'Go and have a cuppa, mate. I feel like an early start. The next train's not till ten past.'

As early-morning passengers arrived, a few looked twice at the young man in uniform. George sensed a reaction, and even heard their comments. Then the bold ones confronted him.

'Like your picture in the paper, mate,' or 'Nice to have a famous porter at my station.'

The SM arrived and George looked at him with a timid eye. 'In your break,' said Fred in a subtle way, and George was glad of the attempt at privacy.

Later he stood in his uncle's office.

'Take a seat,' said the SM.

'I'd rather stand, Mr Carmody.'

Fred snapped. 'Sit George, and cut the Mr Carmody routine.'

As Fred spoke, a person tapped on his door.

'Not now,' bellowed the SM and George's nerves kept jangling.

'Okay Porter Miracle, what's done is done. Right now you're facing a choice. Scurry back up to Norwich and resume your old duties, or act like a man and work here until a transfer or promotion presents itself. So, is it Norwich or London?'

George spoke without hesitation. 'I'd rather London, please.'

'Good choice. Now, go back to work, and where's your Military Medal?'

'It's in my locker.'

'Pin it on your uniform and wear it whenever on duty. If people are going to talk about you, at least let them know they're talking about a man who showed extraordinary bravery in the field of war.'

George felt a flush of happiness. 'Yes sir.' At the door, he stopped.

'And borrow one of those flash walking sticks in Lost Property.'

'Borrow, Uncle? Isn't that stealing?'

'It is, you're right, f'get it. But George, I want you to learn the best form of defence is attack. Show the passengers and staff you've achieved success in your life. Stand tall. Tell the world you're proud to be a returned serviceman and an honest railwayman.'

Fred pointed to the exit and George, feeling light on his feet, departed.

Christmas 1917 crept closer. The air raids on London with horrific casualties were still on everyone's minds. In Wood Green, the disappointment of missing out on the move to Chelmsford slowly faded and the usual excitement of the Advent season gathered pace.

George continued his porter roles at Liverpool Street but always kept the Hampstead murder in the back of his mind. On duty in Lost Property, he was again interrupted by a young woman dressed as a lady of means. Her youth and beauty grabbed his attention. His mood rapidly changed when she spoke.

'Excuse me but are you Mr George Miracle?'

Not again.

He nodded but refused to speak.

'I'm Valerie Smythe-Taylor and the fiancée of George Carruthers.' George Miracle's dander came alive.

Oh yes and the sister of Victoria Ward no doubt?

'George saw the newspaper article about his late father with an illustration of you, and sent me on a mission, so here I am. He hoped you'd still be working at Liverpool Street.'

To George, this seemed less of a trap. 'I see,' he said quietly. 'And how is your fiancée?'

'He's bearing up well, thank you. He was wounded in France and is now back home in London recuperating after his operation.'

Even more credibility seeped into the conversation. 'May I enquire about his condition?'

'Yes, he lost his right leg.'

George lost his hesitation. 'I'm sorry to hear that.'

'George would very much like you to call on him in hospital; if you can spare the time of course.'

'I'd be glad to visit him. Which hospital is he in?'

'It's the Edmonton Military Hospital in Middlesex. Visiting hours are pretty flexible and I know he'd be delighted to see you again.'

George lost all anger and suspicion. 'I'll pop out after work this afternoon. Please give him my best.'

Her smile made the Lost Property room much brighter. 'Thank you, kind sir. I'll give him the good news in person. Goodbye.'

When his shift ended, George went looking for his uncle finding him on Platform 10 arguing with his new ASM. Fred spotted his nephew.

'You want me?' he asked.

'Yes sir.' George asked his uncle to tell Connie he wouldn't be home for supper. He was to visit a fellow soldier in hospital. Fred agreed and went back to his lively discussion.

George caught a train to Silver Street. He wore his GER uniform with his Military Medal firmly pinned to his jacket and the walk took about 10 minutes. He'd taken to acting the role of a dandy by using his walking stick as a sort of prop to pretend his damaged hip could not interrupt his go-ahead lifestyle. In short, he was vain and desperate to prove he was as fit as the next man.

The Edmonton Military Hospital, a former workhouse, looked impressive as did the circular drive with its blossoming garden.

'Good afternoon,' he said to the receptionist. 'I'm here to visit Private George Carruthers.'

'Do you mean 2nd Lieutenant, Lord George Carruthers?'

Porter George Miracle stood corrected. 'I'm sorry. Yes, I do.'

'Second floor, turn right at the top,' she said pointing, and the

George with all limbs intact set off for the stairs. He carried his stick and walked without relying on it, pretending his hip didn't hurt, disguising his vanity.

This was not like his hospital stay in East London. There were fewer beds and almost all beds came with covered frames allowing those with missing or mangled limbs a little privacy. Chairs were few as getting in and out of bed without one or especially two legs didn't often happen.

A nurse approached George. 'Can I help you, sir?'

He went to say the patient's lengthy name and title when the fiancée with the dazzling smile switched it on again, stood and waved.

'Thank you,' said George, 'I can see my friend.' He set off and, when close, Valerie stepped forward, stood on tip-toe and kissed the visitor on his cheek. He looked stunned as shock, surprise and joy came alive and his name was called.

'George, my dear fellow,' said Carruthers extending both his hands. George the visitor stepped around the young lady and both men shook hands warmly. 'Thank you so, so much for coming to see me. How kind you are.'

'Nonsense, I'm delighted to visit a fellow soldier.'

Carruthers pointed. 'Grab a chair, old man.' The porter did. 'Now sit and tell me all your news.'

George offered the chair to the young lady.

Thank you, no,' she said moving. 'I can sit on the bed. George has left me plenty of room on his right side.'

The lovers smiled but George found it difficult. 'I'm sorry to hear of your misfortune.'

Carruthers scoffed. 'No choice, old man,' he said. 'I picked up trench foot anyway. Now tell me, George, do I spy a Military Medal on your splendid GER jacket? I cannot believe you won that for sweeping Platform Number 1 at Liverpool Street.'

George didn't blow his own whistle but Carruthers and his fiancée kept asking about his life in recent times. They genuinely congratulated him making his heart swell with pride.

It took Valerie to prompt her fiancé to announce he too had been awarded a medal, the Distinguished Service Order, a DSO.

After a spot of lively chit-chat, George didn't see the signal but Valerie did and stood. 'Please excuse me a moment, gentlemen, I must speak with the matron.' She left and George resumed his seat. Carruthers changed his expression, body language and voice.

'Listen, my friend,' he whispered. 'I'm to blame for all the crap you've copped about my father's death.' George went to interrupt. 'No, please, let me finish.' He paused. 'I believe I know the truth about my father's death but when I went to the police and told them everything, the investigation went nowhere. I think I know how to get the case re-opened but my running days are over. You helped me out before and you know my family. Are you up to getting the press off your back once and for all, and becoming the hero who cracked the case?' George Miracle found breathing tricky. 'Are you up for the challenge?' asked the titled gent.

Porter Miracle struggled. *What the hell is going on?*

Chapter 15

As George Miracle pondered the plan suggested by George Carruthers, Christmas 1917 dawned cold and crisp and even. This wasn't 1914. Between the trenches on French battlefields, this Christmas didn't find Fritz and Tommy singing carols, sharing presents and, with a football having a kick-around in no-man's-land. This Christmas they exchanged shells sans wrapping paper.

The relentless grind and butchery went on. Yes, the finish line appeared as a tiny prick of light at the end of the tunnel named 1918, but as winter bit hard, the stagnation and slaughter continued.

The Miracles pushed aside their disappointment of not moving to the country and prepared gifts for one another. George sat on his bed and made notes. What did the one-legged soldier tell him? The porter scribbled as he remembered their chat in the Middlesex hospital.

A very much married Lady Carruthers was once in love with a wealthy man, and conducted a discreet affair with him over many years. Sir Percival Gregory owned a vast estate and wallowed in old money. He and Cuthbert, George's father, were friends from their days at Eton. The rules for infidelity in the upper class meant you could frolic and fornicate provided you were discreet.

Lady Carruthers played by those rules. Her son sensed the affair and in the pre-war years when home from school, spotted Sir Percival behaving in an ungentlemanly way. The lad hesitated in raising the matter with any of the three adults, and lived to regret his inaction ever since the brutal death of his father.

Around the time he joined the army, George Carruthers overheard his mother on the telephone making a strange comment. 'Find someone to do it, Percy and soon. I won't wait forever.'

Young Carruthers believed the robbery at Hampstead was a ruse to cover the real intention; murder. Hearing the deliberate disturbance, Lord Carruthers came downstairs whereupon the homeowner was murdered.

After his father's death, his son told the police all he knew about the discreet adulterous affair between his mother and Sir Percy. Nothing happened. No arrests were made and still to this day, the crime remained unsolved. Why? At the very least such inaction suggested a cover up.

So now, on instructions from a fellow wounded soldier, for one last time, George Miracle agreed to try and force the police to take action.

In his next lunchbreak, and having told nobody of his plan, he went to the nearest police station wearing his GER uniform with attached medal and ribbon. 'Yes sir,' said the officer on the front desk impressed with this member of the public. 'How can I help you?'

'I have information about a crime in which Lord Cuthbert Carruthers of Hampstead was murdered in 1916.'

The policeman's ears stood to attention. This wasn't a report of a stolen watch or damage to a grave in the local churchyard. This report was stamped *serious*, *important* and *priority*.

The desk sergeant took the details. 'And your place of employment is Liverpool Street Station?' George nodded. 'I'm sure you'll soon be contacted by a detective, sir. Thank you for the information.'

At work, George told nobody. He knew if he blabbed, word would get out and his once often-discussed reputation might take a battering. The illustrated story about him in a tabloid newspaper did him no favours and set many tongues wagging.

At any moment, he expected a detective, possibly two, to enter the Lost Property room and start with, 'Mr George Miracle?'

A few hopeful passengers popped in looking for a hat, gloves, umbrella or handbag but no police arrived.

Surely they must follow up my report about the murder.

When it came time to knock off, he put the log book away, made sure the cupboards and safe were secure and locked, closed the main door and doubled-checked it too was secure. He headed out of the station building and along the platform.

A train from Cambridge arrived and George admired the locomotive as it slowed to stop. It was about twenty yards from him and the buffers when out of his peripheral vision he saw a blur. Then a burly man crashed into him, shoving him to the edge of the platform and into the path of the locomotive.

It all happened in a flash. Instinctively dropping his stick, George threw out his hands and one latched onto the attacker's straggly hair, with George clinging on for dear life.

If I'm going under the train, he's coming with me.

Passing passengers saw the commotion and yelled or screamed.

The attacker had built up a head of steam. He shoved George to the edge of the platform but the porter maintained his grip on the man's flowing locks. As George was about to crash onto the tracks and be killed, the attacker unintentionally joined the party.

Being much heavier and not anticipating his extended journey, the assailant panicked and hugged his victim. The bulky brute hit the tracks first and so cushioned the flying porter.

The driver sounded the whistle and kept sounding it while throwing all his weight into making an emergency stop. With only a few yards to go, it wasn't difficult but even a slow-moving locomotive can't stop on a sixpence.

The straggly-haired monster screamed as the front wheels of the 2-6-0 engine slid against his body. Hidden amongst the loco sounds, came the horrific crack of ribs being squashed.

Accidents draw a crowd and this one pulled them in from everywhere. The SM was told of the accident but didn't know his nephew played a leading part. As he arrived, a porter broke the news.

'It's your nephew, Guv'nor. He's on the track.'

Fred nearly died. The footplate crew were in shock. 'They jumped off the platform right in front of me,' repeated the driver to everyone.

George was helped up and shook like a leaf struggling to believe he was still standing. His shrapnel-decorated hip prepared to scream. His attacker moaned non-stop but screamed in agony when ambulance officers arrived and tried to lift him. The slightest move sent his nerves into orbit.

Both men were taken to London Hospital. Police attended two beds. What could George say? He told the truth and every witness supported the porter's story. The police inspector concentrated on the moaner who, as they say, was known to police. His injuries were savage. Getting parts of your insides crushed promises death.

'So, Luigi, what's your story this time?' asked the officer.

'Piss off, I'm dying.' Luigi coughed and blood trickled out of his mouth. The doctor made a face at the police officer who had no sympathy for the criminal.

'That's the first truthful thing you've ever said, Luigi, but before you kick the bucket, why don't you give Pascal's wager a fly.'

Luigi hadn't been inside a Catholic church since his confirmation, and knew nothing of the 17th century French philosopher or his idea. In short, it states if you're about to die, you've got nothing to lose if you confess your sins and become a believer in the Almighty. The pain in his chest told the professional criminal his lawbreaking days were over so, why not confess?

He looked at the inspector. 'Okay, I'll tell ya.' He paused. 'I done the Lord.'

This fascinating confession meant nothing to the police and besides, how did it relate to the attempted murder of a humble porter at Liverpool Street Station?

'What Lord? What are you talking about?'

Luigi coughed and groaned in pain. 'The toff in Hampstead.'

The inspector gasped. 'Lord Carruthers?'

Luigi struggled to nod. 'I got big dough to pretend it was a burglary gone wrong. I ...'

He couldn't speak but winced and let out a sharp cry of agony. Then silence. The doctor and detective thought he'd died. The doctor felt for a pulse but jerked backwards when Luigi lashed out.

'Not yet,' he spat. 'I ain't dead yet.'

The others were spellbound as Luigi struggled to confess.

'Percy Gregory paid me, and his cousin, your boss Superintendent Gregory, sent the cops up a blind alley.' He looked at the inspector who froze. 'You got a note of all that?'

The stunned detective tried to nod.

'When that porter I shoved off the platform went to the cops with new information, Percy told me to kill the story once and for all.'

'And you alone murdered Lord Carruthers?' The criminal nodded. The inspector felt faint then recovered. 'Good man, Luigi. St Peter will give you time off for good behaviour.'

'Ha!' shouted Luigi who groaned and five minutes later died.

Fred followed his nephew to the hospital, checked on his condition and sat by his bedside. 'So, not content with winning a Military

Medal, you go and solve a murder case involving the aristocracy and a high-ranking corrupt police officer.'

'It all happened, Uncle, because I offered help to a passenger travelling on the Great Eastern Railway.'

Fred leant in and squeezed George's hand. 'We're all doubly proud of you, George.' He stood. 'Now they're keeping you in overnight and I don't want to see you at work in the morning. I'll pop along and tell your mother and Em about their hometown hero.'

He left and George felt terrific. The inspector came and sat by his bed. 'I understand my sergeant has filled you in on the details.'

'He has, sir.'

'You did a mighty job, sir.' George couldn't believe the inspector addressed him as sir. 'Now this advice is free. Look out for the press. They'll want to put you on the front page.'

'Ahead of your superintendent, sir?' asked George.

The detective shook his head and expelled air. 'Indeed and the establishment will be well and truly rocked.' He stood. 'Get well and thank you,' he said and walked away.

A nurse arrived and adjusted George's pillow. 'All comfy are we, sir? Is there anything I can get you?'

'Would you have a notepad and pencil I might borrow?'

Half an hour later, George finished his version of what happened with particular mention of his friend, 2nd Lieutenant, Lord George Carruthers DSO who lost a leg in fighting for king and country. The ward was quiet. George Miracle slipped out of bed, picked up his shoes and uniform and tiptoed to the lavatory. A nurse stood to intercept him. Hiding his clothes, George pointed to his supposed destination. The nurse smiled and George disappeared.

He headed to the office of the *New London Telegraph*. The man at the front desk thought he was playing a practical joke.

'Well if you don't want the scoop on the unsolved murder in Hampstead, I'll take it to *The Daily Mirror*.'

The bloke on reception jumped. 'No, please wait, sir.'

When a senior journalist was called, George soon found himself in the editor's office drinking tea and being feted. They knew who he was. His face appeared in the opposition's paper.

Once they agreed to his conditions; viz., his photo would not appear, and Miss Victoria Hall from the *Mirror* was to be thanked for all her help in solving the case, George gave them his notes.

'But she didn't help you,' said the editor, 'and she lied to you.'

George sat there saying nothing. The editor twigged and he and his journalist smiled then laughed. They agreed with sincerity aplenty.

'Now that's what I call revenge being best served cold,' chuckled the boss. 'You have stitched her up like a kipper, Mr Miracle.'

'I hope there are journalists who keep their word,' said George and stood. 'Now, gentlemen, I have an appointment in Middlesex.'

They escorted him to the street, summoned a taxi and paid the driver in advance as George climbed aboard. In half an hour he walked quietly into the Edmonton Military Hospital. The receptionist was not happy to see any visitor after hours.

'Well please send a message to Lord Carruthers.'

'George,' cried a female voice as Valerie floated down the stairs. She was on her way home but turned around and, using her bewitching smile, escorted the porter to her fiancé's bedside.

George Miracle told George Carruthers everything. Valerie wept and the soldier minus one leg could not stop being grateful. Mind you, he was heartbroken to have gone public with the fact about his mother being part of the conspiracy to murder his father but now he and Valerie would put it behind them and marry.

'George,' said the patient, 'I know this is outrageous but I have one more request to ask, and promise it will be the last.' The porter could not believe the Lord would even think about asking another favour.

Carruthers looked straight at his new friend. 'George Miracle, will you do me the great honour of being my best man?'

The nurses on the ward failed to stop the celebrations.

It's difficult to explain the reaction of Miss Victoria Hall when, next morning, she picked up a copy of the rival newspaper and saw the story that hooked the whole of London.

'That's my story, mine!' she fumed. But when reading the copy and seeing the line, "Mr Miracle insisted on thanking Miss Victoria Hall from *The Daily Mirror* for all her gracious assistance in helping solve the case," her heart came close to exploding.

Chapter 16

It was a Christmas dinner like no other. The story of the aristocratic wife conspiring to have her husband murdered, bounced around a million turkey, goose and chicken-topped tables and even more mutton and sausage-decorated ones.

In Wood Green, three days after the incident at Liverpool Street, George's heroics headed towards old news with Connie on another topic, beside herself with worry.

'How can you afford a morning suit and top hat, George?' she moaned. 'And is the bridesmaid a titled lady? She's probably been to the Palace. You'll be stood next to a princess.' Connie picked at her lunch.

Fred didn't and enjoyed a roast potato. 'Give it a rest, Connie. Take pleasure knowing your boy has made you and his Dad proud.'

'And his sister,' protested Emily.

'And his sister,' repeated Fred.

George stayed out of it.

Connie cracked on. 'But it'll be in all the papers; a society wedding with the groom in a wheelchair. What if there's a Royal there or even two?'

For once, Emily stood up to her mother. 'Ma, George will not be in a wheelchair. He's brave and proud and will use his stick and walk like the railwayman and hero he is. Now could you please pass the Brussel sprouts?'

Mind you, George did have second thoughts about agreeing to be best man. He didn't feel inferior to those who lived in wealthy homes or wore a title as easily as he wore a tie but he didn't want to look foolish and stick out like a sore thumb.

A big wedding in a big church—surely not a cathedral—would be a first for the young porter. *Any* wedding would be a first. The groom promised to send George his invitation with details.

When it arrived, George laughed. Talk about a fuss over nothing. George and Valerie were to marry in a register office in London in a room which seated eight. It meant six guests not counting the bride and groom; four not counting the best man and bridesmaid.

Everyone will be seated, and especially so for the sake of the groom. George handed his mother the invitation.

'You can rest easy, Ma. The King will not be heading to the Chelsea Town Hall.'

Connie studied the invitation. 'I suppose with his family scandal, a big wedding is out of the question.'

'And George gives me the choice of wearing my GER or army uniform complete with medal. You did a great job resurrecting my army kit, and we'll look pretty spiffing in our military uniforms with two medals, two crutches and a walking stick between us.'

Connie smiled. She knew she'd overreacted. The love and pride she carried for her son was so great she wanted everything to be perfect.

'Well with eight in total at the wedding, I hope you get a photo for your dear old mother.'

'Old? What's this *old* business?' ribbed her son.

'And you need to write your speech and practise it for the family.'

It was George's turn to laugh and soon everyone joined in the excitement. But not everyone sparkled. Fred paid another visit to his doctor and again was told to take it easy, to slow down.

'The sooner you're out of your busy station, Mr Carmody, the better. What happened to the quiet station in the country?'

Fred explained the Chelmsford situation to the medical man but said nothing about his health to those he loved.

The wedding could not have been better. The setting, service, guests and reception made it a warm and wonderful occasion. It took character and courage for George Carruthers to carry off his marriage duties with panache knowing his horrific family situation and his catastrophic war injury but it was obvious the couple were madly yet sensibly in love.

George Miracle loved being back in military uniform and thought the bridesmaid to be as pretty as the bride. The women were cousins and before the big day, George suffered serious training from his mother in the art of social discourse and gentlemanly behaviour.

Apart from the four in the bridal party, the guests were Valerie's parents, her young brother, and the groom's late father's brother, his Uncle Edward.

The reception involved all eight seated at a round table. George sat between the bridesmaid and the mother of the bride. Talk about a thorn between two roses.

The food and drink were what you might describe as basic; understandable in this, a time of war.

The best man's speech, expertly edited by family members, followed the "brevity is the soul of wit" rule and pleased everyone.

As guests with legs to stretch, stretched their legs, George found himself chatting to Uncle Edward.

'Thank you for everything you've done to help my nephew. I've been told of your involuntary involvement in my family's wretched affair, and can only apologise to you becoming entangled in the whole sordid mess.'

'Please sir,' said George, 'it's all forgotten and today has been a wonderful occasion.'

'It has and many thanks for your splendid contribution.' Edward handed George a card. 'I'm an MP, the member for Great Yarmouth. If there is ever anything I can do for you, I shall be offended if you do not ask for my help.'

George expressed his gratitude and pocketed the card.

'I believe you work for the Great Eastern Railway at Liverpool Street.' George nodded. 'Are you aware of the rumblings about the plethora of railway companies in Britain?'

George struggled with the word *plethora*. Even understanding its meaning, his answer would still have been no.

'I haven't a crystal ball,' said the politician, but I should not be surprised if the government, of whichever stripe, seeks to reduce the number of companies once this damn war is done and dusted.'

Panic slipped inside George's brain. 'I hope that doesn't mean I could be sacked, sir.'

'Good Lord, I'm not suggesting that. Fewer railway companies will not necessarily mean fewer trains but it will remove duplication of services. I mean there are companies running on the same tracks competing for the same passengers; it's lunacy.'

George pondered those comments. 'I plan to make my career with the Great Eastern Railway, sir. My uncle is the station master at

Liverpool Street.'

'So steam runs in the family,' said the MP trying to smile.

George spoke without thinking. 'Sadly he may have to retire due to ill-health. He and I were due to move to the country, to Chelmsford in fact, but alas the vacancy fell through.'

'I wish you both well.' The MP held out his hand. 'I'm pleased to have met you, young man and do remember my offer.'

They shook hands and the wedding party broke up with George receiving three kisses and four handshakes. He liked the kisses. They were not the same as a kiss from his mother and sister.

His entire family was waiting when he arrived home. Questions were fired thick and fast, especially from the fairer sex.

'Okay, don't rush, one at a time,' he said being served a cup of tea by his mother and a piece of carrot cake baked by his sister.

'Where did you get this flour?' he demanded knowing how everyone struggled to find enough food.

Emily gave as good as she got. 'Stop asking questions and tell us again what the bride was wearing.'

The war continued to dominate. Devastated families received the dreadful news their son, brother, father, cousin, neighbour or friend was killed overseas or listed as missing. For so many there was no body and no grave to visit. A funeral without a body meant the grief came with double the pain.

George and Fred continued their work at Liverpool Street with the SM maintaining his vow of silence on personal matters of health. His reason was simple. What good would it do to share his medical prognosis with his family?

He looked at the daily mail delivery and one from the GER head office caught his eye. He removed the letter and felt his ageing heart start to ache.

The Great Eastern Railway Company
Bishopsgate

27 January, 1918

Mr F. M. Carmody
Station master
Liverpool Street Station
London

Dear Mr Carmody

The position of station master at Whittleton will become vacant at the end of March, 1918. The Board of Directors wishes to offer you this position to commence on April 1, 1918.
Please be assured this is not an April Fools' Day joke.
Your nephew, George Miracle, is offered the position of porter.
The job comes with the use of the station house, and you are entitled to free Rail Removal for household effects.
Kindly reply at your earliest convenience and inform me of your willingness to take up these positions.

Yours faithfully

C. J. Jenkins
C. J. Jenkins
Company Secretary

Pain throbbed in Fred's chest. He wasn't sure if shock, pleasure or disbelief took over his mind and body. He walked around the office. He stared out the window at the station below. His doctor's words bounced around his brain.

Avoid stress, Fred. Retire or God will retire you permanently.

He telephoned the GER head office and asked to speak to a mate, the man who signed the letter he still found difficult to read.

'Clarrie, it's Fred Carmody.'

'Hello Fred, how are you? Did you get my letter?'

'I did and thank you.'

'Don't thank me, old boy. Our masters made the decision and insisted your nephew, your famous nephew no less, be part of the move. Have you told him?'

'Not yet. I'm still wondering how it all happened and why so fast?'

'Oh Fred, surely you know how business works. It's not what you know but who.'

'Of course but you'll need to fill in the gaps.'

'Well when a member of the House of Commons and a director of the Great Eastern Railway are members of the same golf club, wheels within wheels begin to turn. Powerful people wield power, Fred, you know that, and you've moved from a stopping train to an express.'

'I'll be honest, Clarrie, I'm still in shock.'

The company secretary laughed. 'Whittleton is quaint, busy without being rushed, has a lazy branch line and the cottage is a smidgeon shorter than a cricket pitch from the SM's office.'

Fred's eyes went all moist. 'It sounds perfect.'

'Good place to retire from. I take it you want the move?'

'Silly question,' said Fred. 'I'll tell the boy and reply immediately.'

'Good man,' said Clarrie and the call ended.

With letter in hand, the SM headed to Lost Property. His nephew was accepting a briefcase from a woman. 'Thank you, madam. I'm sure the owner will be most grateful.'

She departed. George looked at the SM. 'Good morning, sir.'

'Finish what you have to do,' said Fred and waited as the case was stored and the log book entry completed.

George looked at his uncle and waited for him to speak. The SM said nothing but removed the envelope from his pocket and handed it to the porter.

The company name on the envelope kick-started George's heart.

'Read the letter,' said Fred.

George did so but showed no outward emotion. He handed back the letter. Inside, his emotions were bubbling.

'Thank you,' said George quietly excited.

'It's nothing to do with me, my boy. Apparently that MP you met at the wedding belongs to the same golf club as a director of the GER. This is all down to you, George. You offering to help a young soldier out there on Platform 1 two years ago has made all this possible. It's called reciprocity.'

George didn't know the meaning of the word.

Fred departed but called. 'I'll leave you to tell the ladies.'

Once the SM left, George clenched his fists, raised his arms, and shouted, 'Yes!'

He hopped out from behind the counter and, without his walking stick, fell into a unique style of dancing. Well, moving around to celebrate the news.

He felt a right ninny when he turned and saw his relief watching the celebration.

'I fort you 'ad a bung leg, George,' said Sid from Lewisham.

George grinned. 'Only on a Tuesday, Sid. Toodle-pip, old bean,' he smiled departing, 'toodle-pip.'

Chapter 17

The family went to check out their new home, by train of course. It was a Sunday and the visit to Whittleton was planned well in advance. Emily bubbled with excitement. 'How far are we from the sea? Perhaps I could learn to ride a horse, Ma.'

Having lived her entire life in busy London, a new life in the countryside meant Emily's cup of anticipated pleasure overflowed.

The current station master replied to Fred's letter signing his name simply as A. Gardiner. 'Do you know him, Uncle?' asked George as they hopped aboard the 10:08 Down from Liverpool Street.

'Never heard of him,' said Fred. 'I asked around and found nothing. I have no idea if he's retiring, resigning or relocating.'

'What about the branch line?' asked George who already knew the stops; three stations and two halts. This short line was unlike any of the services in London or Norwich where George worked before.

He worried. *Do they need another porter? Is the company being generous because my uncle has been a faithful employee for nearly 50 years, and I brought good publicity for the GER?*

Their train passed through lush countryside and even the SM looked out to admire the scenery.

George had drawn a map of the line and Emily checked each station as they stopped. Half an hour after they set off, she began to announce. 'We're coming to Brinkley and then Hopetown Heath and after that it's our new station.'

'It's Hopetoun Heath, Em, with the *toun* pronounced *tun*.'

'You'll get there,' said Fred impressed by his niece's enthusiasm.

'I can't wait till we get to Whittleton,' she purred. The young woman looked at her mother and worried. 'What's wrong, Ma? Don't you want to live in the country?'

Everyone looked at Connie. 'Of course I do. I told you it'll make a nice change for all of us.'

She didn't convince, her body language not matching her words as opposed to her children who were super keen.

The train slowed as they approached Whittleton. George stood well before the train stopped. His heart pumped faster. They arrived. This station stood ready to meet its new station master and his offsider.

Passengers alighted and a couple boarded heading along the line. The quartet from London gathered and waited as a strange voice bounced along the platform.

'Stand clear, train now departing, stand clear.'

The quartet stared seeing no-one. Hidden behind departing passengers stood a person wearing a cap with *Stationmaster* but this master was a mistress; he was a she.

Fred and George looked at one another. The woman approached. She barely stood higher than the hand trolley she pushed, and her mass of red curls might have even been on fire.

'Good morning, ladies and gentlemen. Welcome to Whittleton. I'm Audrey.' She looked at Fred. 'You must be the new SM.'

Fred struggled to get over his surprise. 'Fred Carmody and this is my sister, Connie, my nephew, George and my niece, Emily.'

'How do, folks. Now I reckon the ladies would like to see the station house. Am I right?'

Connie nodded and Emily smiled. 'Yes please,' she said.

'Good-o, well why don't you gents proceed to the signal box and introduce yourselves to Terence Montague Chives, a.k.a. Monty, who knows far more about Whittleton than I ever will. Okay?'

What could the new arrivals say? They agreed.

'This way, ladies,' said Audrey heading to the Up platform.

George and his uncle looked around the station taking in everything then walked to the signal-box. 'Let him do the talking,' said Fred and George understood. At the stairs, Fred called. 'Ahoy there; permission to come aboard.'

After a long pause, the signalman appeared. He could never be described as young, well-dressed or clean, and, even from a distance, his collection of teeth displayed vacancies on main and branch lines.

'Howdy,' called Terence. 'Is you the new Guv'nor?'

'Fred Carmody,' said the SM as he led the expedition skywards. At the door to the box, Fred introduced the young man. 'This is my nephew, George, porter at large.'

'Call me Monty, everyone does.'

They shook hands and entered the signal box. To be fair, Monty may have easily won Scruff of the Year but his work place was immaculate. The levers, work desk, telephone, bells and clock faces shone; the whole place gleamed. Even the cloth he used to keep his sweat off the pristine levers was fresh from its daily wash. Monty never needed a mirror being able to check his junkyard whiskers and vandalized teeth via his clock.

He addressed his visitors. 'So wotcha wanna know, gents? There ain't much happnin' at Witty I ain't seen, done, fixed or broke.' He grinned and the breeze rushed in and out of his mouth.

Witty? thought both visitors. *Whittleton is Witty?* They didn't get much of a chance to ask anything or make a comment such was Monty's garrulous personality and superior knowledge of "his" station and its surrounds.

Fred spoke. 'I gather you've been here more than a week.'

Monty cackled. 'When I started on the rail, Stockton t'Darlington was still a gleam in George Stephenson's eye, and Adam was catchin' the Up Cambridge for Wisbech Grammar.'

George's excitement at being a porter in a picturesque station—he adored the island platform with the branch line on one side—and his general high anticipation of a new start in the country, took off with interest once he met the larrikin with the levers. Working with Monty promised fascinating times, and if he was the icing on the cake, the sponge must be pretty darn terrific.

'What about the branch?' asked Fred. 'Keep you busy does it?'

'It's a doddle,' said Monty pointing. 'The 11:21's comin' in now.'

The new staff moved to watch an 0-6-0 loco, the Whitty Flyer or the Crabbie, built in Stratford, arrive pulling the smallest consist either men ever saw. It was a one train line so unless the cows decided to travel under their own steam, there was no need for a staff exchange.

'I don't fink the comp'ny's gunna get rich on the branch. I know all the passengers' birfdays and most of the livestock's inside leg measurements.'

Fred and George exchanged glances. They struggled not to laugh out loud. Monty didn't try to be funny, his humour rolled out sans effort.

'So what advice would you have for a new SM and his offsider?'

Monty turned and looked at them. He sniffed. 'Jus' remember, the passenger's your boss, and never be late.' He brushed past them. 'Scuse me.' He headed towards the door.

The visitors looked at one another. George, who already knew the timetable for the Whittleton branch, especially on a Sunday, shrugged then mouthed. "There are no trains due".

On the landing outside his door, Monty stood and yelled. 'Jus' put it there, luv. I'll be down in a minnie.' He turned back to his visitors. 'It's me better 'alf wiv me elevenses.'

Fred moved. 'Well don't let us keep you, Monty.' He beckoned to George. 'We'll be starting next week and thanks for the guided tour.'

'Yes it's much appreciated,' said the porter. They shook hands and George added, 'May I fetch your tea, sir?'

Well now, was the signalman impressed or what? The porter offered to collect Monty's cuppa *and* called him sir. This first meeting went well for all concerned.

They spotted the gatekeeper, Desmond, coming out of his shed and another meet and greet took place. He too was part of the Whittleton furniture.

Back on the far side of the island platform, Fred approached the crew on the little loco in from Crabbwell, the terminus of the branch line. Driver and fireman were salt of the earth railwaymen and pleased to meet the new SM and his offsider. George could tell their kind greeting to him was tinged with a little caution. *Is this fella with a bit of a limp a porter? How does he manage big parcels?*

Fred and George moved back to the Up platform and were in time to meet the returning ladies. Audrey led them but stopped to introduce the incomers to Eric the porter who was twice George's age, no, three times as old. He and Monty were the two longest-serving employees on the station with Desmond a close third. Eric excused himself to deal with a passenger.

Connie and Emily looked like they wanted to start hopping from one foot to the other. Their smiles were spontaneous.

'The station house is lovely, Fred,' said his sister.

'It's great, Uncle,' added Emily, grinning, 'and George your bedroom is the shed out the back.'

George knew his sister was teasing him and delighted in her

happiness but still made a face of mock rage.

Audrey studied George's movement. 'You got a mobility problem there, my lad? There's a step or three around here.'

'Thank you, Miss, but …

''Missus,' snapped Audrey. 'My old man was SM here before he said no to an exemption and went off to die for his country.'

The mood turned dark. 'I'm sorry for your loss, Missus,' said George. He patted his shrapnel hip. 'I cop a bit of gyp around Christmas but mostly I'm fine.'

Audrey forgot the topic and George's family were proud their boy didn't mention his hip was a war wound, a result of serving king and country.

'Well, what would you like to do next?' she asked.

Connie and Emily were keen on a trip to the village. Fred wanted to inspect his office, leaving George to ask about the branch line. To his delight, Audrey yelled to the footplate crew.

'Oi, Madge, how's about you take the new porter and show him the delights of Crabbwell?'

'Be a pleasure,' shouted the driver; name William Conker, hence his nickname. William Conker to William the Conqueror to Your Majesty, shortened to Your Maj to Madge. His fireman copped the same rural logic. His name was John Smith who happened to be a fine exponent of watercolour painting especially of flowers. Fireman Smith was likened to John Constable, the famous artist from East Anglia. So the fireman who painted a la Constable became Bobby as in Robert Peel's bobbies. George was yet to learn this local dialogue and held on as Madge and Bobby "fired" the Crabbie.

As the ladies went window-shopping and sticky-beaking, Fred poured over the books, and George, contrary to company regulations, climbed aboard the footplate for the next service on the branch. It was infrequent most days and even more so on the Sabbath.

There was no room for dancing on this footplate with the 0-6-0 tank engine. There was no tender as the coal and water were enclosed within the locomotive. It was a light railway and the words *express* and *branch line* were incompatible. There were three stations and two halts. Often the halts were ignored because the crew knew everyone who hopped on or off at these places, and being stuck out in the middle of nowhere, a one-eyed drunken sailor could see the platforms were empty even in the middle of the night in a rain storm.

The station buildings on the branch were basic. The waiting rooms were old carriages. One halt, Pickling, boasted three fire buckets on the wall of the lavatory with the fire buckets used more inside than out.

George chatted away with driver and fireman. These were one of the train crews he would work with, who knows for how long?

The single-carriage train departed sans people and arrived at the end of the line sans people. Crabbwell and Liverpool Street shared nothing in common although, to George's great surprise, he met the SM. Well, he called himself the SM but in reality he was a porter.

Trying not to be rude, he wondered aloud how such a small station in such an isolated rural setting could keep a station master busy.

'Oh we're busy here, boyo,' said Owen Griffiths, revelling in his native Llangollen accent. 'It's the three P's I'll be telling you; passengers, parcels and pigs. We're so busy on certain days I haven't got time to scratch meself.'

He said "we're" so busy. Who's we?

George again politely enquired, this time about parcels.

What parcels? Who sends parcels to and from this backwater?

'Would you believe last Christmas we sent 23?' explained the pretend SM. 'It would have been 24 if Harry Ribble hadn't got his old mare stuck in the mud, and didn't get here till Boxing Day.' George saw a cup heading his way. 'All for you, boyo.'

'Thank you,' said George accepting a cup of tea brewed by the self-proclaimed SM. George noticed the footplate crew drank their own brew, and even tossed bread and eggs on a shovel and thrust the lot in the firebox. He understood why as soon as he sipped his tea.

It tasted bitter, seriously so. He tried to control his reaction but found himself spitting the brew on the platform. The footplate crew grinned like Cheshire cats and Owen took it all in his stride.

'You'll get used to it, boyo. Steep it for an extra ten minutes is what I say, and you get the tannins to come alive.'

'Thank you,' said George, 'I'll try to remember.' He pretended to sip then pointed towards the distant village. 'Is that the village of Crabbwell over there?'

Owen walked towards the end of the platform; it wasn't far. 'Come and I'll show you.' As George followed, he emptied his cup on the track against the loco. The crew gave him a thumbs-up.

'This is the problem,' said the SM. 'They built the station nowhere near the village. There's the river, see, but they reckoned it would cost a king's ransom to build a rail bridge so here we stop and here we stay. It rains here every day with a y in the name, and who wants to traipse along muddy tracks and fields to catch a train? Our passenger numbers would take off with another half mile or so of track.'

Sitting as it did on a small hill, the station gave passengers a view of Crabbwell but that's about all. A few locals reckoned it was quicker to walk than catch the train.

'There you have it, boyo.'

Talk about an education. Having explored the basic station, its goods shed and observed its faraway village, George shook hands with the singing station master, and told the footplate crew he'd try the passenger experience for the return journey and travel inside the solitary carriage. As the sole passenger, he climbed aboard the Crabbie Sunday special heading back to Witty.

The loco ran around the carriage and chugged along in reverse for the trip home. With no tender, the crew had a grand view ahead.

The countryside gave George's heart a lift, and when he saw a young woman who waved as she rode her horse in a nearby field, he instinctively waved back. This move to the country just got better. *People wave to you, even pretty girls. That never happened at Liverpool Street where everyone rushed past, always in a hurry.*

Back at Whittleton, he thanked the crew, waved to Monty and looked for his family. Uncle Fred appeared deep in conversation so he left the station and headed to the village. Unlike Crabbwell, this one was much closer to the railway.

Coming towards him were his mother and sister. They bubbled with happiness. Emily especially couldn't stop talking.

'It's wonderful, George. There are shops and cottages, a village hall and a pretty church. What was your village like?'

'I'm not sure. The station is about a mile away.'

'Well whose clever idea was that?' asked his mother.

George shrugged. He wished he knew.

'I met a young man outside the bakery,' said Emily. 'He doffed his cap and wished me good day.' Her eyes sparkled as she spoke. 'Whittleton could be the nicest village in England.'

Connie directed her children back to the station. 'What time is the next London train, George?'

He looked at his watch. 'Twenty-two minutes, Ma but I don't know if Uncle Fred will be ready in time.'

She rounded up her sheep. 'Come on, we'll make him.'

And they did. Audrey waited with them on the Up platform.

'I'll be off the Tuesday after you start but I'll vacate the station house before you get here next Sunday.'

'Thank you,' said Fred, 'and for all your help today.'

The rest of the family supported him. The train rolled in and the visitors boarded the first carriage. Emily and George took a window seat each with George facing the locomotive.

Audrey gave the guard the nod and the Londoners were away. Next time, they would be back to stay.

Chapter 18

That Saturday morning, their last in London, Fred and George did the rounds at Liverpool Street saying goodbye to everyone from the paperboys to the new SM. Fred had served as station master here in London for 17 years. This normally upright and proper chap even shed a tear when a few staff members gave him a hug.

Despite his much shorter time at Liverpool Street, George too enjoyed a strong following. His war wound, medal, murder mystery, and as the victim in an attempted homicide, helped make and maintain his reputation as the popular porter. Many drivers, firemen and guards wanted to shake his hand.

'Now don't you f'get the crews what taught you everyfin', young fella,' said more than one railwayman. Camaraderie ran deep within the staff at this big and busy station.

Taking the train home, uncle and nephew said nothing, their thoughts remaining private. They were about to spend their last night in London. Would either ever return?

Next morning the local carrier Smedley, his dray and horses were early and ready for action at Wood Green. 'You wait there, Mr Smedley,' said Fred. 'We'll do the fetchin' and carryin'.' And they did.

George, Connie and Emily took the boxes, cases and a few sticks of furniture placing them in the street while Fred and Mr Smedley stacked them on the cart. With the load made fast, the railwaymen hopped up beside the driver and, waving to the ladies, headed into town.

Being a Sunday morning, traffic both foot and vehicular was light and they entered the road into the station and pulled up beside their platform. Porters came from all directions to help their former boss place belongings in the goods van.

Connie and Emily arrived and three of the family of four took their seats. The guard bounced along the platform to give Fred a friendly shove as a few station staff wanted a final handshake. Finally he flopped in his seat.

'Delaying a train, Uncle, is an offence under the Regulation of Railways Act 1889. You could have been fined,' reprimanded George while sporting a large grin.

Connie and Emily joined in the teasing and Fred threw up his hands. 'Never again, I promise.'

They arrived in Whittleton on time and were the only passengers getting off or on. Audrey and porter Eric were waiting on the Down.

'Welcome one and all,' said the SM and before anyone could say or do anything, Monty bounced down his steps and onto the platform.

'Happy days, Guv'nor,' he cried shaking Fred's and then George's hand. 'Welcome, welcome one an' all and lemme give you a lift.'

Audrey was having none of it. 'Monty,' she snapped, 'the Crabbie's due in three minutes.'

Monty didn't see the need for any fuss. This was because the branch line crept in alongside a farmer's field beside the island platform and never troubled the gatekeeper or the signalman.

'So it is,' said Monty, grinning to display his lack of dental care. 'I'll catch you all later. Tally ho,' he cried shuffling off to his eyrie.

Back on the Down, the senior porter and gatekeeper gave a hand and the transporting of the goods from London took no time.

Boxes and bags were placed on the platform trolley and Eric, with nigh on 30 years' experience, steered with ease. So with two SMs, two porters and a gatekeeper, moving goods took no time. Emily and Connie carried their personal cases, and Connie held tight to the carry case with Trixie the cat inside not sure what was happening.

Emily took off but dropped a handkerchief. Despite the size of the trolley and its weight, Eric spotted the object and called.

'Oi, Miss, you dropped somethin'.'

The porter forgot the new SM's niece was deaf, and Audrey gave Eric a quick and soft reminder. He nodded an apology to Connie who scooped up the fallen item.

The shortest walk in the village was long enough to pull a crowd. As the trolley and new arrivals reached the cottage, nearby neighbours were in their garden, on their doorstep or, for the pushy ones, in the street outside the station master's cottage.

One woman, known locally as Busy Lizzie, who made it her

business to know everyone else's business, stepped forward. 'Mrs Carmody, I'm Elizabeth Hutchinson, and would like to welcome you to our village, and I hope you and your husband and family will be very happy here.'

Most of those being politely nosy, added support. They and Lizzie copped a slap when Connie replied.

'Thank you for your kind words, Mrs Hutchinson but I'm Mrs Miracle, a widow. The station master, Mr Carmody, is my brother.'

Fred knowing the importance of keeping sweet with the locals, and killing prompts for unwanted gossip, added his two bobs' worth. He pointed to family members as he spoke.

'We're delighted to be in your charming village. My nephew, George Miracle, is the new porter, and his sister Emily, and my sister, Connie, are looking forward to meeting you all.' Those details set minds racing and tongues preparing to wag. 'But now as you can see we have a bit of unpacking to do.'

The locals nodded and disappeared. Eric and Audrey gave the incomers a hand and soon the luggage finally settled inside.

'Your stove was lit an hour ago, Missus,' said Audrey. 'You're good to go. Now, Eric and I have a train in four minutes, so please excuse us.'

All four new arrivals voiced their thanks and George followed the two staff to the door. 'That'll be the 11:37 Up London stopping all stations to Liverpool Street, if I'm not mistaken.'

Audrey smiled and Eric nodded his approval. 'I like this boy,' he murmured.

They left and the family exhaled, pulled out a chair each and sat.

'Well,' said Fred, 'we made it but before we relax, let's unpack.'

'No,' contradicted his sister. 'Let's eat first.'

'Eat?' queried Fred. 'You'll take an age to find things and …'

She opened a case and produced a packet of sandwiches she made in London that morning. 'Kettle please, Emily; stove please, George.'

Fred gawped as Connie found a table cloth, George stoked the fire and Emily filled the kettle and popped it on the stove. In no time, Fred's family enjoyed their first meal in the station house, Whittleton.

Unpacking went well with everyone pitching in. With only three bedrooms, two would have to share. George and Fred set up in the same room, although George inspected the shed in the back garden and reckoned a spot of basic carpentry could create an annexe for the porter. He said nothing for now.

Once the unpacking was finished, the family gathered in the kitchen for afternoon tea. Connie's baking produced wonderful smells and her scones went down a treat. As a second cup of tea was being enjoyed, the front door knocker came alive.

The older siblings groaned as one. 'Not already, Fred,' said Connie. You don't start work till tomorrow.'

Discovering the visitor news, Emily stood. 'I'll go.' She opened the front door and met a cleric who raised his hat.

'Good afternoon,' said the Reverend Ernest Small.

'Good afternoon,' replied Emily, her eyes fixed on the man's lips.

'I'm your vicar and want to welcome you to our village.'

'Thank you, please come in.' He stepped into the narrow passage and, not facing the hostess, he spoke. 'And you are?'

Emily, despite sensing vibrations, struggled to understand and so didn't answer his question. She indicated the front room and the vicar, slightly offended, stepped inside.

'I'll fetch my uncle,' she said and disappeared.

Whispers filled the kitchen. 'The vicar?' groaned Fred. 'How many priests ever came calling in London?'

Connie shushed him. 'This is a village, Fred. Go and introduce yourself,' she ordered.

Fred rarely entertained visitors at Wood Green. 'A station master's home is his castle,' he whispered but left the kitchen to enter the front room. 'Good afternoon, sir,' he said and they shook hands.

After exchanging names, the vicar repeated his welcome then moved in for a spot of proselytizing. 'I do hope we can have the pleasure of the company of you, your wife and children at St Michael's and All Angels.'

The vicar and Busy Lizzie were in sync.

'I have no wife or children, sir,' said Fred causing the priest to wonder if a godless family had fallen from the sky. 'Connie,' called Fred and an uneasy silence settled in the front room.

The family arrived as one, and the front room needed a *No Vacancy* sign. Introductions followed and the vicar's pulse resumed normal service. He kept pushing for a sale and mentioned that

Evensong would start in a few hours. Connie spoke for the family.

'It's been a long day, Vicar, with lots of unpacking, and ...'

'Of course, how silly of me,' he apologized. 'Well I'm so pleased to welcome a new family and I'm sure we'll see one another if not in the village then at the station. Goodbye. Goodbye.'

The vicar navigated the packed front room and left with many forced smiles on show. The family fell into the hand-me-down furniture-suite donated decades ago by a previous SM.

'The problem with village life,' said Fred, 'is if you don't go to church, your absence sticks out like an elephant at a tea party.'

'Em and I will go, won't we?' Connie now found her daughter needed a different way of handling. Nearly 16 and no longer a child, the girl's confidence and curiosity grew at an ever faster speed.

'Yes, Ma,' she said then froze as the others reacted when the front door knocker came alive—again.

Fred groaned. His sister shushed him again. 'Let's pretend we're not here,' whispered the station master.

'Fred!' snapped his whispering sister. 'George, see who it is.'

The porter stepped into the passage and opened the door.

'Good afternoon,' said a besuited middle-aged gent who, like the previous caller, raised his hat. 'My name is Godfrey Grantley-Smythe, chairman of the parish council. Do I have the pleasure of addressing the new station master?'

In the front room, the others heard everything. Fred rolled his eyes, his sister smiled and his niece giggled at the adults' facial expressions. Fred rose and spoke. 'Ask the gentleman in, George.'

Another round of introductions followed after which the chairman, on behalf of the parish council, welcomed the new arrivals.

Fred, in his usual avuncular style, expressed his thanks and promised to assist the locals with anything to do with the railway. A link was established and the chairman took his leave.

The family retired to the kitchen with quips and comments aplenty about their new found status. They were about to finish whatever little unpacking remained when that damn front-door knocker sounded another rat-a-tat-tat.

Everyone laughed. 'The door,' mouthed Connie to her daughter.

'It's your turn, Uncle,' said Emily, grinning from ear to ear.

Fred gave a low growl and set off up the passage. He opened the door to another villager wearing a hat. Being a female, the woman kept her headwear in place.

'Good afternoon,' she smiled. 'Are you the new station master?'

'Frederick Carmody,' he said. 'How can I be of assistance?'

'I was hoping I could speak to the lady of the house.'

'You most certainly can,' said a relieved and grateful SM. 'Do come in.' He called. 'Connie, there's a lady to see you.' To the visitor he said, 'Come on through to the kitchen.'

The lady of the house appeared holding a tea-towel. 'Can I help?'

In the kitchen, the visitor, Fanny Albright, met the family.

'I'm one of the village sewing-circle ladies. We meet on Thursdays in the church hall where we knit socks for our boys in France. If either of you ladies would care to join, you'd be most welcome.'

'I've started to knit,' said Emily. 'Could I go, Ma?'

Fanny beamed and even more when Connie spoke. 'Of course you can. We'll both go.'

Their third visitor departed full of gratitude. Fred waited till the front door closed. 'Right, how about I put a sign out front, "Last train has departed".' He headed for the door. 'I'm going for a walk and I require the porter to accompany me.'

The men left and Fred headed away from the station. Down the High Street they went where the few locals stopped and stared. Fred nodded and George copied his boss.

'Keep moving,' mumbled the SM and they did.

Beyond the village they reached a path which lead to the local mountain. In Snowdonia or the Grampians, this mountain would be described as a field. East Anglia did a nice line in being flat.

They stopped by a fence and looked over their new county.

'Here we are, George, for better or worse. How are you feeling?'

'I'm excited, Uncle. I love the station with its pretty platforms, solid gates and fascinating branch line. I think we'll be happy here. I certainly hope you are coming from busy Liverpool Street.'

Fred grew pensive. 'I shouldn't need to tell you this but the words of wisdom we heard in the signal box from Monty when we visited last week are the truth and nothing but the truth.'

'Yes, Uncle, and I agree.'

Fred repeated Monty's advice. 'The passenger is our boss, and we must never be late.' George watched his boss and relative. 'The difference between working here and in London is we live among the passengers. We stand next to them in the shops, in the pews and on the platform.' He looked at his nephew. 'Any questions?'

'I have only one, Uncle.' He paused. 'Do I have to learn to knit?'

Their laughter rolled around the farms as they strolled home.

'Oh, and one other thing,' said Fred. 'If we lose a parcel or cause a passenger to miss their train, or do anything to upset our customers, we can't avoid the critics. In London, irate passengers wouldn't come knocking on our front door. In a village, everyone knows where we live. Understand?' George nodded and they walked home in silence ready to start a new life in the morning.

Chapter 19

First morning, first shift and Fred and George were at the station early. Fred suggested they work together initially to get to know the routines and give a good impression from the first day.

Many passengers spoke to the staff and at length. George found this a major change from life in busy London.

After a few trains arrived and departed on both platforms, and the branch departed on its first run, Fred was busy in his office and looked up when he sensed a person enter. Fred stood.

'Good morning, sir. How may I help?'

'Fitzsimons, *Lord* Fitzsimons,' said the visitor.

Fred knew about Ripley Hall, the nearby manor house and its owner. The SM touched his cap. 'I'm station master Fred Carmody, your Lordship.'

'I use the trains from time to time. Send and receive livestock, pop up to London, have friends down for a shoot, and so on. I expect the best service at all times. Is that clear?'

Fred displayed suitable humility. 'Indeed it is, my Lord.'

'Good show,' said the toff, tapped his thigh with a riding crop and strolled out of the station.

George saw the gent departing and, making sure he was long gone, approached his uncle. 'Was that the Laird of the Glen?'

Fred flared. 'Don't even think of trying to be funny. Keep your thoughts and wisecracks to yourself.' George understood and muttered an apology. 'Now what are the numbers this morning?'

George knew without looking. 'Best this year, Mr Carmody.' Their modest friction settled. 'And there are parcels on the next Up.'

'Have Eric help you. I'll be in the signal box and then I have a mountain of paperwork to tackle.'

The train to London pulled in and George asked Eric to collect the few tickets. Waiting beside the guard's van, George greeted the guard.

'Good morning, I'm George the new porter.'

'Dave,' said the guard. 'I'm new too and your goodies are here.'

From the van, Dave brought out three parcels, none of which was big or heavy. 'Only the animal to go,' he said entering the van, picked up the carry case and yelled. 'Oh no!'

'What?' yelled a worried George scrambling to see.

'It's gone?'

'Gone?' asked the porter with an explosion in his pulse.

'It's pushed open the cage door and … there it is!'

Both men saw a small black and white puppy as it bolted out of the van and raced along the platform heading towards London. Without a ticket, it may have been fare-evading.

George grabbed the carry case and ran. Well, ran is a relative term. For a chap who at times used a stick to help his balance when walking, chasing a young dog came close to being a hopeless task.

George set off and the train soon passed him. 'Sorry and good luck,' yelled the guard putting away his flag.

The platform sported a fence along its rear and end with a sign warning that trespassing on the line was illegal. Both fences were not constructed with puppies in mind. By the time George reached the end of the platform, the dog could not be seen. The porter panicked.

There were wide fields to George's left, and ahead the cutting for the railway meant the canine would be unlikely to have run that way. George tried calling and whistling. No sign of the pup. Cursing his luck, he hurried back to the station with the empty dog carry case.

'What have you got there?' asked Eric.

'A major problem,' replied George. 'Can you please collect those parcels over there?' Eric grabbed his small trolley.

In the office, George searched for the documentation. The puppy's age and description were stated and then George felt sick. The addressee was Mr Godfrey Grantley-Smythe, the chairman of the parish council, the gent who introduced himself by calling at the station house yesterday. The Additional Notes included the following:

> Dog not to be shown as is a surprise
> present for granddaughter of addressee.

George squirmed. *Oh great! I've lost a parcel on my first day; a lost living, breathing parcel for a little girl, the granddaughter of the most important person in the village. Wonderful.*

Eric arrived with the parcels. 'Everything okay?'

'No,' said George, 'and I need you to say nothing to my uncle.'

The look on George's face startled Eric who willingly agreed.

George, with the animal carry case in one hand, looked at the goods on Eric's trolley. 'I need to deliver one of those parcels,' he said. Scooping up the lightest one, he left.

He took the parcel as a cover for his quest to find the lost dog. Hoping against hope, he planned the rescue of the century. If it meant combing the fields and woodland, so be it.

The smaller parcel was to a man he didn't know—he knew almost no-one in Whittleton—and in a daze, he set off for the address.

Could I have made a worse start, a worse impression than this?

He'd made a simple study of the streets in the village—it didn't take long—and reached the address of the recipient of the small parcel and knocked on the door.

From inside came an elderly sing-song voice. 'I'm coming.' The footsteps were ponderous. 'And yes, I know, so is Christmas.'

George felt a flicker of happiness in his hour of despair but knew he needed to deliver and run. The puppy could be in trouble. *So am I.*

The voice grew closer and louder and began to wax lyrical.

'There was an old lady fantastic
Who tightened her drawers with elastic
She huffed and she puffed and with effort she stuffed
Feeling chuffed with her knickers monastic.'

George grinned and was still grinning as the door opened.

'Good morning,' said the limerick creator with the whitest whiskers in Whittleton, probably the county.

'Good morning,' said George. 'I have a parcel for Mr Septimus Oldmeadow.'

The gent raised a finger. 'One moment and I'll see if he's in.' Using a loud voice, he called into the cottage. 'Are you there, Septimus?' Then a grin appeared as he looked straight into George's eyes. 'He is in and stands before you.' He thrust out a hand. 'How d'ja do?'

Confused and amused, George put down the dog carry case and

shook hands with his first customer. 'Your parcel, sir.'

'Ah, my books, my beautiful books. Thank you, kind sir. Now, come away in and partake of some liquid refreshment.'

George froze, in a mild panic. His problem remained unresolved with no time to dilly-dally, and certainly not to consume alcohol when on duty. He needed to find the runaway puppy. Instead an eccentric gentleman offered him a homemade brew. George had left his post to hobnob with the locals.

Uncle Fred will have me shunting wagons by hand.

George paused before sipping the concoction. Memories of another eccentric, the Welsh self-appointed station master at Crabbwell, and his inky black tea bursting with acrid tannins flooded back. But no. Surprisingly this sweet, fruity liquid warmed his throat.

'Your honest assessment, sir, I pray,' said Septimus.

'It's ... delightful, Mr Oldmeadow.'

The man's whiskers smiled. 'Splendid, excellent,' he purred. 'Now drink up, there's plenty more where that came from.'

George knew his visit must end. 'Sir, I regret I must decline your generous hospitality as I have a most important mission to complete.'

'Oh?' enquired the now fascinated host, 'and what pray tell would that be?' His eyes gleamed. 'I do so hope you're not about to commit a murder but if so, may I please tag along to observe? I'm a novelist, don't you know.'

George indicated the carry case. 'I've lost a puppy. It escaped from the train and ran off the platform. I'm in a spot of bother if the little creature can't be found.'

Septimus changed to deadly serious. 'What breed?'

'I'm sorry.'

'Describe the dog—Jack Russell, Dachshund, Terrier, Whippet or all of the above?'

'I only know it was black and white.'

'Are you sure?'

'Yes, I'm certain.'

'I mean could it have been white and black?'

George hesitated. *He's mocking me.*

'Well young man, this could be your lucky day. Let me get my hat.'

He set off through his cottage, out the back door and into his garden. With carry case in hand, George followed.

'Should I lock your door, sir?' asked the porter.

'Whatever for? Locks are to keep out honest people. Come along.'

There was a gate at the end of his garden. Septimus stepped into a field and watched as George followed. 'Close the gate, there's a good chap, we can't let the little folk escape.'

As George followed the book loving, limerick-reciting, home-brew making, novel-writing, fairy-believing eccentric through a farmer's field, he pondered two thoughts.

I'm dreaming and this is the best time of my entire life.

They headed into a small copse of trees and once out the other side spied a farmhouse. Septimus waved and called.

'Hello, Mrs Brown, hello!'

A middle-aged woman wearing enough clothes to fill a dress shop, waved with difficulty as she scattered seed for her hens.

'Good day to you, Mr Oldmeadow. Who's your friend?'

Septimus stopped. 'This is ... bless my soul, I've neglected to learn your name, sir. Please do forgive me.'

'George Miracle, Mrs Brown, I'm the new porter at the station.'

'So he is and with a problem which you, Mrs Brown, may be able to solve.'

'Anything gentlemen, even for an incomer.'

'How is your bitch? Did she have a decent litter?'

George's heart pumped faster then accelerated.

'Come an' 'ave a look,' said the farmer and they followed her into the barn.

George's heart went wild. There, amongst the hay, was a mother dog and her litter of pups. They were about the size of the missing puppy and, heaven be praised, they were all black and white.

Mrs Brown pointed. 'Take your pick, Mr Miracle. I won't announce them till Sunday so you can have first choice.'

George wanted to cry. 'This is extremely kind of you, Mrs Brown. How much do I owe you?'

The locals laughed. 'How much?' mocked the farmer. 'Where is you from, young man?'

'I'm from London, ma'am.'

'You have much to learn, Mr Miracle,' said Septimus. 'Out here in the country we help one another. You have a need, we do our best to

142

meet your need. Please, payment is not required.'

George shook his head and struggled to speak. 'Thank you.'

'Now they don't need their mother's milk no more, so take the one you want,' said Mrs Brown.

George didn't get to pick, he was the one being chosen. A puppy with a tail causing a draft stood in front of him, looked into George's eyes then placed its front paws somewhere near George's knees. He as good as said, "I'm the one you want; please take me."

George popped the puppy in the carry case, made sure even Houdini couldn't escape therefrom, and again thanked his two new acquaintances.

'Where are you heading, Mr Miracle?' asked Septimus.

'To the station, sir, although I do need to call on the chairman of the parish council today.'

'Ah,' said Mrs Brown. 'Go along my drive and turn right. The lane will take you past Mr Grantley-Smythe's place and the station is … well you can see it from his place. Look out for Primrose Cottage.'

Gratitude overflowed from George's heart and mouth as he set off with a mixture of whistling and chatting to his new friend sporting four legs. Mrs Brown's directions were spot on and soon the porter stood outside Primrose Cottage, the parish chairman's house.

George opened the gate and was stopped by a woman buried beneath a huge sun hat.

'May I help you?'

'Oh, good morning, madam. I'm delivering a parcel for Mr Grantley-Smythe.'

The woman dropped her basket of flowers and tried to run. It wasn't pretty. 'Godfrey!' she called heading for George. 'Godfrey!' The pitch difference between the first and second syllable of her husband's name was about an octave higher for the second sound.

George panicked. Any neighbour would have thought they heard a response to a major accident but then Mrs Grantley-Smythe was well known for yelling at her husband.

He arrived as his wife began cooing at the puppy. George resumed breathing.

The chairman went weak at the knees and imitated his wife in admiring the puppy. Then the chairman turned to George.

'I say, young man, this is jolly decent of you; home delivery and right on time. Well done, well done indeed.'

George found his emotions threatened to explode. 'I'm glad to be of service, sir. If I may, the pup is very lively so I would not release it until you're safely indoors.'

'Excellent suggestion,' said the husband who lost out to his wife as custodian as she set off with carry case in hand.

George wanted to depart. 'I'll be off, sir, and good luck with your wonderful gift.'

It was difficult to know who felt happier; George, the grandfather, the grandmother or the pup. George felt tempted to skip as he headed back to the station. *Damn that sliver of shrapnel in me hip.*

Fred came out of the SM's office. 'What's this leaving the station in order to deliver a parcel?'

'I'm sorry, Uncle, sir but I wanted the chairman of the parish council to have his live parcel, and as you stressed the need for keeping the locals happy, I thought ...'

'Yes, yes, all right, but don't go making a habit of it. Now the next Down is due in five and has a parcel. Hop along and collect it.'

George felt fantastic having avoided a disaster. He crossed the tracks and stood near the far end of the Down platform as the train approached around a slight bend. There was a modest gradient which encouraged the driver to open the regulator a touch while at the same time prepare to slow for the station—good driving skills required—as the train arrived.

'You must be the new porter,' said the guard. 'I heard you were young but I never thought you'd still be wearing short trousers.'

George grinned. 'Please don't tell the headmaster.'

'Henry Burton,' said the guard handing over a large box.

'George Miracle,' said the youthful assistant.

Henry signalled and the train pulled out. 'Make sure you finish your homework,' he yelled and George couldn't control a smile.

The parcel seemed too heavy and more so for a bloke with only 1¾ fully functional lower limbs. He was about to head back for the small trolley when he heard a sound. He looked around and saw nothing. Then he heard it again. It sounded like a child crying.

George wandered towards the London end of the platform, looked around and nearly died. On the other side of the tracks beneath bushes, hiding and looking terrified, crouched a puppy. It decided running away was not such a good idea after all.

'Hello,' called George. 'I've been looking for you.'

Climbing off the platform was illegal but George didn't hesitate. Stepping off the ballast, he crossed the tracks and pulled himself up the embankment towards the bushes. The dog didn't move.

Soft words and no sudden movements made George a natural. He patted and chatted and when he went to pick up the pooch, it happily rested against the human's body. Back down the embankment slid George and, in the process, decorated his uniform; another black mark on his report card.

Actually the soil wasn't black but a rich local tan.

He took a risk by placing the puppy on the end of the Up platform while he dragged himself aboard. The puppy sat stock still. The last time it ran away, the world became scary.

George left the parcel and headed back to the station. Eric and Fred came out of the office as George and his new "parcel" arrived.

'What have you got there?' demanded the station master.

'It's lost or been dumped, sir,' said George, surprised at how easily and naturally he lied.

'What about a collar and details?'

'None,' said George. 'Shall we revert to the practice we employed at Liverpool Street?'

'What practice?' asked Eric.

George obliged. 'In Lost Property, Eric, we put hats on high shelves so they weren't flattened, all books went into tins for protection against moisture and dust, and all coats were wrapped in brown paper to stop moths from having a nibble.'

'What's that got to do with lost animals?' asked Eric.

'Oh staff took them home until the owners came forward.'

'No,' said Fred. 'Your mother won't have a bar of it doing its business in the kitchen corner and Trixie has not been consulted.'

'But sir, the garden shed is a perfect home and your niece the perfect guardian. I'll drop it off between the express and the next Up.'

Eric proved a pal. 'There's a box in the shed, the right size.'

He fetched it, Fred frowned and George patted man's best friend.

The end of this adventure, George's first as the new porter at

Whittleton, produced an interesting two-part epilogue. Emily found her heart singing at the sight of George's surprise package, and immediately claimed the pup as her own. She called him Spike and the bed George made for the dog in the shed became irrelevant as the pup much preferred Emily's quilt. Connie surrendered once Trixie the cat declared a truce.

The second issue occurred when the president of the parish council bumped into George in the High Street the following Saturday. After polite greetings, the grandfather revealed the huge success of his gift.

'Mind you, it's the first dog I've seen have a pee by squatting.'

'It must be from London, sir. They have life back to front up in town.'

More laughter and bonhomie before George slipped away. Spike he knew was male but only now did the porter realise Mrs Brown's gift was a bitch.

Chapter 20

Christmas 1914 – Ripley Hall, Whittleton

L ord Fitzsimons fumed. 'What do you mean you refuse? It's your duty. I served, my father served. You must serve.'

'I'm sorry. Father, but I won't,' said his 20 year old only son and heir, Stephen.

'We're at war, man, your country needs you. Every fit man from the village has joined or is planning to do so. You're not only a disgrace to your family but to the village. If you were any younger, I'd thrash you.'

The boy's mother, Lady Fitzsimons, heard every word from a nearby room. She bit her lip and fought to hold back tears.

'I oppose war, Father, this and every war. Why should helpless citizens, women and children be driven from their homes and worse, be attacked and slaughtered because grown men reckon they've been slighted.' The silence was deafening. 'Well, what's your answer?'

The father glared, his face puce. Spittle crouched ready to fly.

'Get out!' thundered his Lordship. Nearby, his wife wept.

'If it's what you want, I'll go. May I say goodbye to Mother first?'

The fury inside the knight threatened to boil over. 'Never would I believe my son would become a coward. You are no longer my son.' He pointed and screamed. 'Leave my house and never return!'

Stephen moved quickly to find his mother who was a mess. They embraced. She wept without stopping. His heart broke.

'I love you, my darling boy,' she managed between sobs, 'and always will.'

'Stay brave, dear Mama. I love you and will never stop loving you.'

He kissed her forehead, turned and left.

Lord and Lady Fitzsimons didn't speak for nearly two days and then it was purely perfunctory. 'I'm going to my sister's,' she said. He grunted. There was another type of war in Ripley Hall, Whittleton.

Stephen knew about conscientious objectors, those men who chose not to fight and were known as conchies. Many people despised them. He never spoke of his stance and remained steadfast in his beliefs.

He moved to London, found work in a warehouse in Bethnal Green and took a bedsit nearby. Poverty thrived. He kept seeing posters with General Kitchener's face and pointed finger calling for men to enlist. Stephen never wavered. The rift with his father ate away at him, and remembering his mother in despair broke his heart. But still he refused to enlist.

The war was definitely not over by Christmas and continued well into 1915. One night Stephen stood in line at a soup kitchen when a man beside him asked if he'd enlisted. Stephen took the risk of speaking the truth.

'No, I'm a conchie.'

'Me too,' said the other chap, 'but I've joined the FAU.'

Stephen looked at him. 'I've never heard of the FAU.'

'It's the Friends' Ambulance Unit. The Quakers started the ball rolling but anyone can join. We serve at home and behind the lines overseas doing basic medical work for wounded soldiers.'

'You don't fight?'

'Not with weapons, only bandages. It enables conchies to make a vital contribution. Are you interested?'

Stephen sensed the hairs on the back of his neck rise up as one.

'I am, most interested.'

'Mind you if the sight of blood worries you or having blokes dying in your arms doesn't appeal, I'd stay well away.'

Stephen felt fantastic. 'How can I join?' he asked.

His first training took place in Buckinghamshire. The FAU came under the control of the Red Cross and trainees became efficient in the basic treatment of wounds and injuries. Soldiers fought, doctors treated the wounded, and the Friends' Ambulance Unit members helped transport the sick, the wounded and dying.

In France and Belgium, many FAU volunteers were attached to trains which became a hospital on wheels. They were known as an AT (Ambulance Train) with a number. The Great Eastern Railway played its part donating whole trains, with loco and tender, plus 16 GER carriages divided into various sections—cots meaning beds, sitting and service. Doctors and nurses operated in the service carriages supported by many orderlies. The FAU volunteers would lift, carry and help the wounded from a station to a train to an ambulance and help with any basic medical needs.

As the war refused to end, casualties kept mounting. The work of the FAU volunteers became invaluable.

Artillery was not always accurate, in fact constantly inaccurate, and as guns became more powerful, many an AT came under fire. Any Red Cross signage on an AT did nothing to ward off long-range shells.

Working as a volunteer, Stephen Fitzsimons distinguished himself many times rescuing and caring for his fellow countrymen. During the horrors of the Somme, his AT, already chock-a-block with wounded and dying victims of the slaughter, set off towards the French coast but found its way to safety blocked.

Their only escape route meant going back whence they came, back towards the front line. The train came under enemy fire.

They reached their departure station and found new casualties, seven men, lying helpless on the platform. The train slowed. Stephen and a fellow FAU mate leapt from the now crawling train and helped lift every man aboard.

The station scored a direct hit. Shattered timber, glass and shrapnel smashed against the carriages. Orderlies helped load the men and Stephen was the last to board as the locomotive steamed into the French night.

When aboard, a doctor noticed Stephen looking wretched. His back was blood stained where glass and shrapnel attacked his flesh. He was slowly bleeding to death.

'Catch that man!' shouted a doctor as the "coward of Whittleton", the courageous FAU volunteer collapsed.

By 1918, the attrition factor became apparent. Both sides had engaged in trench warfare for years. With America declaring war on Germany in 1917, and having troops fighting in 1918, the allies received a boost.

On the German side, both soldiers and citizens grew weary. Starving Berliners wanted the war to end as did their demoralized troops. In the German army, resignations from the top and desertion from the ranks delivered the surrender and so ended the war.

Announcing the date produced a poetic sound. At the 11th hour of the 11th day in the 11th month, 1918, World War One officially ended.

Much celebrating took place particularly in England, and certainly in Whittleton, as trains arriving or departing and on the branch from Crabbwell, sounded their whistles with no regard for safe working or company policy.

When they heard the news, the SM and his nephew embraced. 'Thank God we're safe, George,' said his uncle. 'Thank God it's over.'

'Should we decorate the station, Uncle?'

'Of course we should and at the very least, the Union Flag.'

George and Eric jumped to it. Every passenger, coming or going, greeted staff with a smile. The world was at peace and in Whittleton even the trains huffed and puffed their happiness.

A week later when the midday train on the branch arrived, driver Madge called to George.

'Hey George, Freda wasn't on the Pickling halt. Did she come to town another way?'

'I haven't seen her, Mr Conker. Could it be she was late?'

'She ain't never late and she never misses visiting her sister on a Wensdee. I tell you, she might be in trouble.'

George thought about it. 'Could I run out with you on the next Down and check on her.'

'Good idea but if she's hurt, we really shouldn't wait.'

George pondered his next move. 'I'll have a word with the SM.'

Fred was unimpressed. 'George, we can't check on every passenger who misses their train. That's a job for the police. Anyway, have you tried using the telephone?'

'She's never had one.'

'Well what about a neighbour or the porter at Crabbwell?'

'We're about equidistant, Uncle, six of one.'

Fred waved him away. 'You deal with it.'

So George found Eric and told him. 'I'll be checking the branch for an hour or so.'

'What's wrong?'

'Madge saw an object on the line. I won't be long.' Two more lies.

He set off along the side of the line beside the ballast where the ground was easiest for walking. Walking on the sleepers didn't suit his hip. Shortly after Marlowe station, deserted of course, he left the track and headed into the fields. Sheep scattered. George knew a path of sorts used by horse riders.

He reached the dirt road which led to Freda's smallholding. By going cross-country, he saved a fair distance than by walking to the Pickling halt where Freda always waited and then heading inland.

He cursed himself for not bringing wet weather gear as the clouds called a meeting and moved a motion, passed unanimously. At first the drops were soft and social before the big 'uns arrived, and he copped a drenching. He tried running, more a quick hobble, and reached the cottage. Banging on the door, he wanted shelter as much as finding the missing lady.

'Are you there, Freda? It's George from the station. Hello?'

He listened but the rain on the roof drowned out any response. He opened the door—it was never locked—and called again. Without waiting for an invitation, he ducked inside dripping water on the ancient floor.

'Hello, Freda!' Then a response. A spectacularly large cat having regularly enjoyed the richest cream and milk in the county approached, meowing. It wasn't a greeting rather a demand for luncheon.

'Where's your mistress?' More creamy requests came from the cat.

George felt nervous. *Will I find the lady dead in her bed?* He moved through the cottage speaking the owner's name. Nothing. He opened the back door and peered through the rain.

He yelled loudly. 'Hello, Freda!'

Back came a faint voice. 'I'm in here!'

For George there were only two possibilities—the barn or the privy. They were a decent distance apart so he didn't want to brave the rain twice although he could hardly get wetter. He thought of a plan.

'Are you in the barn?' he shouted.

Back came the answer. 'No, I'm in the privy.'

This was not George's preferred answer.

If she's in the lavatory, she must be trapped or stuck. How does a male porter attend to a woman in such a situation?

At Liverpool Street, there were female members of staff for such an occasion. His choices seemed limited, *were* limited. He felt confident he could make a rescue but worried about subsequent versions of the tale. How did rural mockery measure up to that in London? *Stop thinking, George.* Head down, he ran.

Half way to his goal, a magnificent rugby tackle sent him flying to the ground. Rufus, Freda's much loved Irish wolf hound, saw his friend from the railway station and did what he always did.

'Hello George!' was his regular greeting which involved front paws on George's shoulders and a lick to remove whiskers, warts and whatever else appeared on display. Freda would have him on a lead in the village but at this particular moment, she was otherwise engaged.

The rain maintained a steady downpour. Rufus cared not at all for the precipitation. He wanted to greet and lick his friend, the chap who always patted and spoke to him in Whittleton. Dogs remember.

'Rufus!' shouted George.

'Rufus!' shouted Freda. She knew his every move and anyway, could see the action through cracks in the privy walls. It had never been nominated for any architectural or construction awards.

George struggled to his feet and slipped and slid the remaining ten yards to the privy door. Rufus joined him. It was difficult to say who looked worse.

'I'm here, Freda,' yelled George.

'Congratulations,' yelled Freda.

The heavy rain on the tin roof sounded like gunfire. Shouting became essential.

'Are you stuck?'

'No, I'm knitting, have dropped a stitch and can't find it.'

He ignored the sarcasm because of his perceived ethical dilemma. 'Is it okay if I open the door?'

'Well how else in God's green acres can you get me out?'

George exhaled. *This would never happen at Liverpool Street.* 'Okay, here goes.'

The door opened easily and the vision for both humans proved interesting. George looked like some creature from a primordial swamp and Freda looked, well, downright ridiculous. Her feet, wearing unconventional farming footwear covering homemade socks made of wool from sheep sheltering about 50 yards away, pointed to the tin roof. Her posterior, which should been resting on the recently cracked and now larger seat above the pan, had disappeared south, hidden from view. Her knees tickled her chin. Hmmm, tricky.

Her arms were free but the more the woman tried to extricate herself, the more entrapped she became.

'Thank you, George,' she said and meant it. 'I've been here since breakfast. Thank you for thinking of me and thank you for coming. Tell me, do they have umbrellas in London?'

He loved her wit, said nothing and tried drying his hands on his soaking clothes; a waste of time. He stepped forward and took her hands. 'Let me try and pull you free,' he said not fancying their chances. He pulled, she heaved. If she moved, it was in the region of fractions of an inch. He stopped.

'Wait; there must be an easier way.' He pondered the situation. From behind, he could place his hands under her armpits and lift. In theory it appeared sound. But to arrive in a lifting position, he would first have to stand above her on the frame of the privy, bend his knees and lift. Interesting from both a physics and a personal relationship point of view. Dripping water everywhere wouldn't help.

Freda survived as a smallholding farmer by being practical. 'Get a rope from the barn.' George hesitated. She snapped. 'Do you need a railway memo in triplicate?'

He ran, slipping en route. The barn was actually a shed but what's in a name? Rufus fancied a game and followed his mate. George returned with rope hoping Freda's plan, whatever it was, would work.

'Slip one end through the gap at the top.' George looked up and understood. Threading a needle when the eye was out of reach meant another trip.

He slid to the wood pile and picked up the stump Freda used as a chopping block. As a way of congratulating him on his hard work, the heavens changed gears and the rain moved to "Cop that, Muggins".

With the chopping block in position, George stood thereon and shoved the end of the rope through the gap. The lintel looked sturdy. Fingers crossed. Once the rope dropped, Freda reached up and grabbed it, pulling both ends to her.

'Right, my hero,' she said trying to waggle herself ready for lift off, 'lean in and give me a hug.' George froze.

'I'm sorry?'

'I'll pull and you link your hands around my back and lift. Ready?'

She didn't pose a question but rather stated a command as in "get on with it, Sonny Jim".

Freda's sinews came out to play. She strained on the rope as George hugged the woman and heaved. Success. She moved. Not a mile but definitely in the right direction. 'Fall backwards,' she shouted and George needed a while to comprehend her command.

'Fall backwards,' she screamed.

George thrust his shoes against the stone floor of the lavatory and pushed with all his might. Their respective centres of gravity changed. Freda's scream echoed around the fields despite the weather. Sheep, huddled under trees, turned in the direction of the great lavatory liberation.

George did fall backwards with Freda pitching forwards. The porter saw little point being worried about his inappropriate intimacy with the passenger as Freda stretched out atop his youthful body. The rain became less intense for George as Freda took on the role of a ground cover. Rufus thought all his Christmases had come at once as he jumped on top of his mistress and barked.

A passing photographer would have salivated.

In the farmhouse cottage, George was ordered into the spare room with a second command of "strip". He was down to his long johns when a towel, trousers, shirt and jacket sailed into the room.

'They were me Daddy's 22 years ago so there might be the odd moth and spider. Mind how you go.' As he dried and dressed, he heard the Down branch chugging towards Crabbwell.

Freda's dad was a big boy and George looked like a puny child, the recipient of his big brother's old clobber.

The porter enjoyed a cracking lunch with eggs so fresh they were still clucking.

'I can't thank you enough, young man,' she said doling out more food. 'You coming out 'ere on foot jus' f'me, I reckon it makes you a right gentleman. An' t'think you is a war hero an' all.'

George explained how Bill noted her absence.

'Who's Bill?'

'The driver.'

'You mean Madge.'

'Yes, Madge, sorry.'

Freda changed topics. 'Now George, my hero, the rain's gonna stop and you can catch y'train in twelve minutes.'

George frowned. *How does she know the rain is going to stop? How does she know the train timetable?*

By now, George should have learnt how country folk know a lot about nature, life and important matters such as timetables. Freda was right on both accounts. She led him to the door then gave George a huge smacker on his lips. It tasted different. George recovered.

'I want you to know, Freda, I'll not discuss your unfortunate accident with anyone.'

'What!' she exploded. 'I'll be tellin' half the county. I'll dine out on this whole bloomin' business f'months.' She cackled again and George saw her eyes sparkle. She laughed at his stunned expression. 'Well how can you keep it a secret when you step off the train lookin' like a prize-winnin' turnip crossed with a scarecrow?'

George did look a sight. Freda's father was built like a brick privy and George lost his hands in the jacket sleeves and wore the biggest trouser cuffs in England.

He smiled and set off waving to Freda and Rufus while the cat continued to meow for more cream.

The Up was delayed at the Pickling halt as the footplate crew couldn't stop laughing. George was grateful the carriage was empty but died of shame when the crew constantly sounded the whistle as they approached Whittleton causing those within staring distance to stare, wondering what was so special.

It turned out to be the sheepish porter in ridiculous fancy dress.

Next Wednesday when Freda and Rufus arrived at Whittleton, the farmer made a point of seeking out her hero and repeating the kissing routine. Rufus joined in the celebration and slobbered with élan.

Chapter 21

In 1919, Britain and elsewhere, countries resumed a semblance of normality, although the loss of so many millions still haunted families and individuals. Lord and Lady Fitzsimons in Ripley Hall, the manor house at Whittleton, existed rather than lived. The casting out by His Lordship of his only child, due to the young man's refusal to enlist, left a gaping wound in the hearts of the property owners, especially and more so Her Ladyship. The married couple rarely spoke to one another, only when necessary and usually through an intermediary, a servant.

'Tell Her Ladyship, I shall be going to London for a few days.'

'Very well, my Lord,' replied the compliant manservant.

What a life.

George survived the constant ribbing from several Whittleton station staff thanks to his valiant rescue of one of the branch line's favourite passengers, and in time began to enjoy his new-found fame. His happiness bloomed when he received a letter, an invitation for a reunion of his WW1 unit from his fighting days in France.

It was to be held in London on a Sunday afternoon allowing men who lived outside the capital to leave in time for a homeward train.

'It'll do you good to see your old pals,' said Connie.

'I wish I could come,' said Emily feeling a soft spot for London and her former life.

It was George's shift on Sunday but his uncle didn't hesitate to offer cover. 'It'll cost you a report on the Liverpool Street staff,' said Fred.

George smiled. 'You want me to spy on your old station, Uncle?'

The merriment flowed and when the day of the reunion arrived, all three family members admired George in his military uniform.

'Thanks, Ma, it's come up a treat,' said George as his mother took a brush to add the finishing touches.

'Where is your medal, George?' asked his sister.

He produced it.

'Wear it,' said Connie in what sounded like an order. She took it and pinned it on his chest. He felt proud, the womenfolk more proud.

As he entered the platform his uncle appeared and gave him the once over. 'You'll do,' he said. 'Enjoy yourself and remember my request.'

Eric came up to George and admired his colleague. The Up branch pulled in and Madge gave whistle blasts when he spotted George.

'What's wrong with your scarecrow suit?' yelled Bobby.

Desmond the gatekeeper and Monty the signalman both poked their heads out to get a look at the war hero. The Up London arrived and George received a send-off to remember. He took his seat and enjoyed every mile of the trip to London.

As soon as he set foot on the platform at Liverpool Street, a porter of old yelled.

'George!' he cried running to the passenger. 'Are you coming back to work here?'

Passengers looked at the man in military uniform. ASM Rogers was two platforms away and heard the yelling. By the time he arrived and shook George's hand, three other members of staff had surrounded the former London porter. Two lad porters had never met George but knew of his exploits.

'Great to see you again, George,' said ASM Rogers. 'How are you and how's your uncle?'

It was like old home week with George being offered tea, handshakes and news. He felt bad to decline but wanted to be on time for his reunion. He descended to the Underground, caught a Central Line train and a few minutes later hopped out at Holborn. From there it was a three minute walk to the Grand Connaught Rooms where people first gathered in 1775.

Steps were few and George's excitement at thinking about meeting former comrades pushed any hip jingles from his mind. He entered the mighty foyer.

Will I remember names? Will they remember me?

The sound of excited voices hit him as soon as he stepped inside. Reunions were bubbling in various rooms. Men, who hadn't seen former comrades for months, even years, were catching up in style.

No-one turned to look at him when he entered. An orderly with

157

knowledge of military divisions approached.

'Good afternoon, sir. Your reunion is in the room through there.' He pointed and George thanked him and departed. He entered the room where again everyone chatted away. Then a voice rang out.

'It's a Miracle!' George knew the voice and Captain Alan Laidlaw strode towards him providing the firmest handshake this year. 'Bloody good to see you, George. How are you? How's the leg? You're looking terrific. Back playing trains I suppose.'

George finally found a chance to speak. 'I'm fine, sir, and yes to playing trains.'

'Come and catch up with the boys.'

He did and loved most of the reunion. Finding out men he knew were killed gave him a kick and worse, hearing of those who survived but were now limbless or mentally shot to pieces hit hard.

George believed in what he called the insanity of war and here his opinion was reinforced. He loved the good tales—there were happy times despite the mud, blood and death—and he found leaving a pain. He could not even guess at the number of handshakes he made.

Walking through another room on his way out, his name sounded loud and clear. 'George Miracle!'

He knew the voice and face of the man who called. Using crutches, expertly mind, George Carruthers, headed his way. Delight shone from both their faces. Their embrace, crutches and walking stick notwithstanding, was warm and skilfully done.

After the usual questions about health and families, George Carruthers took control. 'Come and meet a friend of mine. They walked to a table where they sat beside a young man who wore a suit, not a uniform. 'Mr George Miracle meet Mr Stephen Fitzsimons.'

The three found it easy to talk about the war. The porter knew little of the FAU but the amputee seemed to know everything and heaped praise upon Stephen who replied.

'His Lordship exaggerates. I was one of many doing the best we could for the sick and wounded.'

'His Lordship,' remarked the porter in surprise and delight. 'Have you inherited your father's title?' The young aristocrat nodded, the mention of his father hitting hard. 'Congratulations, my Lord.'

'Enough about me; tell me your news. Are you now the station master at Whittleton?'

'Whittleton?' said a surprised Stephen and the others took note.

'You know it?' asked George the untitled.

'My father is Lord Fitzsimons.' The conversation hit a brick wall. 'May I ask about the health of my parents?'

'As far as I know, they are both well.' George the railwayman ventured into dangerous territory forgetting his mother's advice about personal questions. 'Have you not seen them of late?' Oh dear.

Stephen took it all in his stride. 'Not since 1914, shortly after the outbreak of war.' The others were shocked. Stephen felt a need to explain. 'Being a conchie I refused to enlist to my father's anger and shame. Not to put too fine a point on it, he disowned me and asked me to leave.'

The others wondered about the full meaning of "asked me to leave". Was it a euphemism for dismissed and disinherited?

Lord Carruthers pushed the point. 'But does he not know you joined the FAU and saved countless lives risking your life every day?'

Stephen shook his head. 'I ... I don't know.'

The porter volunteered an offer. 'When I next see him at the station, would you like me to say we've met?'

'Thank you but no,' said the disinherited son. 'I often think of my parents, especially my mother, and would be grateful for news but I do not wish to cause them distress.'

His Lordship snorted. 'As one Lord to another, I would take great delight in describing the magnificent bravery my son displayed for years on the Western Front.'

Silence amidst the chatting saw all three men breathing deeply not knowing what to say. George Miracle stood.

'Gentlemen, I bid you farewell. A railwayman must never be late.' Handshakes were strong. 'It's been a delight to be in your company.'

Lord Carruthers urged his best man to return to London and journey out to Hampstead. 'I know your memories of the house are shocking and terrible, George, but Valerie and I would love to see you. Oh, and please do bring your wife. What's her name by the way?'

Both men sparkled with laughter and porter George left in the highest of spirits. All the way home he thought of many people and events, not least the former FAU member, his extraordinary bravery and the local Whittleton residents, the parents estranged from their son, their only child.

A few days later, George helped Eric load parcels into the Up London train. It was a popular mixed goods as the locals produced quality agricultural products much sought after by Londoners.

Train gone, George wandered back to the office when he heard loud voices. His uncle and the local squire were going at it hammer and tongs.

'Don't you take that tone of voice with me,' snapped Lord Fitzsimons. 'I know exactly what I paid for and I tell you there are several items missing.'

'I am not disputing your claims, my Lord, simply advising you of company procedure.'

'I haven't come all this way to complain but to obtain a guarantee my lost or stolen items will be returned or replaced.'

'And I repeat I will do all in my power to get to the bottom of the matter.' Fred wanted to raise his voice and tell the toff to get lost. As always, he kept his professional hat on and followed procedure with a reasonable and courteous tone throughout.

'You haven't heard the last of this, my man,' snapped Fitzsimons and, storming out, almost collided with the young porter.

George touched his cap with his index finger. 'Good day, my Lord.'

A growl was the reply and the angry man left not knowing he'd dropped a glove.

'My Lord,' cried George collecting the glove. Fitzsimons turned and saw the offered item. He waited for the lesser mortal to come to him, the higher mortal.

Surely a growl would not be the reply this time. Would His Lordship slip in a grunt? George moved forward and as the glove was handed to the irate gent, George spoke.

'I met your son last week, my Lord.' His Lordship stopped as if shot, his expression changing by the second, as he craved details but could not bring himself to ask. George explained.

'We were at an Army reunion in London and I must admit your son's war service puts mine to shame.'

Now the Lord looked like he'd been stabbed as well. He could only remain standing because the bayonet thrust into his belly was not withdrawn.

His voice croaked. 'My son served in the war?'

'He did with exceptional bravery under enemy fire, my Lord. As a

Quaker, I suppose he keeps his light hidden under a bushel.'

The father needed to leave. The pain he suffered was difficult to describe. But even more agony struck when he thought about having to tell his wife. He'd avoided her like the plague simply because he disinherited their son. Now, out of the blue, he discovered his son was not only not a coward but in fact an exceptional war hero.

Having to speak reasonably to his wife would be excruciating. Having to tell her his news would be unbearable.

George bowled into the SM's office where Fred looked awkward trying to control his rampant blood pressure. The whole point of moving away from stressful Liverpool Street was to give his heart a break.

'The nerve of the fellow,' said Fred. 'I've met a few awful men in my time and believe me, the worst are all bloody toffs.'

'Relax, Uncle. You won't have any more trouble from his Lordship.'

Fred's face changed. A minute ago the man's abuse and rudeness flooded his office. Now his nephew claimed to have flattened the Lord. Fred panicked.

'What have you done?' he gasped thinking the worst.

'I've broken a promise, Uncle. A young man asked me not to broadcast his bravery, and especially not to his family, and I have ignored his kind and reasonable request.'

'Tell me,' said the SM and George did.

When finished, Fred shook his head. 'What a wonderful and fantastic story. But I've never heard of the Friends' Ambulance Unit.'

'Join the club, sir.'

'And you say His Lordship looked shocked?'

'No, shattered. I'll be mightily surprised if he shows his face in here ever again, or at least not for a very long time.'

'His good lady will. She booked tickets for the 10:29 Up tomorrow. We'll soon see if she knows about her boy.'

Lady Fitzsimons would make a good poker player. She gave away nothing. Travelling with her maid, she entered the platform and nodded to the staff before heading to a bench to wait.

From a polite distance, George addressed her. 'The train is on time, your Ladyship, another eight minutes.'

She nodded and her maid returned with their tickets. George slipped into the office. 'Well?' demanded the SM in a whisper.

'Nothing,' said George. 'I've never seen the woman smile, not in all the time we've been here.'

Fred shrugged and went back to work. George slipped back to his roots at Liverpool Street and swept the platform. Eric was on the Down doing the same.

The Up pulled in and George was ready. He moved to Her Ladyship's carriage and opened the door. She nodded to her maid. Such an order of entry was unusual. Following her servant, Lady Fitzsimons paused as she was about to enter the carriage.

'Next time you see my son, please tell him I've always been proud of him.' She looked hard at George and smiled then mouthed the words, "Thank you". George, thanks to his sister, could lip read well. He nodded, returned her smile and closed the door.

When Fred heard the news, his heart enjoyed a moment of relaxation.

Chapter 22

Life rattled along in Whittleton with trains running up and down the line and the branch doing its usual business or lack thereof. The war would never be forgotten but in 1920, people started to resume their lives with a sense of normality. One day after the Branch arrived with the last train for the day, and the fire was killed, Madge popped into the SM's office.

'Evenin' guv'nor,' he said.

'All good?' asked the SM.

'Still have sheep problems this side of Pickling Halt. We ain't exactly the Express, and a few blasts on the whistle gets 'em movin' but if there's ever a decent breakout, we could come home with a few mutton sandwiches.'

'I'll have a word with the farmer. Phillips isn't it?'

'Silly Philly we call 'im.' Madge dropped a newspaper on Fred's table. 'Wotcha reckon to this?'

Fred looked at the article. The heading was *Government Proposes Rail Amalgamation*. 'It's been coming, Madge. It seems like forever there's been more than 100 Railway Companies fighting for the same passengers and freight. There are even competing companies running on the same tracks.'

'So what'll happen? And will we lose the branch?'

'Your guess, my friend, is as good as mine.'

'Now come on, Mr Station master, tell us what you know not what you think.'

'I don't know anything but I'll have a small wager on the government forcing more than a hundred companies to join forces, and if the GER has to amalgamate, you can be darn sure your poky little enterprise will be swallowed whole.'

Madge produced mock outrage. 'Poky little enterprise?'

Fred smiled. 'Sorry, I meant your majestic mainline extravaganza.'

Madge worried, turning serious. 'We won't lose our jobs will we?'

Fred shrugged. 'Write to your local MP. Ask him.'

'But I'll be retired before I get a reply.'
'Dead more like.'
The men laughed, Madge picked up his paper and left.
'Goodnight Fred.'
'Goodnight Madge.'

The SM pottered around, his habit of "everything in its place and a place for everything" keeping him in his office. There was a freight train on the Up due to pass through in an hour.

At this time of night the usual plan was for Emily to deliver a hot bowl of soup and a crusty cheese sandwich while the officer on duty waited for the last train. However, life changed for the residents at station house when Emily began walking out with a local beau.

He was the son of a farmer on a property a mile or so from the village. The courting couple met at church, and after one Sunday service, Bertram, always Bert, plucked up the courage to ask Connie if he might escort Emily home. With the as-the-crow-flies distance being about 50 yards, and the road walking distance about twice that, Connie could hardly refuse.

The young man knew all about bovine and ovine breeding but lacked any intimate knowledge or hands-on experience in the human equivalent. In London, Connie gave Emily the facts of life in a direct explanation which only heightened her daughter's interest.

Things progressed from that first romantic encounter. A meeting at the church was planned for that night where prayers would be offered and letters written to encourage the missionaries the parish supported in their African endeavours. Due to an acute shortage of cinemas, dance halls and cocktail bars in the village, the prayer meeting offered an ideal opportunity for young romantics to meet and greet.

Hence Uncle Fred's supper at the station being delivered by his nephew standing in for the niece/sister delivery service.

George decided to stay and chat with the SM mainly because the heavens opened and the short trip home could still cause a soaking.

'What do you think of this government proposal to close most of the lines?' asked George.

'Oh for pity's sake, George, get your facts straight. There's a big difference between close and amalgamate.'

'Sorry but I wonder what you think will happen?'

'You're the second fellow who has asked me that today?'

George waited for his uncle to answer. Before he spoke, they heard a sound, apart from the driving rain. Both looked to the platform.

'Help!' sounded a female voice.

The men hurried to the platform and George caught an exhausted woman limping in soaked to the skin.

'It's okay, take it easy,' said George helping the woman into the office and placing her in a chair beside the fire.

'What's happened?' asked Fred.

'We crashed. Our truck's blocking the line.'

The railwaymen were instantly alert, even afraid. 'Whereabouts?' Fred remained calm but his nerves started to jangle.

'It's this side of Blackmore Junction. We skidded, went through the fence, crashed down the bank and flipped ending on the tracks.'

George knew his geography. 'It's before the Up signal.'

'My husband is trapped in the truck. It rolled over. I managed to climb out but he's stuck. Please help because he's lying right in the path of the train.'

Eric popped his head in to say goodnight but didn't go home.

'Grab a red lamp, Eric, and get moving towards Blackmore Junction,' said Fred. 'The Up freight is heading this way with a crashed truck blocking the line. Go!'

With lamp in hand, Eric ran. He was nearing retirement and not the fastest runner in the world. 'I'm faster than him,' said George looking at his uncle.

'That's why you must get detonators on the track. If Eric doesn't make it in time or they don't see the lamp in this rain, or the signal, they'll hear the detonators. Now go!'

George grabbed a box of detonators and fled. Fred handed the woman a rug and encouraged her to sit still in front of the fire then he too joined the running railwaymen. Off the Up platform he dropped, across the tracks and up onto the Down. He screamed as he moved.

'Monty! Monty!'

No response from the signal box. Plenty of response from the SM. He climbed the steps but felt a pain ping in his chest.

Bugger the belting rain. Damn my heart.

'Monty!'

This last cry roused the signalman who opened his door and saw the desperation on Fred's face.

Monty scrambled down the last few steps and helped Fred inside.

He gasped. 'Stop the freight, there's a blockage on the line.'

Monty sprang into action. He hit the bell to contact the box beyond Blackmore Junction. He moved the lever to STOP. Then he grabbed the phone and rang the next box.

The signalman saw the unusual action and heard his phone.

'What's up?' was all he said.

'Harry, stop the freight. The line's blocked.'

'She's gone; on time she went through a minute ago.'

'Well spread the word, mate. We may have a derailment close to my box.'

Monty rang off and worked the levers. The signal between Blackmore Junction and Whittleton switched to STOP.

'Will he see it?' asked Fred having trouble breathing.

'Certainly not if it's behind him and maybe not if this rain gets any worse. What else have you done?'

Fred explained about Eric and George but Monty was worried looking at the SM's face. 'Are you all right guv'nor?'

'I've been better.'

'Here, take a seat.' Monty handed him a tot of brandy. 'For the rheumatism.'

Fred nodded and tipped the liquid down his throat.

'Ring the police and tell them to bring help.' Fred felt serious pain.

Eric struggled. His age didn't help. The gloom plus the rain made vision tricky. Moving too fast invited an accident *before* the accident. He picked his way along the line stepping from sleeper to sleeper. The all-important lamp, glowing red, he guarded with his life.

He slowed, even stopped at one stage to catch his breath. He strained listening. Was that the train already? Silence. On he went. A second Whittleton station worker felt a pain in his chest. Forget the impending crash and derailment; two locals were in big trouble here and now.

Eric didn't see the fallen tree till he tripped over it. A branch reached over the outer rail. Removing the branch was easy but tripping and landing on the rail meant he fell, twisted his ankle and whacked his knee. Bloody hell, it hurt as pain shot up his leg.

He lay beside the track keeping the lamp safe. But it was useless here on the Whittleton side of the crashed truck. Lifting his soaked and now throbbing body, he limped north.

Then a noise scared him witless. It came from behind. He turned to see a person heading straight for him. He knew the voice.

'It's me, Eric.' George reached his colleague. 'How are you?'

'Terrible.' He offered the lamp. 'You'll be faster.'

'I have the detonators and need to go as far beyond the truck as possible. You keep going. Once the detonators are on the track, I'll come back for you.'

'I can't go on,' groaned Eric. 'My ankle's a mess.'

George took immediate action. 'Okay,' he said taking the lamp. 'Keep well clear of the tracks.'

George disappeared into the night. Eric stumbled off the tracks.

George never thought about his hip. He too stuck to the centre of the track. He too strained to hear the train. He knew the consist; it was long and heavy, the weight of the freight meaning stopping would be slow and take a long, long piece of track.

He rounded a bend and saw a shape. Closer, he discovered the truck. It was lying upside down covering most of the Up track.

'Hello,' bellowed George. From the dark shape came a weak reply. 'Hello.'

George knelt on the ballast and peered in the cabin. He used the red lamp giving the wretched driver a red glow. The engine of the truck finished up inside the cab pinning the driver. George tried to comfort the man.

'There's a train coming. I need to stop it. Once I do, I'll be back.' He stood, rounded the truck and set off, calling. 'Your wife's fine. She told us everything and help is on the way.'

'Thank you,' called the feeble voice of the injured and frightened driver. Thinking about a train bearing down crushed his spirit.

George knew the instructions for the placement of detonators. Move well beyond the potential obstruction. Place three detonators 20 yards apart. He was attaching the third when he heard the train.

Weather conditions for warning any train were terrible. It was dark and bucketing down. The locomotive sounds grew louder.

It was climbing a slight gradient and working hard. George placed the remaining detonators away from the track, grabbed the lamp and hurried forward. He could hear the locomotive well before he saw its beam.

He stood between the Up and Down tracks hoping at least one of the men on the footplate would see the lamp. He held it at head height and waved. Not thinking, he muttered, 'Please God, make them see me.'

The beat of the engine grew louder and the power of the headlight lit up the world. On the footplate, the shovelling fireman worked hard. The driver peered into the blackness seeing nothing but eerie shapes of trees lit by the beam on his locomotive. Then he saw it.

'Christ, what's that?'

The fireman leapt behind the driver. 'It's a red!' he screamed but the driver was already in emergency stop mode. The fireman yanked on the whistle cord playing a message for the guard who jolted into action and frantically spun his brake in the van.

The brake on each fully-laden wagon was only used when they were being stabled. Anyway, there was no-one on the wagons.

The train loomed towards George. He stepped aside as the fiery steel horse hissed and screamed, straining to slow yet still passing him at speed, its sound and draft knocking him over on the Down.

On the footplate, the regulator was attacked with a vengeance and shut. The aim was to stop the supply of steam. The brakes were applied but the leaves on the wet track did all they could to frustrate the crew.

Bang! A detonator exploded. Bang! Another detonator exploded. The squeal of metal on metal screamed into the night air. The heartbeats of the crew added to their panic. In his van, the guard couldn't apply his brake another fraction of a turn.

His fear was the unknown—what lay ahead—a tree, a broken rail, a vehicle, livestock, people—what?

Bang went the third detonator. The train screamed in agony at the pressure being applied. Sheep, settled in for the night in nearby fields, heard the detonators explode. Farmers in their beds or in armchairs with stuffing straining to break free sat up in surprise.

George limped with purpose. He'd abandoned the remaining detonators and now the lamp. Hands free helped propel him forward. The train rushed past. Then he saw it; the glow of the red lamp on the rear of the guard's van. He gained on it.

The train continued to slow as George continued to move. He saw the guard gripping his van in case of a collision and sudden stop. The men stared at one another in the darkness.

'A truck on the line,' yelled George as he continued along the wagons. *How many more wagons?* he thought as his slow speed still exceeded the slowing train.

The pressure exerted by gravity kept rising. George's mind told him the wagons might buckle and burst off the tracks. He could be smashed by an enraged fully-laden wagon. He kept moving.

The sound of the massive train straining to end its journey sounded dangerous. The locomotive hated this type of exercise. The men on the footplate stared forward and could now see the problem. Hitting the upside down truck at speed would send the vehicle into scrap. If anyone was aboard, they were dead. But worse, the impact might dislodge the locomotive or a wagon or wagons and then the laws of gravity would rule the world. A derailed train could mean horrific injuries or death to those on board.

The idea of jumping flashed into the minds of the crew but their work in braking before last Christmas, thanks to George Miracle, enabled them to watch the finale in slow motion. Slow being the operative word as the buffers inched closer to the blockage.

Slipping, sliding, slowing, stopping and then ... clunk. The truck was struck with a gentle even friendly bump. The trapped driver's heartrate matched the combined heartrates of the crew.

George, gasping for air, arrived at the side of the loco. He wanted to weep. Dropping to his knees, the ballast hurt his limbs and caused his hip to cry out in pain. To the crew, he appeared to be praying.

'Bloody hell, George,' exclaimed the driver. 'Haven't you got anything better to do on a Wednesday night?'

The crew climbed down and, taking an arm each, helped George to stand. His head slumped as much from relief as exhaustion. He muttered. 'There's a bloke trapped in the truck.'

The crew released George who stumbled and staggered as the others ran to the truck. They'd not been working a minute to try and free the driver when two local policemen arrived and scrambled down the embankment.

George dropped and sat on the Down track knowing trains were not due until morning. He looked up as footsteps were heard and Eric stumbled out of the night.

'You did it, George, you did it.'

Eric dropped to the ground sitting beside his fellow porter.

'You carried the red, Eric. I've heard of the Lady with the Lamp. Now I've met the Porter with the Lamp.'

They smiled in the rain.

'I heard you were a hero porter when you worked in London. Now you're a hero porter in the sticks.' He placed his hand on George's shoulder. 'It's been an honour and privilege to work with you, George Miracle.'

The driver of the truck was placed on a stretcher and carried along the track until the embankment disappeared before being placed in an ambulance. The driver eventually recovered. Alas not so his truck. That night, the freight was fifty-four minutes late.

The story of the near disaster ran around the traps. The Whittleton staff members were all commended by the GER Head Office with the name George Miracle underlined.

Later, at the station house, in front of the kitchen stove, Connie worked hard filling the tin bath with kettle and pots of boiling water. With the right temperature in place, George sat awaiting his turn with the soap and flannel.

All members of the family thrilled to the tale of the adventure.

'We should actually be praising Em,' said her brother. His family looked confused. 'If she wasn't out making whoopee with her true love, she would have taken Uncle Fred his supper and I would have been relaxing here at home. I might have even been sitting in this bath.'

'So?' asked his mother, 'what's your point?'

'Well by the time Em ran back here to rouse me, I would have lost two minutes before starting to run along the track, and those two minutes would have seen the train hit the truck and who knows, a major derailment and possibly several deaths would have happened.'

'Good on you, Em,' said Fred. 'There's a lot to be said for romance.'

'Says the world's most confirmed bachelor,' laughed his sister.

Emily tingled with a mixture of embarrassment and happiness as the others teased her about matters of the heart.

Connie clapped. 'Right, bath time, George Miracle, come on, strip.'

'Thank you, Ma. I'll manage in my own time when you lot have gone to bed.'

As the others left, he copped an even bigger ribbing than the one Emily received a minute before.

When he did slide into the bath, the hot water and soapy suds caressed his body. He lay back, luxuriated in aches and pains being soothed, and ran a film of the night's activities through his head. He re-lived the terrified wife, the race along the line, the waving of the red lamp, the detonators, the strain and sounds of the locomotive in an emergency stop, and finally, the train stopping with a gentle nudge of the overturned truck. No fatalities. No derailment. A disaster was averted not far from the Whittleton station.

Chapter 23

B ritain's railways, the first in the world, began in the early 1800s, and it's easy to describe their growth at the time. In a word it was chaotic. Money, or rather the chance to make money, drove rapid development. Investors, in awe of the machinery, which could whip horses and canal boats into a cocked hat, flung bank notes at any opportunity to build a line and purchase rolling stock.

By the time the twentieth century came around, Britain saw more than 100 railway companies transporting people and products up, down and across its green and pleasant land.

And when you throw in metropolitan trains steaming through tunnels beneath a city, England was bursting with public transport rail services.

Several companies made money, plenty struggled and some derailed. For every investor who made a killing, there were many with holes in their pockets or fingers badly burnt. Crazy decisions saw lines built on inhospitable land and a few companies running on the same lines competing for the same passengers. Lunacy.

Most lines ran on a gauge of 4 feet 8½ inches but one wonderfully named chap, Isambard Kingdom Brunel, reckoned a track where the rails were a smidgeon wider than 7 feet was the way to go. Not so good for sharp corners mind. This lead to companies running trains on different gauges or tracks and thus requiring three rails. More expense, more madness.

With important persons, even politicians, on the boards of railway companies, it wasn't long before the government became involved and waved a red flag. They remembered World War One when the government took over the railways. It worked well then. Why not return to those days? The business of railways needed to change and anything would be better than the current mish-mash of competing companies. Things were about to change.

The idea was to amalgamate most companies. Instead of 120+ companies operating separately, it was decided to have only four meaning more than 100 companies would be absorbed, would disappear inside one of the huge companies, to be known as the Big Four.

Fred and George worked for the Great Eastern Railway Company, and despite being a large operation based in London and serving East Anglia, it too was to be amalgamated. Its trains and lines and staff and everything else belonging to the GER would become part of the LNER, the London and North Eastern Railway, one of the Big Four.

The tiny branch line to Crabbwell was soon to be a miniscule part of the behemoth as all GER services became part of the LNER.

For the staff it meant keeping their jobs but there would be a new company name, new logo, uniforms and timetables yet still the same service for people and freight and on the same lines. New locomotives and rolling stock were being planned.

The newspapers were full of the government's ideas and then the legislation. The times they were definitely a-changing.

Fred Carmody moved slower. His joints creaked. He often thought about death but equally about retirement. He reckoned his retirement might increase his longevity. To Fred, the perfect time to take the last train would be the day the Great Eastern Railway was amalgamated.

He wondered about where he would live. Losing the station master position would mean he would lose the station house. If the new company agreed to current staff continuing, George would have his job as porter but the station house would go to the new station master. Where would Fred and his family live?

One perfect idea was floated. If the new SM was single, he could board in the village allowing the Miracles, plus their elderly uncle, to rent the station house. It would be ideal for the young porter.

Alternatively, Fred, Connie and George could rent a small cottage in or near the village with the new SM and his family in the residence.

Emily looked like becoming a wife, married to a local farmer meaning she would be looked after in her new life on the farm.

But George could possibly throw a spanner in the works. Would he want to stay on at Whittleton if the new SM was a bit of an ogre? If George wanted a transfer, what would happen to Connie and Fred?

The big-wigs of the GER had given George many a Gold Star, and his future seemed assured. His war heroism and his good works within the community marked his future as rosy. But if the new company, the LNER wanted change, what might happen to George? Where would the young porter go?

The legislation, The Railways Act 1921—also known as the Grouping Act—went before parliament and passed into law. Soon the GER would be no more. Did the new company directors, those running the LNER, know anything about Fred Carmody's pending retirement and his nephew George and his work record? Did they care?

Fred told George they needed to have a chat. The nephew tried guessing the topics but missed one.

After the last train, they sat in the station house front room. Fred drank his stout while George settled for a brew. The nephew waited for his uncle to start proceedings.

'Not all amalgamations are the same, George. I reckon our new group might have problems and if so, you may want to look elsewhere.'

George froze. *What? Is he telling me to jump ship?*

'Apart from the London Midland and Scottish, the LNER is the biggest, and when you have big companies like us, the Great Eastern, the Great Northern, the Great Central, and others, all being lumped in together, people will disagree. Big boys won't be pushed around.

'But not with say the Great Western. It's basically them and a few small Welsh lines so the GWS should be plain sailing with no in-house punch-ups.'

In shock, George responded. 'You're suggesting I join God's Wonderful Railway?'

'I'm suggesting you become aware of the facts. If the LNER has in-fighting about who's the boss, which locos to use, about staffing levels and how promotion and job allocations will work, you might want to work for another of the Big Four and especially the GWS.'

George didn't reply. This was unexpected and knocked him off his horse. Then the shocks continued.

'And I have an announcement,' said Fred.

'A station announcement, Uncle?' asked George meekly trying to lighten what was obviously a serious mood.

Fred ignored the so-called joke. 'I've decided to retire.' The news was no surprise but hearing such words from the SM gave George's heart a pinch. 'By retiring from the GER, I'll have my pension guaranteed. Staying on into the LNER might see me pushed out and that's not for me.'

'You should be proud of your magnificent career, Uncle. Very few men have achieved as much and done it as well as you.'

George's sincerity stood out and Fred appreciated the comment.

'Thank you but the question, young man, becomes what is best for thee?'

'I've been thinking ...'

'I haven't finished,' said Fred and George lapsed into silence. 'You could stay here as porter or look for a move elsewhere. The women should be fine. Your mother can move in with me in another house in Whittleton, and Emily should have a husband to take care of, and he her.' He paused and, like he always did, wanted to hear the other person's point of view. 'So tell me, what would you like to do?'

'I like it here, the staff members are all wonderful people, and most of the passengers and farmers are the salt of the earth.' He hesitated.

'But?'

'But if the new SM is a no-hoper or a bit of a tyrant, I'll be as miserable as sin. I've been spoilt with only two remarkable SMs.'

'Okay but if you choose to stay, where will you live?'

'With you and Ma or there are plenty of locals who would offer me board and lodging but it's the unknown I'm worried about. Before I decide, I'd like to know who the new SM is going to be.'

'Fair enough, it's your life and your decision.' Fred revealed his plan. 'I'll put in my retirement letter this week. It might give the new company a push to find my replacement quick smart. When he arrives, you can decide if you'll stay or look for another place. Okay?'

George nodded. 'Thank you, Uncle, thank you for everything.' He looked at his mentor. 'Have you told Ma and Em?'

'Your mother's probably listening right now from the kitchen.'

The sound of a chair being moved forced the men to smile.

Once the word spread about Fred retiring, the Whittleton station numbers shot up. Passengers and people collecting goods popped in but there were folk who simply wanted to wish the old boy a happy retirement. Several women brought cakes and a few men brought home-brewed concoctions capable of growing hairs on your chest.

'Now you listen to me, Mr Carmody,' said the widow McPherson, 'my old man worked himself into the ground then retired and then he dropped dead. Let's be havin' none of that with you. Y'hear me?'

'I do, Mrs McPherson and thank you for the marmalade. It's the best in the county.'

The widow squinted. 'I heard you said those exact words to Mrs Burnley only last month.'

Fred laughed and waved away one his favourite regulars.

The GER accepted Fred's wish to retire and sorted his pension. He was told his replacement would be decided by the new parent company, the LNER.

Fred and Connie looked for a place to live. They loved Whittleton and saw no reason to leave the village or the area. And with Emily's romance, if not on the boil, then simmering, staying put made further sense. If George chose to remain in Whittleton, he too would need a new place to live.

Fred's last day was a Sunday. He would work until the last train passed through Whittleton with the next not due until Monday.

The crew from the Branch, Monty in the signal box, Desmond the gatekeeper, and Eric the porter would all be there for Fred's final send off. Even Audrey, the station master during the war and Fred's predecessor, willingly agreed to return. As for the locals, well the expression, "a bumper crowd" seemed appropriate. There was a buzz in the village.

For most people, the station master, particularly in a small town or village, was a VIP. He was looked up to and appreciated. He could hold a train for an out-of-breath struggling passenger. He could retrieve your lost property, tell you the time of the next train without needing to look up anything, and best of all, he remembered and always used your name.

'Should I make a speech, Ma?' asked George when Uncle Fred was outside.

Connie was baking. 'Of course, but keep it short. With all the food and drink on the platform, people will be keen to partake and not have to listen to you or Mr Grantley-Smythe prattle on forever.'

'I heard a few members of staff from Liverpool Street want to be here when "old Fred", as they call him, waves his final green flag and blows his final whistle.'

'How will they get home if the party's after the last train?'

'The family of one of the porters lives in the next village.'

Connie reminisced. 'I can remember when Fred first worked on the railways. Dressed up as a lad porter, he couldn't stop grinning the day he left home for Liverpool Street.'

'So is it true Whittleton is the only other station he's worked at?'

Connie nodded. 'All those years he almost lived at Liverpool Street. SMs who started as a lad porter, worked their way up the ladder and stayed at the same station for decades are getting to be a thing of the past.'

'The railways are changing, Ma. Can you believe we're about to have only four railway companies in the whole country.'

'Well your uncle's the old and you're the new, George. Have you decided if you'll stay on as porter in Whittleton?'

'I'm not sure I'll have a choice. This new company with a new board of directors may have their own ideas.'

The mother found herself a bit teary. 'For you railwaymen, this is the end of the line. Apart from your time in Norwich, you are about to leave the family home for good.'

George realized. 'So I am. You've finally managed to get rid of me.'

She didn't laugh. 'Your father would be so proud of you.'

Tears appeared and George went to put his arm around her. 'I miss him too, Ma.' He broke free. 'Now I must write my farewell speech for the station master about to retire.'

On Saturday night, George entered the station house. It was late with the last train long gone. He moved quietly with the house silent. The women retired but in the kitchen, the about-to-retire SM sat pensively by the stove.

'Uncle,' whispered George. 'Why are you not abed? It's your big day in the morning.'

'I've been up before dawn more times than you've had breakfast, my boy, and tomorrow will be no exception. Everything all right at the station?'

'Yes sir. The last Down was late because the gates at Newton got struck by some toff in his new Bentley but nothing else of concern.'

'Good-oh,' said Fred and stood. He poked the ashes as he always did before retiring. 'I'll see you in the morning,' he said and left.

'Goodnight Uncle,' said George watching the man who became his surrogate father and gave him a start in the railway world all those years ago. It was indeed a changing of the guard.

Why is the old boy still up? Does he not want to retire?

George slept well. He'd trained his body to wake on command. Forget about roosters and clock alarms. Sleeping in trenches in France helped train his body. He rolled over and in the dim pre-dawn light saw his uncle's empty bed.

He's on form even on his last day.

George sat on his bed and stretched. He needed a pee so headed outside. The stars sparkled and streaks of daylight were like searchlights on the horizon. The backyard walk was a doddle although with bare feet he felt the cold.

'Oh, good morning, Uncle' he said recognizing his uncle standing against the back fence.

Fred said nothing and George paused then panicked. He ran all of six and a bit yards and saw the old man's face twisted, his eyes opened wide, wider than wide.

'Uncle,' gasped George as his heart raced and his throat constricted. 'Uncle, no, no, no!'

On the day he was to retire, the station master in the Whittleton station house, retired permanently. His heart finally said enough was enough. He'd fallen against the wood pile and because it wasn't flush, he didn't slump to the ground. He was propped on the kindling.

In France under fire, George knew a lot about death. He saw many men die. It was a natural thing to close his uncle's staring eyes and gaping mouth. Having made the old man comfortable, George did what he came to do then unpegged a towel from the clothesline and draped it gently over Fred's head.

Calmly he returned inside and dressed. He chose not to cry although his heart was broken. He must not allow his mother or sister to go outside without being told. He tapped gently on his mother's bedroom door. She was awake. 'What is it?'

He opened the door. The weak daylight was enough for both to see the other's face. She saw pain or danger or seriousness. 'What's happened? Is it Fred?'

George didn't need to speak. His gentle nod spoke volumes. His mother gasped. He closed the door and waited till she emerged.

'Where is he?'

'Outside. I think it was a heart attack.'

'Have you told Emily?' He shook his head. 'I'll tell her. You make him respectable.'

They separated and when George came back to the kitchen the women were quiet. Emily moved to her brother and hugged him. She sobbed. George tried to comfort her and didn't know what to say.

'He became my father,' she cried. 'He looked after me all my life.'

'I know, I know,' said George.

'He needs to be brought inside,' said Connie trying to be calm and practical.

'I'll get Monty. We'll put him in his bed and then I'll ask about an undertaker. I've covered Uncle Fred with a towel so you can go outside.' He hugged Emily again then kissed his mother and left.

The women went outside to the lavatory. Their grief took a hit. Spike, who loved the old man with a passion, had jumped up onto the woodpile and in so doing the towel put there by George had been dislodged. Spike was licking the deceased.

'Spike,' hissed Emily and her dog hopped down.

Connie replaced the towel before the women returned inside with dog in hand.

Monty looked shocked. 'Jesus,' he said, 'and on his last day. Course I'll come.'

When George and Monty arrived the women were dressed and Monty offered his condolences. The men lifted and carried Fred carefully and put him back on his bed. With the blankets drawn up, he looked asleep.

Monty took over. 'I'll telephone Clarence Beers, the undertaker.' Monty pointed at George. 'But young man, you, me and Eric have a station to run. I'll have the vicar come round so you ladies needn't worry about nothin'.' They looked stunned as the bewhiskered signalman brought a sense of calm and purpose to their lives.

And so in Whittleton on a Sunday morning, it turned out that Fred

Carmody missed his final day at work.

It will come as no surprise to learn it was the first time in his 53 year railway career he took sick leave, although it could be said that being dead is probably not one of the ailments one can suffer to be considered ill.

The news raced around the village. If the station master died, it would have been news. But to die on the day he was to be celebrated and thanked on his retirement, meant it became shocking news.

People kept arriving at the station to offer their condolences to George and the other staff. The door to the station house was opened on a regular basis.

A telephone call to London saved the friends of the former SM from making the trip. The cakes already baked and beverages already brewed would be consumed in a sombre setting.

The Reverend Small behaved in a gentle fashion. 'I know Mr Carmody was not a churchgoer, Mrs Miracle, but to me and to so many in the village he was a tower of strength. I would be honoured to conduct his funeral service and, if you so wish, to have him buried in the churchyard.'

'Thank you, Vicar,' said Connie.

'Thank you, Vicar,' said George and Emily as one.

And so it was done. Fred didn't care where he was buried. He was asleep dreaming of an August Bank Holiday as Liverpool Street platforms were packed with day trippers clutching their parasols, buckets and spades and heading to Felixstowe or wherever.

Management sent a relief SM who found being billeted with Monty and his missus far more interesting than life on the station.

After the funeral, with George exhausted, Connie posed the question. 'When do we have to leave? When will they send a permanent station master?'

'If I knew that, Ma, I would tell you. The new legislation putting the GER into the LNER has been approved and comes into effect in January, 1923. I guess appointments are not the top item on their agenda but until the new man arrives, we carry on. Two porters and a relief SM are enough to steady the ship.'

And they did. The trains kept running. George felt pressure to pressure Head Office about the permanent SM. His uncle would know who to contact in London. George knew no-one high up in the GER and not a single soul in the new company.

His concerns troubled him more each day. *Will I hate having to work under the new SM? Where will my mother and sister live once we move out of the station house? I'll be fine. I can bunk down in the Goods Shed.*

The 09:12 Down pulled in a minute late and the guard shouted to George. 'Morning George. Here's the mail.'

George approached. 'Thank you, Henry,' he said, taking the letters. He glanced at the front of the first envelope and didn't recognize the official logo. It read *London and North Eastern Railway.* He stared at the envelope not thinking about his proximity to work colleagues.

'Ouch!' he cried as the blast from the guard's whistle disturbed George's hairstyle and equilibrium. He headed to the SM's office as the train pulled out.

'For you, sir,' said George handing the envelope to the relief SM. He opened it and looked at George.

'Not for me, young man, it's for you.'

He handed the letter to George who looked puzzled. He started to read the missive then squinted. He misunderstood and struggled to comprehend. Surely he misunderstood. He read again, this time aloud so as to be certain of the meaning.

> Dear Mr Miracle
> The new management of the LNER wishes to offer you the position of station master at Whittleton. Please advise your intention in this matter at your earliest convenience.
> Yours faithfully
> *C. J. Jenkins*
> C. J. Jenkins
> Company Secretary

Eric wandered in and saw the expression on George's face. 'What's happened? You look like you've seen a ghost.'

George said nothing but handed the letter to the porter.

He read it, looked at the relief SM and then George. 'Bleedin' Nora. That's worth standin' up for.'

'Why?' asked George. 'I'm not even 25. It's like having a lad porter running a mainline station.'

Eric spoke his mind. 'Hardly and I think you need a lesson in blowin' your own trumpet, Mister. They reckon you're up for the job, I reckon you're perfect for the job and so does the village.'

'I second that,' said the relief SM

George struggled to respond. His shock kept growing. 'I don't think Lord Fitzsimons would agree.'

'Okay, not His Toffyness,' said Eric.

'Or the farmer from Hell or Mrs Bradshaw with her cats or ...'

'Oh come on, George, stop looking at the teeth of the bloody gift horse. You're in, my son. It's a brilliant career opportunity. Grab the offer with both hands. Your uncle would be over the moon.'

George understood. He saw Eric grinning and extending a hand. They shook with a firm grip which grew in strength. They pumped hard and grinned harder and only stopped when a passenger knocked on the ticket-box window and shouted, 'Shop'.

When George walked into the station house kitchen, Connie was sewing and Emily thumbing through a magazine of bridal dresses.

'What are you doing home?' asked his mother.

'Good news, Ma, we don't have to move.'

Both women stopped what they were doing, looking confused. The smile spreading across George's face surely didn't mean bad news.

'What's happened?' asked Connie more curious than Alice.

He sounded superior. 'I think you mean, what's happened, *sir*.'

'George!' snapped his sister, tired of the game.

He handed the envelope to his mother. She opened it with Emily by her side in an instant. Emily read the faster and screamed, her mother likewise a second or two later.

The letter fell to the floor as both hugged the new station master, the youngest in the land. Spike barked with happiness and their celebration woke the slumbering Trixie.

The Stationmaster Miracle Series Book 2 ~ *The Miracle Branch Line*

The Detective Joanna Best Mysteries

www.cenfoxbooks.com

Joanna Best is the youngest homicide detective in town. Smart, feisty and gorgeous, she's brilliant at cracking cases and rubbing people up the wrong way. Some jealous colleagues are desperate to undermine her. Certain criminals want her dead. Juggling a career with Victoria Police, having three men madly in love with her, and a strange family,

Jo Best's adventures will drag you in. Her second banana is an Australian born Chinese IT guru who makes computers sing. Her best pal is a female 60ish police surgeon, a forensic genius and chocoholic.

I could not put this series down. The characters, plots, settings, kept me reading. I really liked the word comedy phrasing. A couple of characters I wanted to smack. **Amazon**

Sherlock Holmes

The great man is soon to retire. On his last night at Baker Street, the loyal landlady drops a bombshell. Holmes is staggered. Mrs Hudson has done what!? Sherlock Holmes never panics—until now. Dr Watson arrives and is stunned. It's their greatest challenge. Sir Arthur Conan Doyle is furious. A famous author turned WW1 counter-intelligence spy is on the case. *The Strand Magazine* smells a scoop. Inspector Lestrade from Scotland Yard plans revenge, and at stake is the brilliant reputation of the world's most famous consulting detective. His only hope is to 'play the game'.

www.cenfoxbooks.com

A delightfully imaginative pastiche. Recommended. **Peter Blau BSI**
An extraordinary book, one of the most enjoyable pieces of Holmesian fiction I've read in a long time … a complex, ingenious and deliciously funny story of intersecting realities, and the conclusion is entirely satisfactory. I love it! **Roger Johnson**
Commissioning Editor: *The Sherlock Holmes Journal*

The Detective Joanna Best Mysteries

www.cenfoxbooks.com

Joanna Best is the youngest homicide detective in town. Smart, feisty and gorgeous, she's brilliant at cracking cases and rubbing people up the wrong way. Some jealous colleagues are desperate to undermine her. Certain criminals want her dead. Juggling a career with Victoria Police, having three men madly in love with her, and a strange family,

Jo Best's adventures will drag you in. Her second banana is an Australian born Chinese IT guru who makes computers sing. Her best pal is a female 60ish police surgeon, a forensic genius and chocoholic.

I could not put this series down. The characters, plots, settings, kept me reading. I really liked the word comedy phrasing. A couple of characters I wanted to smack. **Amazon**

Sherlock Holmes

The great man is soon to retire. On his last night at Baker Street, the loyal landlady drops a bombshell. Holmes is staggered. Mrs Hudson has done what!? Sherlock Holmes never panics—until now. Dr Watson arrives and is stunned. It's their greatest challenge. Sir Arthur Conan Doyle is furious. A famous author turned WW1 counter-intelligence spy is on the case. *The Strand Magazine* smells a scoop. Inspector Lestrade from Scotland Yard plans revenge, and at stake is the brilliant reputation of the world's most famous consulting detective. His only hope is to 'play the game'.

www.cenfoxbooks.com

A delightfully imaginative pastiche. Recommended. **Peter Blau BSI**
An extraordinary book, one of the most enjoyable pieces of Holmesian fiction I've read in a long time … a complex, ingenious and deliciously funny story of intersecting realities, and the conclusion is entirely satisfactory. I love it! **Roger Johnson**
Commissioning Editor: *The Sherlock Holmes Journal*

Three World War Two Thrillers

In 1939 Germany is smashing through the Low Countries and the British, Belgian and French forces are trapped at Dunkirk. Louise Wellesley is a gorgeous and aristocratic young Englishwoman desperate to become an actress. But her upbringing demands she go to finishing school, the Buckingham Palace debutante ball and remain at home until the right chap comes along. Such young ladies most definitely do not cavort semi-naked upon the wicked stage. But war brings change. People tell lies. Rules are broken. So when you're in a foreign country and living by your wits while facing arrest, torture and death from the French police, Resistance, Gestapo and a double-agent, you bloody well better remember your lines, act out of your skin and never ever bump into the furniture. Oh and it helps if your new best friend is Edith Piaf.

A Plum Jewel is the third in the series about a beautiful young actress turned spy. In the opinion of this reader it may be the best. Cenarth Fox has loaded this tale with so many twists and obstacles the reader may feel the need to take notes. Mr. Fox's knowledge of the working of wartime Britain and France is remarkable. The reader is right in the middle of the action. I can't recommend this book strongly enough.
Scott Skipper

The Plum Trilogy – www.cenfoxbooks.com

A Sweeping Saga

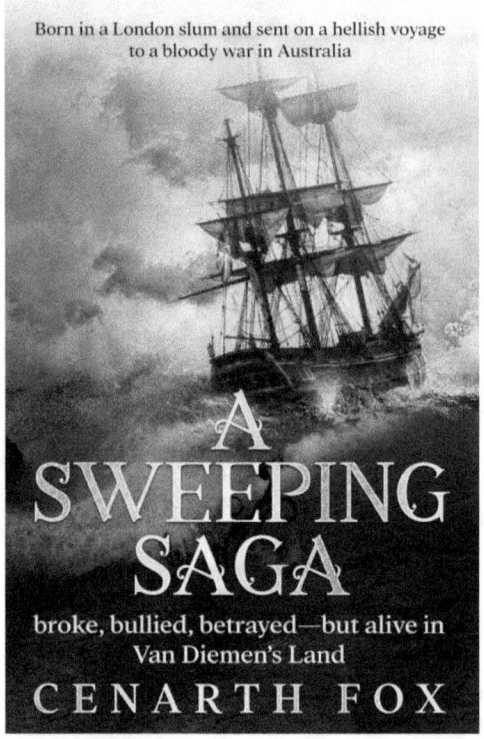

Born in a London slum and sent on a hellish voyage
to a bloody war in Australia

A
SWEEPING
SAGA
broke, bullied, betrayed—but alive in
Van Diemen's Land
CENARTH FOX

Jonathon Sweeping became Oliver Twist before Dickens was born. In a
London slum, his young parents battled poverty, disease and heartache.
Forget schooling. Shove the child up a chimney. Make young Sweeping a
sweep. Threaten him, injure him but under no circumstances pay him.
No wonder death and stealing dominated society when even children
fronted the Old Bailey. What hope for the boy? Jonathon moved from
prison hulk to convict ship to the other side of the world where Van
Diemen's Land with its stunning natural beauty became a war zone. It
was kill or be killed as genocide exploded. The boy became a man
fighting injustice, cruelty and bushfires. He started a family and together
they lived, loved and built a new nation in what became Tasmania. This
is Jonathon Sweeping's sweeping saga.

*A combination of fine scholarship and effective prose make A Sweeping
Saga a great pleasure to read.*
Emeritus Professor Michael Roe University of Tasmania

A Man of Sorrows

Patrick Bronte, father of the famous Bronte sisters was a truly remarkable man. He gave Job in the Old Testament a run for his money in the suffering stakes. His Irish birth and background, his ancestors lived fascinating lives. When Patrick asked a famous novelist to write a biography about his famous daughter, Charlotte, the priest was pilloried without mercy. "Patrick Bronte should be taken into the garden and shot," wrote one critic. Nice. The criticism was woefully untrue and yet the gentle man forgave his enemies. Discover the truth about the patriarch of an amazing family.

I thoroughly enjoyed Cassocked Savage, an excellent mix of fact and fiction which took me on Patrick's fabulous, and unfortunate journey from poverty in Ireland to the Yorkshire I know and love. It deals sympathetically with the Gaskell episode and the dialogue between Patrick and Maria brings the story to life. The chapter on Thornton and Hartshead is wonderfully evocative.
Steve Stanworth
Chairman of The Bronte Birthplace trust